Having achieved his heart's desire at a high price, Prince Colin of Sendorra and his fiancé, Nobel Prize winner Alain de Gris, find themselves at the epicenter of a twisted plot. Colin's cousin, Drake Bradford, and his grandmother Maura, the high priestess of the Bradford Coven, have conspired for years to bring down the royal family.

Resembling his cousin in features and coloring, Drake, the soulless rat, has been using their similarities—and black magic—to his advantage. Princess Charlotte, Colin's ex-girlfriend, is unwittingly drawn into the feud, blissfully unaware she's been sleeping with an impostor.

In this anticipated sequel to *A Tangled Legacy*, Colin and Alain, along with their fearless group of witches, ghosts, and familiars, embark on a convoluted journey to save the people they love and ensure the royal succession.

A Noble Cause

Legacy, Book Two

Mickie B. Ashling

A NineStar Press Publication

Published by NineStar Press
P.O. Box 91792,
Albuquerque, New Mexico, 87199 USA.
www.ninestarpress.com

A Noble Cause

Printed in the USA
First Edition
August, 2019

Print ISBN: 978-1-951057-32-9

Also available in eBook, ISBN: 978-1-951057-31-2

Warning: This book contains sexually explicit content, which may only be suitable for mature readers, and scenes of graphic violence.

I dedicate this story to my good friend and staunch supporter, Jeannie, who takes my first drafts and turns them into something worth keeping. She's been along on this journey from the beginning and deserves all the recognition. I couldn't have done it without her. Thank you!

Prologue

CHARLIE'S HEAD LOLLED back against the leather seat of the BMW as Drake Bradford, still in his disguise as Prince Colin of Sendorra, navigated the crowded streets of Biarritz before merging onto the toll road heading toward Paris. He'd cast a sleeping spell on his "fiancé" to avoid the interrogation he was sure would follow once she realized they were on their way out of town. He needed privacy to confer with Granny Maura to formulate a new plan while the royals were busy drawing up countermeasures to deal with him.

Drake grew impatient as Granny's phone rang and rang. Like many seniors, she didn't have her mobile at her fingertips, defeating the whole purpose of instant availability. Finally, after the seventh ring, she picked up.

"It's about bloody time."

"I couldn't find my phone," she replied apologetically.

"We've already talked about this on several occasions," Drake scolded. "Put it on your kitchen counter so you know where to look."

"What's the problem?" she asked dismissively.

"I've managed to kill off the dowager and Colin in one fell swoop."

"You *what!*"

"They should have stayed out of my business," Drake defended.

"Tell me exactly what happened," Maura ordered tersely.

"Plans started to unravel the minute Colin showed up unexpectedly. He wasn't due home for another couple of days, and Charlie and I would have announced our engagement by then. There was nothing he could have done to stop us from marrying, but then it all went to shit."

"Where are you?"

"Driving to Paris."

"Is Charlie with you?"

"Of course she is," Drake snapped. "She's mine and I have every intention of marrying her. Plus, she's carrying my child."

"Don't come to Paris," Maura advised. "It's the first place they'll look."

"What do you suggest?"

"Let me find you an apartment in Prague."

"Why there?"

"It's a good place to hide in plain sight."

"Get back to me with details once you've made the arrangements."

"It might take a few hours."

He grunted. "Doesn't matter, Granny. This is going to be one long-ass drive."

"All right."

Drake gunned the engine and put the car on cruise control the minute he was on the toll road. He was still seething at having been foiled—by an incompetent witch, no less—and wasn't the least bit sorry he'd destroyed a dynasty. The only downside to this turn of events was figuring out how to deal with Charlie and her parents. He'd have to use her pregnancy and his powers of persuasion to convince her he was a far better choice than Colin could ever be. Granted, he didn't have a kingdom to lay at her feet, but he and Charlie had great chemistry, and the girl melted into a pliant fool the minute he laid hands on her. He'd keep her so sexed up she wouldn't dream of rejecting him.

His phone rang an hour later, and he was stunned by Maura's news.

"Colin isn't dead."

Drake slammed on the brakes, and the car fishtailed to a stop on the shoulder, narrowly avoiding a six-car pileup.

"Impossible!" he thundered. "I stopped his heart."

"Isabelle Simon and her son managed to bring him back to life," she deadpanned. "The coven has already received a lengthy email demanding retribution."

"Or what?"

"We'll have a war on our hands, Drake. I'm not sure I can get the other members to stand by our side when your actions were completely unjustified."

"Fuck the coven," Drake snarled. "I don't want their help. And need I remind you this was your plan all along? What about the dowager?"

"She's dead."

"So, you got what you wanted," Drake pointed out malevolently. He sucked in air through his clenched teeth and gripped the steering wheel. "Now it's my turn, and you'd better back me up."

"I'll see you in Prague."

Chapter One

ANDREW MATERIALIZED INTO the apartment located off Karlova Street in the historic center of Prague. Bibi, the snowy owl who was Isabelle Simon's familiar, was his prickly companion on this mission to locate Colin's ex-fiancé, Princess Charlotte of Navarre, aka Charlie. Unlike the easily recognizable bird, Andrew was invisible, one of the few benefits of being dead.

Older than his identical twin by minutes, Andrew had been stillborn, but his bond with Colin continued beyond death, and he'd been by his side as companion and confidant ever since. Recent events propelled him to take on this new role as familiar, and he was learning on the job.

Colin's supernatural gene had been largely unexplored due to Prince Emile, Colin's grandfather and defunct ruler. Emile's irrational fear of witchcraft had inadvertently started a disastrous chain of events that resulted in the recent death of the Dowager Princess Alexandra.

Alain, the only son of Isabelle, the high priestess of the Simon Coven, and a powerful gray witch in his own right, was slowly teaching his young lover, Colin—and Andrew by assimilation—the finer points of witchcraft. He'd explained how a familiar, whether astral or physical, would help to enhance Colin's power through direct manipulation of natural energy and could warn and defend him against danger. Andrew had been doing most of this already, but the magical element was new.

What had prompted this midnight reconnaissance was a conversation the twins had the night before the state funeral, two days ago, when Andrew had intercepted Colin in the palace kitchen.

Why are you up at this ungodly hour?

"Dammit, Andrew! You scared the fuck out of me."

Seriously, bro. You should be in bed with the love of your life.

"He mentioned a snack earlier, and I thought I'd make up a tray in case he wakes up hungry."

Did you forget you were a prince? Pick up the phone and order your servants.

"I didn't want to disturb anyone."

You really are growing up.

"Stuff the commentary."

I gather the royals approve, or Alain wouldn't be in your bed.

"They've been surprisingly chill."

Hard to believe.

"But—"

"Ah...the invariable objection. Alain can't make a baby."

"Exactly."

Such a buzzkill.

"I know."

What's the next step in this vendetta with Drake?

"Apparently there's protocol to follow, even if he's a murdering psychopath."

You need a hunting license?

"Isabelle wants to avoid an all-out war between the covens. If we do this without a nod of approval, there will be hell to pay."

My friends and I can literally scare him to death.

"We're not dealing with an ordinary witch, Andrew. Drake is a warlock, and you weren't successful the last time you confronted him."

Unless he's got a personal relationship with Satan, we can bring him down.

"Who says he doesn't? He seemed invincible the other night."

We were caught off guard, but I'll be ready next time. Bibi and I should reconnoiter to see what he's got up his twisted sleeve.

"It can't hurt."

Any idea where we should start looking?

"Not a clue."

Has anyone heard from Charlie?

"No."

Drake seemed pretty confident she'd run away with him.

"Things will change once she learns he's my doppelganger."

How can you be sure?

"Her parents will intervene, for one thing, and I know Charlie. She'll flip out when Drake shows his true colors."

Remember Drake's parting shot? He says she can't get enough of him.

"How could Charlie be fooled so easily?"

Maybe he's a fantastic lover?

"Gross."

When was the last time you slept with her?

"Andrew, stop!

I have a bad feeling, Colin. Do you think he'll hurt her if she rejects him?

"I don't know what he'll do. We've got to find her," Colin stressed.

Hopefully, Bibi won't lead me astray.

Andrew disappeared and materialized in Isabelle Simon's foyer. He'd been there once before, the night Colin asked him to be his familiar, and had toured the palatial residence, including the turret Isabelle used as her workshop. The high priestess had warmed to Colin, even though he was a member of the Bradford family, sworn enemies of the Simons for decades, and the last person on earth she would have chosen for her only son. Colin revealed the unbroken connection with his dead twin, and the need to get Andrew up to snuff as his familiar, so Isabelle offered Bibi's services.

Tonight, Bibi let out her usual annoying screech when she spotted his ghostly presence. Isabelle appeared shortly after, looking remarkably composed in a lace-trimmed peignoir with her silver hair tumbling around her shoulders. She looked damned good for a woman in her late sixties. Although Isabelle couldn't see Andrew, she felt his presence and listened intently while he explained the urgent need to find Princess Charlotte. With a nod of approval, she waved them away and the hunt was on.

Andrew didn't have the foggiest how Bibi's tracking device worked, but he had to trust the owl to lead him in the right direction. He questioned her accuracy after they crossed into Austro-Hungarian territory. Wouldn't Drake head toward his place in Brussels, or better still, to Navarre, Charlie's ancestral home? Her royal parents would have to consent to the marriage if Charlie was onboard with his plan, especially if she was pregnant. Then again, Drake's lies had overtaken the truth a while back, and Andrew wondered if pregnancy was just wishful thinking on Drake's part.

In the heart of downtown Prague, Bibi perched on a parapet outside a double-paned window while Andrew slipped into an apartment to explore. The place was small, but well furnished, with all the amenities one needed to survive a long stay. There was a kitchenette with a stacked washer and dryer tucked into an alcove beside the rear exit. A large TV cast a bluish light over the small sitting area, where Drake had fallen asleep on the recliner. Whatever he'd been watching had long since ended, and the only thing on the silent screen was the network logo.

Andrew studied his cousin in repose. Older by five years, Drake's physical similarities to Colin, often described as the golden boy, could be effortlessly enhanced by magic. The same flaxen hair, lean build, and arctic blue eyes were a genetic match, but upon closer inspection, it wasn't hard to tell them apart. Years of privilege contributed to Colin's illustrious appearance, whereas Drake, raised under different and oftentimes difficult circumstances, was a tarnished version of the prince.

At present, Drake looked harmless, but Andrew knew there was powerful evil contained in his serene façade. Drake hadn't hesitated to cast the toxic spell that had killed the Dowager and stopped Colin's heart. If it weren't for Alain, the principality would be minus an heir and thrown into a constitutional crisis. Fortunately, it wasn't the case, but Drake, under his guise as Colin, had managed to convince Charlie to run off with him, and his day of reckoning would have to wait until she was safely out of his reach.

A stifled cry of distress drew Andrew's attention away from the sleeping menace toward the bedroom. He passed through the wall and found Charlie lying on her side covered by a thick quilt. Colin's ex, a perky brunette with an engaging smile and a wicked sense of humor, looked awful. Her eyelids were puffy, and her normally shiny hair lay in dull tendrils around her pale face. There was a plastic bucket on the floor by her side of the bed, which she'd been using to catch the remains of her latest meal.

Andrew grimaced when he watched her throw off the blanket, lean over, and retch spasmodically, backhanding the slimy mess consisting of tears, snot, and ropes of saliva, while pleading for help to no one in particular.

Her voice was croaky from vomiting, and Andrew wished he could get her a glass of water or a cool washcloth, a simple task under ordinary circumstances, but...seeing a tangible object floating in her direction might result in hysterics, which would alert Drake. Andrew had no desire to prove his mettle without reinforcements. All he could do was report his findings and hope the royals would arrive in time to rescue poor Charlie.

She'd been the unwitting pawn in this dangerous game Drake and his grandmother, Maura, had conceived a while back. Colin had unknowingly participated by suggesting Drake impersonate him while he jetted off on a romantic holiday with his new boyfriend. He'd paid for his terrible mistake in ways he'd never anticipated but so had others.

The bedroom door swung open, and Andrew watched Drake walk into the bedroom, eyes darting suspiciously. He knew Drake couldn't see him, but the warlock's sixth sense must have picked up a new presence in the room, and he was instantly on high alert.

"Is that you, ghost?"

Damn, he was good. Andrew didn't engage in any way, but Drake continued.

"Tell my resurrected cousin to back off if he ever wants to see Charlie again."

He knew Colin was alive!

"Who are you talking to?" Charlie asked plaintively.

"No one," Drake replied.

"I can hear you."

"You're overwrought," Drake deflected.

"Please call my parents."

"Not yet."

"What are you waiting for?"

He walked up to Charlie and helped her sit up. "Get in the shower, Charlie. You reek."

"I'm sick," she whined. "I can't keep anything down."

"The doctor said morning sickness is a good sign."

"Good for whom?" she asked irritably. "I see no benefit to any of this."

"It indicates you have the right amount of hormones your fetus needs to grow, and your placenta is thick enough to supply the nutrients. Plus, vomiting removes toxins."

"You sound like a public service announcement," she snapped.

"I read it off the internet."

She flopped back down and wailed. "You promised to take me home."

"Let's wait until you're past the first trimester. This way no one will come up with some stupid excuse to postpone our wedding."

"What the fuck ever," Charlie fumed. "My parents have encouraged our match for years. They would never object."

Drake shrugged.

"Why didn't we go through with the plan to announce our engagement at your birthday party?" Charlie asked.

Andrew frowned. Didn't Charlie know who she was dealing with?

"Your pregnancy is messing with your brain cells. I told you Granny had a stroke and they canceled the party."

"How's she doing?"

"Fine."

Lying sack of shit!

"We should go home, Col. I hate this place."

"Soon," he replied. "Get in the shower, babe. It'll make you feel better."

He walked out of the room and Andrew followed, hoping to get more insight on this current situation. Passing close enough so Drake could feel the change in temperature, Andrew smirked when Drake flung his arm out.

"Out of my way, ghost! You have no power over me."

The fury in his voice belied the fear in his eyes, and Andrew wondered if Drake was treading water now that his scheme to step into Colin's shoes to marry Charlie had failed. Did he have a backup plan or was he simply reacting? He was obviously in touch with Maura or he wouldn't have known Colin was still alive. Was he planning to use Charlie as ransom, or did he still intend to marry her? There were too many open-ended questions, and Andrew couldn't hang around to find out more. He'd report back and await further instructions.

Chapter Two

CHARLIE BARELY MADE it to the bathroom sink before another spasm hit, and with a growing sense of alarm, she noticed traces of blood mixed in with the rest of the muck. Was the incessant vomiting irritating her esophagus, or could this be a symptom of something more serious? If she were back home, a doctor would be consulted, but they were in Prague, a strange city as mysterious to her as Colin's recent behavior.

Crinkling her nose at the unpleasant odor, she discarded her soiled clothes and stepped into the shower, hoping the hot water would wash away more than her physical discomfort. The small enclosure quickly filled with steam, and she poured a generous amount of orange-scented shampoo into her cupped hand, sighing with relief as her fingers scrubbed through the frothy lather. Perhaps a good soak was all she needed to shed some of the discomfort which had been slowly building since leaving Biarritz.

For as long as she could remember, Charlie dreamed of being Colin's wife and mother to his children. She was eight when they were first introduced, and they'd hit it off immediately. Both sets of parents were pleased a solid friendship had been established, and they planned events with the youngsters in mind. With their eyes on the future, Charlie's parents explained the vital role she would play in the succession of Sendorra, the neighboring mountain principality, long an ally to Navarre. Although never officially engaged, an unspoken agreement between the royal families had been forged.

Like any other plan involving children, maturity led to the inevitable reshaping of goals. When thirteen-year-old Colin confessed he was also attracted to men, Charlie was devastated. Instead of seeking advice from one of her parents, who might have advocated patience, she shut down and refused to attend any more royal functions. She and Colin spiraled into sullen and confused adolescents. Boarding school had been a welcome relief for both of them. Now they would only have to see each other during the summer months, and the long stretches in between could be spent growing up.

She tried not to think about Colin hooking up with his mates in school. It made her angry, but not because she was homophobic. Anyone who took Colin's attention away from her was deemed a threat. Nonetheless, his phobia for male pregnancy hadn't disappeared with his sexual awakening, and Charlie had a viable uterus, which automatically placed her at the top of the list of prospective consorts.

With the future in mind, she learned as much as possible about lovemaking—without losing her virginity—to prove she would be a good fit. On her eighteenth birthday, they'd blindly fumbled through their first time, making certain to use protection. Things had steadily improved for a while, and then they'd dipped drastically. She wasn't sure why, and Colin offered no explanation. The chemistry between them never reached the necessary boiling point to sustain them for the long haul. Two years later, they decided it was best to move on, and their spontaneous lovemaking on the night in question had been an act of desperation, a last-ditch effort to keep their connection alive, but it had ultimately failed to bind them together.

Or so she thought. Charlie dealt with her parents' disappointment, and life went on until she missed her period. Once she confirmed the pregnancy, priorities changed and thoughts of marriage and motherhood took center stage once more. But Colin was dating again, and his current male lover was an accomplished scientist, at least a dozen years older and far wiser than she could ever hope to be. Trying to worm her way back into Colin's life would be unlikely unless she told him about the pregnancy, which would be an awful way to win him back. Colin was no paragon, but he did have a strong sense of duty and would never suggest an abortion. Still...Charlie didn't want to force his hand. The romantic in her hoped he'd arrive at the logical conclusion organically. They were meant to be together.

With a reunion on her mind, she texted Colin to secure an invitation to Biarritz, where the royals spent the entire summer. She was overjoyed when he responded enthusiastically. The alleged new boyfriend wasn't mentioned, and Colin agreed with her suggestion she reside in an apartment away from palace intrigue. It was the sensible thing to do if they were to get any privacy. Buoyed by his response, Charlie didn't mention the pregnancy.

Surprisingly affectionate, considering they'd broken up only five weeks prior, she and Colin partied like never before. It was a magical time, and everything was different in and out of bed. It came to an abrupt end when the morning sickness started. She was afraid Colin would be angry once he realized she'd been knocked up all along—

so she left out the pertinent dates—and basked in his excitement when she shared the news. Soon he was making plans for their public engagement and subsequent marriage.

The dowager's stroke couldn't have come at a worse time, not that there was ever a good time to have a life-threatening emergency, but it hardly explained Colin's agitation and almost feverish need to leave Biarritz at once. Traveling without their personal security was unprecedented, but Colin said they'd be hounded by paparazzi if they left town with their usual retinue. It would lead to questions, and he didn't want to downplay the current health crisis by inserting their own joyous announcement. They could lie low in Paris while getting daily updates from the palace.

Except they hadn't stayed in Paris. After an overnight stop at the Ritz, where he'd left her for an hour to confer with some mysterious relative, his mood plummeted.

"What's wrong?"

"We have to keep traveling."

"Why?"

Colin narrowed his eyes. "Because I said so."

"I'm sorry about the pregnancy, Colin."

"Don't be. You know how much an heir means to the monarchy."

"I know, but I was hoping we'd have another year to enjoy our rekindled romance." Stepping forward, she examined his face, hoping to see joy in his eyes instead of wariness. When he didn't reply, she ventured, "We're on the right track, aren't we? Things have never been this good between us."

Colin nodded.

"Do you regret anything that's happened since my return?"

A shadow glided over the familiar face, and for one moment, Charlie was convinced she was looking at a stranger. The feeling passed soon enough, but the sense of foreboding left in its wake was disconcerting. As they traveled farther away from Paris, Colin shed his congenial veneer, and her unease grew in direct proportion to his edgy behavior. Something wasn't right, but she had no way of knowing what it might be.

Done with her shower, and feeling marginally better, she reached for the towel on the rack and jerked back after realizing Colin had slipped into the bathroom.

He handed it to her wordlessly, hungry eyes examining her wet torso and lingering on her breasts.

"Your tits look great," he said huskily.

She shrugged, uncomfortable under his scrutiny. Wrapping the towel around herself, she stepped out of the enclosure and was shocked when Colin reached for the towel and yanked it away.

"Not yet," he muttered.

Wide-eyed, Charlie watched Colin step closer and cup her right breast, fondling her nipple with his thumb. He smiled when the tender skin puckered reflexively. "I've still got the magic touch."

"They're extra sensitive," Charlie reasoned.

"I can't imagine what they'll look like in a few months."

"Probably horrible," Charlie complained. "My bra no longer fits. I feel like a cow."

"You don't look like one," Colin said. "In fact, I rather prefer this to the A cup."

"Can I have the towel back?"

"If you blow me first."

Charlie was taken aback by his request. Colin hadn't touched her since she announced her pregnancy, and even before then, he'd been careful of her feelings. His current language and tone of voice made her feel dirty for some reason.

"Come on, Colin. Stop messing around."

He put his hands on her shoulders and pushed her down. "Do it."

Tears filled her eyes. "What's gotten into you?"

Slowly unbuttoning his fly, he released his engorged cock. "I have an acute problem you can solve in minutes. Now, stop arguing, and do as you're told."

Crumpling under his scrutiny, Charlie sank to her knees. She wasn't overly fond of this act. In truth, she found it demeaning but had acquiesced in the past to make him happy. Doing it in bed as foreplay felt a lot different than getting down on her knees and servicing him like a whore. He tried combing his fingers through her wet hair and grumbled when they got caught in the tangles. Frustrated, he grabbed her by the neck and drew her closer to his groin.

"Let me go," she pleaded.

He looked down at her upturned face and ignored the tears. "Do I have to remind you I'm the father of your child and your future sovereign?"

"And I am a fucking princess," she snapped viciously. "You can't treat me like a goddamn hookup."

"Put your potty mouth to good use so I don't regret my decision."

"I didn't put a gun to your head," Charlie protested. "You wanted this reunion as much as me."

"Keep lying to yourself while I get something out of this. Open up," he commanded, "and don't even think about biting me."

Holding her head steady, he worked his cock into her mouth and thrust savagely. She gagged and tears blurred her vision, but she didn't dare pull away. Fear superseded humiliation and she powered through while trying to make sense of this radical change in the man she'd loved for years. Fortunately, it was over quickly, and he walked out of the bathroom as soon as he spent. Charlie crawled to the toilet and threw up.

She shuddered in disgust, quickly standing to rinse out her mouth and brush her teeth. Wrapping the towel around her shaking body, she staggered back into the room. It was empty, thank God, and she threw on a T-shirt and sweatpants before climbing into bed.

Warm and safe for the moment, Charlie cried softly. Was this the sort of behavior she should expect going forward? She and Colin had their differences in the past, and they'd argued on occasion, but he'd never been disrespectful or shown such a cruel streak. Had he been pretending to be happy about her pregnancy? Did he feel trapped? Was he missing his old boyfriend?

Charlie covered her face with a pillow as her sobs grew louder. She didn't want Colin to find her this way. The next time they met face-to-face, she'd have to resume some semblance of control. He wasn't the only one who could pull the royal card. She might have been a party girl after they broke up and played loose and fast with her affection, but it all changed once she realized she was carrying his child. Her life had purpose once more, and she looked forward to a future by Colin's side.

If he needed to be persuaded to fall in love again, then she'd swallow her pride and let him have his way with her occasionally. Mama had mentioned on more than one occasion that men had certain needs she couldn't hold off no matter the circumstances. Weary of the constant nausea and malaise, Colin must have reached a breaking point. Charlie didn't think she'd win him back by shoving him away. But first things first. She had to get her hands on some medication. It was impossible to feel sexy when she was constantly sick.

The next morning, Charlie forced herself to get out of bed and join Colin in the kitchen. He looked up in surprise when she drew up a chair.

"I want to see a doctor," she announced.

He frowned. "What for?"

"I'm tired of feeling ill. There's a reason you snapped last night, and I have to accept some of the blame. Abstaining can't be easy."

"It's not." Colin studied her curiously and slowly reached for her hand across the dinette. "I'm surprised you're being so tolerant. I was sure you'd be furious this morning."

"I was hurt more than angry, but upon reflection, I realized you're going through a stressful time and needed some release."

"Thank you."

"Please find someone who might have a cure for this morning sickness. It'll solve most of our problems."

Colin nodded. "I've been doing some research, and there's a midwife in the area local women call on for all manner of things. Her name is Maura."

Charlie's spirits lifted immediately. "Will you engage her services?"

"I'll take care of it this morning."

Charlie smiled. "I know this hasn't been easy on you, Colin, but I want you to know you can count on me going forward. I don't want you to regret our reunion."

"I haven't yet," he reassured her. "Can you stomach some breakfast?"

Chapter Three

HAVING JUST LAID his granny to rest, Colin's mood was somber, but it was time to put aside his grief and focus on righting a terrible wrong. Key players were gathered around the conference table in what amounted to a council of war: his fathers, Prince Sebastian, present ruler of Sendorra, and his consort, Duke Errol Maitland, along with Colin's newly proclaimed fiancé, Alain de Gris, and his mother, High Priestess Isabelle Simon. Andrew hovered behind Colin's chair, a ghostly presence only visible to one, while Bibi watched over the proceedings from a spot high in the rafters.

The immediate concern was finding the safest way to extract Charlie. Going by Bibi and Andrew's report, she was definitely pregnant, and still in the dark regarding the person sharing her bed. The warlock's parting shot referencing Colin's inadequacies, in and out of the bedroom, left a bitter aftertaste and a surge of jealousy that was surprisingly inappropriate. Colin had no right to feel territorial—they had broken up over six weeks ago—but Charlie had been a fixture in his life for as long as he could remember, and the news of her pregnancy had shaken him. Drake had willfully destroyed his grandmother, and luring Charlie into his bed under false pretenses was beyond reprehensible. To his mind, it was tantamount to rape, and death by hanging or lethal injection was a fitting punishment.

Colin addressed Isabelle. "Have you received a reply from the Bradford Coven?"

"They deny any involvement in this plot-gone-wrong."

Alain snorted derisively. "What did you expect them to say, Maman?"

Isabelle smirked. "History has proven them to be a cowardly family."

Colin resented the blanket statement and was determined to show his future mother-in-law that at least one member of the Bradford family wasn't going to flee from the challenge. The bad blood existing between the clans went back several generations. It was a tawdry tale of illicit romance and vengeful acts of violence that had no business encroaching in present day history—but it had.

After his grandmother had learned he was romantically involved with a Simon, name change notwithstanding, she'd sought help from her estranged sister, Maura, who convinced her Colin was bewitched. The only way to break the connection was through magic, but Colin was woefully unschooled in his craft. Alexandra had gone along with Maura's suggestion to invite Drake, her beloved grandson—who'd learned witchcraft at her knee—to serve as Colin's tutor. She never realized Maura would use this opportunity to extract revenge for all the slights she'd supposedly endured since Alexandra had become a royal.

Colin had resisted the suggestion at first, but after meeting Drake, who'd presented as agreeably charming, and secretly supportive of his new relationship with Alain, he'd been lulled into a false sense of security. Some would argue his Granny got what she deserved, but neither she nor Colin had any idea submerged slights would surface with astounding viciousness.

He didn't know what had transpired between his granny and Drake during his absence, but Colin wasn't blind to her faults. She could be meddling and prone to histrionics, but she'd always loved Colin unconditionally. He found it hard to believe she'd done something drastic enough to Drake, who was posing as Colin, to merit the insidious attacks that had destroyed her health.

The duke addressed Isabelle, breaking through Colin's thoughts. "May I ask a question?"

"Of course."

"Who confirmed Charlie's pregnancy?"

"Bibi."

The incredulous look exchanged between the royal couple wasn't lost on anyone.

With a raised eyebrow, Isabelle clarified. "I realize you're unfamiliar with the ways of magic, my lord, but you'll have to trust me on this. If my familiar says Charlie is pregnant, you can be sure it's true."

"Dear God," the Duke muttered.

"Indeed," Prince Sebastian intoned. "Colin, we have to contact her parents. For all we know, Charlie has already been in touch with them to break the news. They'll be expecting an engagement and a quick marriage to follow. Keeping quiet makes us complicit to this horrendous crime. They'll never forgive us when the truth is revealed."

"They'll demand retribution," Colin concluded. "As much as it hurts to say this, I'm not prepared to offer marriage to save Charlie's honor."

"You have to accept responsibility for this fiasco," the prince determined.

Desperate for support, Colin searched for Alain's hand and took heart when he felt warm fingers twining with his frigid digits.

"Charlie and I broke up long before Drake showed up. There was no way I could have anticipated her sudden reappearance in Biarritz. Nevertheless, I admit this current situation is a direct result of my getaway with Alain, but I'm certain her parents won't insist on a loveless marriage to forestall the gossips."

"I agree with Colin and accept my part in this unfortunate chain of events," Alain interjected, "but I believe full disclosure will go down a lot easier if we rescue Charlie first. Having her back in loving arms will lessen her parents' anxiety, and Charlie can weigh in on any decisions going forward."

Prince Sebastian shook his head. "I still think they'll want Colin to propose. If I were in their shoes, I'd demand satisfaction, and a wedding ring will go a long way to restoring the peace."

"I disagree," Colin stated. "Once Charlie realizes she's been duped, and my feelings for her haven't changed, she'll consider alternative plans."

"You're not seriously suggesting an abortion, are you?"

"It's not my decision to make," Colin said. "Look, I hate what's happened, and it's rather pointless to speculate without her present. What I do know for certain is I'm marrying Alain as planned."

He was met with stony silence. Diplomacy was about to ruin his life, and he didn't know how to circumvent this sudden shift in attitude without alienating his parents, but he'd be damned if Drake destroyed one more person he loved.

"Perhaps the discussion on marriage should be postponed until this current crisis is resolved," Isabelle chimed in diplomatically. "Charlie's situation is dire, but not hopeless. Let me go to Prague with Alain. We'll bring her back safely."

You're not going anywhere without me," Colin seethed.

"There is but a small difference between gallantry and foolishness," Isabelle replied. "Your magic is not fully developed, and Drake will use you as a shield against Alain and me."

Normally, Colin would cede to Isabelle's realistic assessment, but he was in no mood to be agreeable. His future was at stake, and leaving it in her hands, however capable, was as good as giving up.

"Charlie doesn't know either one of you, and she won't fall into step unless I'm there to back up our claim."

"I can be persuasive."

"I'm sorry, Isabelle. This is my fight and I insist on accompanying you and Alain. Charlie is more than a pawn in this travesty; she's my friend. I owe her an explanation in person."

"Is he always this tenacious?" Isabelle asked Alain.

"You have no idea," he responded grimly.

Isabelle wasn't used to being disobeyed and it showed. Shimmering with unconcealed fury, she addressed Prince Sebastian and the duke. "I will not be held responsible if anything happens to your son."

"I'll sign a disclaimer," Colin offered.

"Fat lot of good that'll do if you're killed," the duke pointed out. "I forbid you to go."

Colin's eyes narrowed. "I outrank you, Da. You can't stop me."

"But I can," Prince Sebastian thundered. "You have to listen to reason."

Colin stood abruptly. "Sorry, but I refuse to obey."

He was out the door before they could say another word.

Dude, that was epic.

"You have to help me, Andrew. I can't just sit back and let events unfold without my input. This is my fucking life."

So you said.

"Any idea how we're going to pull this off?

Gas up the Range Rover and grab your BF and his charming mother. We're going to need their powers if we have any hope of rescuing Charlie.

"We'll fly."

On a broomstick?

"Don't be ridiculous," Colin snapped. "I'll hire a private plane."

You will?

"Alain's done it before, and I can persuade him to do it again."

Don't be too sure.

"Then I'll drive."

In his room, Colin threw a handful of clothes into his carryall and braced for Alain's furious tirade. On cue, his fiancé slammed open the door and marched toward him, eyes flashing in anger.

"You are not coming!"

"Try to stop me."

"Dammit, *chaton*. Be reasonable for once."

"No one in their right mind will believe Drake is my doppelganger, least of all Charlie. She's a lot of things but dumb isn't one of them."

"You underestimate my power."

"Casting a spell to turn her into a mindless zombie isn't reassuring. She's already lost so much—I want to give her back some control."

"We don't know if Drake has her under his own spell."

"And the only way to snap her back to reality is with me by your side. Trust me on this, Alain. I promise to follow your instructions to the letter, but I have to be a part of this. Don't ask me to sit by idly when I'm the cause and effect of Drake's diabolical plan."

Abandoning the fight, Alain wrapped Colin in his arms. "Your grandmother started this, not you, but I share your feelings of guilt. It's the only reason I'm giving in to your impossible request."

"Thank you," Colin said softly. "I promise you won't regret it."

"Let's hope not."

"Can we hire a plane?"

"Absolutely."

"You two go ahead," Isabelle said frostily. "I'll find my own way."

Colin jumped away from Alain. "I didn't hear you come in."

Waving him away dismissively, she addressed her son. "You are a fool in love."

"I'll protect him."

"Drake won't hesitate to destroy your boy if he feels threatened. Can you say the same? You've shied away from the darker side of magic all your life. Are you prepared to cross the line if necessary?"

"I'll do whatever it takes to keep Colin safe."

"Then let's get on with it. Meet me under the astronomical clock in the old town square at six o'clock tonight."

Colin gaped. "You'll be there so soon?"

Isabelle actually rolled her eyes.

"How?" he asked.

"Stupid boy," she muttered angrily. "Alain, please enlighten your fiancé. I'll see you later."

She was gone as quickly as she'd appeared earlier, leaving a scent of lavender in her wake. Colin looked to Alain for answers.

"Astral travel," he said succinctly.

"Can you teach me how to fly?"

"It's already on the list."

"Bump it up to the top ten."

"You're impossible."

Chapter Four

THE LOW MURMUR of voices coming from the living room signaled the arrival of the midwife. Charlie contemplated getting out of bed, but the constant vomiting was taking its toll. She tried sitting up, but a wave of dizziness forced her back down. Weak and disoriented, she wished the room would stop spinning. The conversation continued and she flinched when Colin's frustrated query traveled through the thin walls of the small apartment.

"What is wrong with her?"

"Morning sickness is a normal part of pregnancy."

The stranger's standard reply fell on deaf ears.

"Do something about it," Colin ordered, slamming the door and rattling windows on his way out.

"I didn't do this by myself," Charlie whispered. She burst into tears and covered her face with both hands, too distraught to hear the bedroom door open or hear anything but her own hitching sobs.

"There, there," the stranger crooned. "Have some of this tea I brewed especially for you. It should help you sleep, if nothing else."

Charlie ventured a glance through her fingers. The old lady standing over her bed had to be pushing eighty. She had wrinkles over wrinkles and bony fingers clutched the steaming mug in a death grip. Bluish veins showed through the paper-thin skin, and Charlie had to wonder what on earth Colin was thinking by hiring this crone. If she wasn't so miserable, she'd refuse the drink.

"Are you the midwife?"

"Yes, dear. My name is Maura, and I'm here to set things right."

She sounded convincing and Charlie almost believed her, but upon closer inspection, the woman looked so insubstantial, it was hard to imagine her capable of anything.

"Have you been doing this a long time?"

Maura pursed her lips but didn't reply until after she helped Charlie to a sitting position. "I've been a midwife for over fifty years," she said in a voice meant to intimidate, rather than reassure. "There's nothing I haven't seen or done with regards to childbirth."

"I guess I'll have to trust you," Charlie conceded reluctantly. "Do you have anything to stop this infernal queasiness?"

"My special tea is infused with calming herbs," Maura stated, passing Charlie the mug. "The only way we'll know what works best for you is trial and error."

Charlie took a sip and made a face. The darkish liquid was minty, but there were other subtler flavors she couldn't identify. "It tastes like mouthwash."

"That's because of the peppermint oil," Maura explained. "It's effective against nausea and indigestion, as is chamomile, the other herb I included in the brew."

"I've had chamomile before, but this tastes different."

"Perhaps it's the passion flower I added to help you sleep."

"That must be it," Charlie replied. "I suppose I can't throw up if I'm zonked out. Won't this hurt the baby?"

"Certainly not," Maura huffed. "I would never give you anything harmful. Your nausea should taper off when you've passed your first trimester."

Charlie counted weeks in her head. "I'm close."

Scraggly gray eyebrows rose in surprise. "The prince informed me you're barely three weeks along."

"His calculations are off," Charlie said flatly.

"May I examine you?" Maura asked.

"I don't want you shoving your fingers up my cooch."

"I'm just going to listen to the baby's heartbeat with my stethoscope, take your blood pressure, and measure your stomach."

"Isn't that a doctor's job?"

"Midwives are trained to do it as well."

Charlie sighed and handed back the empty cup. She watched Maura go through the motions. The midwife frowned after she took her blood pressure.

"What's wrong?" Charlie asked nervously.

"It's a little on the high side," Maura replied. "Let me take it again."

After putting away the equipment, Maura said, "It was better the second time, but we'll keep an eye on it. You don't want it to get any worse."

"Okay."

"When was your last period?"

"I didn't get one in June."

"So, you're almost eight weeks along, not three," Maura calculated.

"Sounds about right."

"That's why I'm hearing the heartbeat already."

"Was it strong?"

Maura nodded. "Yes."

"I hope it's a boy," Charlie said wistfully. "Colin needs an heir and if I can bang one out on the first try, then my job is done. I have no plans to go through this a second time."

"Won't a girl do?"

Charlie shrugged. "As far as I know, the principality has always been ruled by men."

"You'll know the sex after an ultrasound."

"How soon can that happen?"

"A few more weeks."

"I should be fine by then, right? Walking about and eating normally?"

"Let's cross our fingers."

They both jumped at the sound of the front door slamming. Colin strode into the bedroom and took in the scene. "Are you okay?"

"I'm doing fine," Charlie said. "The baby's heartbeat is strong, despite my sickness."

"That's a relief."

Maura picked up her small bag. "I'll be back to check on you next week."

"All right."

"Try to have another cup of tea in a few hours," Maura advised. "The effect is cumulative, so you should see some good results by tomorrow. I'll leave a bunch of custom-made tea bags in the kitchen for your convenience."

Charlie nodded and watched the pair walk out of the room. She was reluctant to admit it, but she was feeling marginally better. Maybe the old biddy knew her stuff, after all. Colin returned shortly and pinned her with the look she was starting to recognize as a prelude to an outburst.

Alarmed, she asked, "What is it?"

"The midwife says you're farther along than I thought."

"Don't act like this was all my doing," she said defensively. "It was meant to be a farewell dinner, Colin. Not my fault it evolved into a fast and furious fuck. If I had known pregnancy was this awful, I would have never let you near me without a condom."

Colin's eyes narrowed. "What the hell are you talking about?"

Charlie gathered her long hair into a ponytail and reached for the elastic she kept on the nightstand. If they were going to have another argument, she wanted to look halfway decent. Colin was probably in a foul mood because they hadn't had sex in a few days. Men were so predictable, she thought in disgust. Even though Colin was her childhood friend and should be more understanding, he was ruled by his dick. The proof was in the easy way he moved on to guys after their breakup in May.

She wanted to call him out for being a selfish bastard, but she was in no position to take the moral high ground. She *had* lied and had no qualms luring Colin back into her bed, knowing all along she was already pregnant. They never talked about his crush on the scientist—who was kind of dreamy and hard to resist when it came right down to it—but she assumed it had been a rebound thing and fizzled out after the initial thrill. Would Colin have given her a second chance if she'd shown up at the palace with her pregnancy test in hand?

She'd been wrong to keep him in the dark, she thought guiltily. If she'd been honest from the beginning, she'd be in a cushy bed at the Imperial Palace with a ring on her finger instead of in this dump in the middle of Prague.

"Why aren't we back home?" she asked irritably.

Colin gripped Charlie's arm and hauled her out of bed. "What farewell dinner are you talking about?"

"You're hurting me," Charlie yelped.

Clutching her other arm, Colin shook her. "Shut the fuck up and answer my question. What dinner?"

Alarmed, Charlie tried pulling away, but it was useless. Colin had her firmly in place, so she caved, torn between shame and fear. Tears rolled down her cheeks, and her breath hitched as she admitted she was at least eight weeks pregnant.

"You were already knocked up when you sent the first text?"

She nodded. "I didn't want to blindside you with the news since we'd officially broken up."

"You bitch! And then you decided to get back into my bed with a little subterfuge, and I fell for your stupid plan."

"Colin, come on," Charlie reasoned. "I hoped to recapture the feelings we'd shared for years with my impromptu visit. And it worked, didn't it? We had a great reunion, and the sex has been amazing."

"Until the tadpole started screwing with your hormones."

"Sorry?"

He let go of her abruptly and she wobbled. Charlie watched in disbelief as Colin grappled with his temper. A muscle jumped in his cheek while he clenched his teeth. She was afraid he'd crack a molar or worse. Reaching for his hand, she said, "You're frightening me."

He grunted and shook her off.

"Why are you angry?" Charlie asked. "We've secured the monarchy. Our marriage was preordained from the beginning. Granted, it would have been better to wait until after the wedding, but your fathers will be overjoyed to hear I'm carrying your heir."

"Stop talking and let me think," Colin ordered.

"What's there to think about?"

"My future."

"You mean ours, don't you?"

He walked toward the door, then stopped and whirled around to face her. The man who stared across the short distance had brown eyes, not blue, and the icy expression changing his features rattled her composure. Charlie blinked several times and backed away slowly. Colin was evolving before her eyes, like a celebrity meme chronicling the passage of time, going from fresh-faced to world-weary within seconds. He'd been clean-shaven just a minute ago, and now he was a scruffy stranger with a downward sneer to his mouth that made her hair stand on end. Was she hallucinating? Had the morning sickness finally melted her brain? Or perhaps the midwife laced her tea with mind-bending herbs to knock her out.

"You're not Colin," she said in a shaky voice. "Who are you?"

"Your worst nightmare," he replied malevolently.

Even his tone of voice and accent were different. "Did you put drugs in the tea? What have you done to Colin?"

"I tried to kill him, but he wouldn't stay dead."

The horrific reply was delivered without inflection, and Charlie's knee-jerk reaction was loud and accusatory. "You arrogant bastard!"

In an instant, the man lifted a hand in her direction, and Charlie cried out when she felt a sharp pain pierce her gut. Clutching her stomach protectively, she sank to her knees. "Don't hurt the baby," she begged. "*Please* don't hurt us."

"I couldn't care less about that asshole's kid."

"The royals will pay any ransom you demand," Charlie said brokenly. "But you have to keep us both alive."

She looked at him hopefully and could sense a slight shift in demeanor; then it was shattered with his next threat. "Keep your mouth shut, or I'll rip out your tongue."

Charlie bit her lower lip and watched in silence as he stalked out of the room. She had a hard time believing what her eyes and ears had just witnessed. It had to be a side effect of the tea. She vowed to avoid another cup and climbed back into bed. Wrapping her arms around her belly, she fell asleep hoping things would look different after a nap.

Chapter Five

ISABELLE STRAIGHTENED HER long black skirt and wrestled with the top three buttons of her traveling cloak. It was getting harder to navigate astral travel without any mishaps, but at least her issues were simply cosmetic. Her heart rate was normal, and she wasn't in the least bit winded. While most of her contemporaries were either dead or languishing at home, the high priestess was in excellent health, albeit less nimble due to her arthritis, which stubbornly resisted magical healing. The heavy wool eventually parted, and she pushed back the hood. Tendrils of hair escaped the tortoise shell pins holding them in place, and she smoothed them back with steady hands.

Bibi's familiar call drew her attention, and she spied the snowy owl perched on the head of a moving statue decorating the Astronomical Clock, one of Prague's most famous treasures. Isabelle acknowledged her familiar's presence with a brisk nod and watched as she took off toward one of the old apartment buildings edging the town square. She circled around a few times before settling on a concrete parapet outside an upper story window.

First to arrive at the designated meeting spot, Isabelle scanned her surroundings, grateful for the opportunity to reconnoiter without Alain's interference. She loved and respected her only son, but he wasn't thinking clearly at the moment. This love affair with Colin had brought out a side of Alain he'd been keeping under wraps for most of his adult life.

It should have come as a relief to see him finally unleash his preternatural powers, but not when it was for the wrong reasons. As much as she liked the young prince, who had proven surprisingly resolute, he was standing in the way of Alain's destiny—taking Isabelle's place at the head of the coven once she passed. To be fair, Alain had never wanted any part of this legacy, and she shouldn't blame Colin, but now that Alain was fully invested in the principality of Sendorra, due to his ties with the royal family, there wasn't any hope of changing his mind.

Isabelle's offer to help chase down the warlock who'd murdered the Dowager Princess Alexandra, and almost killed Colin, was wrapped up in a heavy dose of personal gain. If she could get Alain to realize it was possible to have the best of both worlds—head the Simon Coven and be Colin's consort—he might step into both roles graciously. Instead, he was using this exigent campaign to justify his current actions. Alain intended to resume his scientific life once this was over. Isabelle had to prove by example that preternatural gifts were not a loathsome yoke around his neck, but a powerful means of protecting the people he loved, namely Colin.

Once again, she thought how different her life would have been if Angus, her second husband and Alain's father, hadn't died so young. She might have had another son or daughter who'd gladly step into her shoes, but Angus had been felled in his prime by an alleged heart attack. She'd never requested an autopsy since it was common knowledge among the covens that the Bradfords had caused his death with a deadly curse to get back at

Isabelle for casting a wasting spell on the youngest Bradford, Laura. The little bitch had started the tawdry chain of events by luring Isabelle's first husband, Rand, into her bed. When they'd been discovered, the Bradford patriarch had killed the cheating son of a whore in a *hunting accident.* Isabelle would have preferred to castrate the lying bastard with her own hands, but never got the chance. Squeezing the life out of Laura in tiny increments hadn't been quite as satisfactory.

It was an antiquated tale of lust and revenge in a repeating loop that had no place in this age of mobile phones and internet. Nonetheless, it had been real at the time, and Isabelle hadn't remarried in case her third husband suffer the same fate. She'd had countless lovers through the years but hadn't thought to have a child out of wedlock. Alain had been so exceptional it never crossed her mind. The first time he'd insisted on distancing himself from the coven, she'd attributed his shocking behavior to teenage angst. He'd compounded his revolt by announcing he was bisexual and having children was so far down on his list of priorities it might as well be nonexistent.

Isabelle gave him wide berth while he was in school and through most of his twenties. Occasionally she'd slip and succumb to matchmaking, but Alain stubbornly refused to be swayed. Any hope she had of gaining a grandchild to take Alain's place in the coven was dashed when he fell in love with Colin.

The young prince—a mere child in her eyes—had his own set of procreation issues to contend with, and like it or not, the biological facts were irrefutable. Sendorra needed an heir and Alain couldn't provide one. She wanted a grandchild and Colin, despite his intersex status, was indispensable and forbidden to get pregnant. It was a horrible puzzle she couldn't resolve, and it made her feel like a failure as a mother, and more importantly, as a high priestess. With hundreds of spells at her fingertips, she couldn't find a way out of this conundrum.

A loud hoot broke through her thoughts, and she glanced up at Bibi who hadn't moved from her earlier spot. Isabelle acknowledged the warning with a hand wave and followed the bird's line of sight. A couple were exiting one of the apartment alcoves. The older woman she recognized as Maura, the eldest Bradford sister, and the young man by her side could only be Drake. His resemblance to Colin was uncanny. It would take the simplest of spells to alter one's perception once he donned his disguise. Poor Charlotte never stood a chance.

Instead of following the pair, Isabelle waited until they disappeared around a corner, and she walked briskly toward the old building. She could feel the protective wards grow in strength as she approached, but the Bradfords were no match for her, and a muttered incantation blasted away the invisible shield with little effort.

She stepped into the foyer and took note of the decor. Prague was a city of architectural contrasts, and many of the grander edifices had suffered during the communist-occupied years. Whoever owned this property had restored the Art Nouveau interior with a keen eye and deep pockets. Marble flooring, intricate light fixtures and etched mirrors provided a welcoming atmosphere, as did the tiny elevator, which saved her from the endless flights of stairs edged by an ornate wrought iron railing. Not that she wasn't capable of the task, but Isabelle preferred to conserve her strength in case there was something more challenging awaiting her upstairs.

She confronted another basic ward and broke through easily. Did they think their simple spells could keep someone like her away? The apartment itself was a disappointment, decorated with transients in mind. Upholstery was chosen for its durability rather than esthetic value. It reeked of stale booze, leftovers, and the unmistakable odor of sickness. Housekeeping must not be part of the rent, she thought with distaste. Underneath Drake's many affectations was a run-of-the-mill pig who probably never washed a dirty dish in his life.

Isabelle made sure to pick up her skirt and avoided touching anything. She was wearing expensive kid leather gloves and sighed with irritation when she realized they'd end up in a trash bin once she finished exploring. There was no way in hell she was taking them off to turn the doorknob. The stench was stronger in the bedroom, and the lump under the covers had to be Princess Charlotte. The room was illuminated by a tiny gap in the window covering, and with a flick of her wrist, the floor-length drapes parted without a sound. Sunlight flooded the room and Isabelle made a moue of disgust at seeing the abominable state of neglect. The girl had been using a tin wastebasket when she couldn't make it to the bathroom, and it was overflowing. Isabelle gagged and quickly muttered an incantation. In the blink of an eye, the room was put to rights, and after she took a breath of clean air, she realized belatedly that she'd broken the first rule of stealth. Once Drake saw the pristine apartment, he'd know there'd been an intruder, and her magical thumbprint was unmistakable.

Unperturbed, Isabelle sat on the edge of the bed and lightly poked the sleeping girl.

"Don't hurt me," squeaked a panicked voice.

"I'll do no such thing," Isabelle retorted.

Large eyes on a pale face peered over the lowered duvet. "Who are you?"

"My name is Isabelle Simon, and I've come to take you home."

"Did my parents send you?"

"No, child. I'm here on behalf of Prince Colin."

"But…"

Charlie's voice trailed off as she tried to make sense of Isabelle's reply.

"I realize things are confusing at the moment, but if you'll get dressed, I can take you to Colin, and he'll explain why we have to make haste."

"He said we couldn't go back to Navarre yet. Is he still angry? Is the engagement off?" she asked, looking perplexed.

Isabelle sighed, hating to be the bearer of bad news, but there was no getting around it. "You've been duped."

"Sorry?"

"Colin is not the man who impregnated you."

Charlie sucked in a shocked breath. She threw off the covers, sat up, and swung her legs off the bed but swayed as she got to her feet. She plopped back down and fell against the pillows. When Isabelle reached out to help, she pushed her away.

"Don't touch me!"

Isabelle retreated, keeping her eyes on the distraught princess. "As you wish."

"You're crazy," Charlie quavered. "I'm not sure what's going on, but I know Colin fathered my child."

"You think he did."

"I was there!" The fear was replaced with anger, and in a steadier voice, she asserted, "We did it on a sofa at the

Imperial Palace the night we broke up. Granted, we were both shitfaced, but a lot of babies are made under the influence. This one is no different."

Isabelle's cool demeanor shifted slightly. "We were under the impression this was a recent event."

Charlie didn't reply.

"Does Drake know?"

"Who in the ever-loving fuck is Drake?"

"The man who's been keeping you locked away like a treasure."

"Are you high?"

Isabelle sniffed loudly. "The only one who's delusional is you. Anyone with half a brain can tell the difference between Colin and his cousin, Drake. I'm surprised you were so easily fooled by the charade."

"You're fucking serious?"

"As the proverbial heart attack," Isabelle responded dryly. "Let me ask you one more time. Do you want to be rescued or not? I couldn't care less what you decide, but Colin seems to think you're worth the trouble."

"Colin sent you?" Charlie asked dubiously. "For real?"

"Do you want to go home?"

"I need my mother."

"I'll take that as a yes. Can you get dressed without my help?"

Charlie nodded and got out of bed. In a stained nightgown with greasy strands of hair hanging down her back, she looked nothing like a princess. Her earlier bravado was nowhere in sight as she inched her way to the bathroom on unsteady feet. Isabelle stayed close but didn't touch her in case she had a change of heart. She did give her a magical boost to help her along when she wobbled.

In the bathroom, Charlie tied her hair back with an elastic band and cleaned her face and teeth. Looking much improved, Isabelle offered to get her a change of clothing.

"Sit here and catch your breath," Isabelle suggested. "You look a little winded."

Charlie nodded and sat on the lowered toilet seat.

"How far along are you?" Isabelle had to ask. It was her duty to verify the accuracy of Charlie's claim, so Colin would understand the gravity of the situation. Alain would resent her for meddling, but the outcome wouldn't change for the better if she kept her nose out of this wretched affair.

"I dunno," Charlie replied dully. "We broke up in late May, and I never saw my period again. Eight or nine weeks?"

"Have you felt the baby quicken?"

"Sorry?"

"Has the baby moved yet?"

"What does it feel like?"

"A flutter."

Charlie shook her head. Looking up, she asked earnestly, "Have you had kids?"

"One."

"Is it exciting to feel movement?"

Isabelle smiled. "It's magical."

"Then this is all worth it."

"Definitely," Isabelle assured her. "I'll be right back."

Isabelle froze upon entering the bedroom. Drake was standing at the foot of the bed, arms akimbo. "Who are you?"

"Isabelle Simon."

"Granny did say you might turn up."

"I'm here to take Charlie off your hands."

"Why on earth would I give up my trump card?"

"Do you know the child isn't yours?"

Drake shrugged. "It only makes the brat more valuable. How much would the royals pay to get them back in one piece?"

"They might let you live."

"You didn't answer my question," Drake spat. "I have no intention of releasing Charlie or her bastard if they don't pay up."

"Really, Drake? You've gone through all this trouble for money?"

"My motives are none of your business," Drake replied tersely. "Your job is to get a message to Colin."

"And if I refuse?"

"You'll end up like the late Dowager."

Isabelle cackled. "Your granny must not have given you any background on me. We can do this easily, or you can play the fool like the rest of the Bradfords and attempt to stop me. What'll it be?"

There was a loud wail from inside the bathroom and a thud.

"Oops," Drake said, raising one eyebrow.

"You bastard," Isabelle snarled after realizing he'd attacked Charlie subliminally. "Leave her alone."

"She'll bleed out if you lift your pinkie in my direction," Drake threatened. "Make no mistake, Isabelle. My only interest in keeping those two alive is monetary. Once they've lost their usefulness, I won't hesitate to kill her. This fight isn't between you and me. Stay out of it or end up collateral damage."

"I don't respond to threats," Isabelle said, adding, "Not in a good way. You've crossed the line, and you'll pay when you least expect it. In the meantime, I'll relay your message. Harm one hair on the girl's head and negotiations are off the table. Make sure she gets some medical help. She's severely dehydrated and malnourished. You won't have to kill the child at this rate. She'll miscarry if you don't do the right thing."

"Blah, blah," Drake said, waving away her concerns. "Granny's got this under control."

"Your gran couldn't find her way out of a box," Isabelle said with disdain.

"Shut up." Like a petulant child, Drake sent a fireball her way.

She repelled it with one of her own, and the carpet around Drake smoldered.

"Don't even think about it," she warned. "I can immolate you before you realize you're dead."

The malevolent glint in his eyes didn't disappear, but he raised both hands in mock surrender.

Isabelle disappeared in a swirl of gray smoke.

Chapter Six

THEY WERE WAITING underneath the Astronomical Clock as agreed, trying to blend into the milling crowd. It was a good place to hide in plain sight, as Isabelle had pointed out when she suggested the location, but it was inconvenient putting up with tourists and their infernal cameras. Alain detested photo ops and Colin didn't care for them either. To avoid recognition, they wore hoodies and dark glasses, looking more like a couple of thugs instead of a prince and his fiancé.

Isabelle materialized and stumbled into Alain who held her in his steadying arms. Thanks to her protective shield, the only one who noticed was Colin.

"Honestly, Maman. Do you always have to make a grand entrance?"

"You'd be a little out of breath, too, if you were trying to outrun a deranged warlock."

"What happened?"

"Let's find a café, and I'll tell you over some hot tea and croissants."

Impatiently, Colin asked, "Did you see Charlie?"

"All in good time," Isabelle replied.

Prepared to unleash an epic rant, Colin hesitated. Isabelle was his future mother-in-law and the high priestess of the Simon Coven. There was no use pulling the royal card if it would only be met with ridicule. She moved at her own pace and, as Alain pointed out many times, was prone to drama. Isabelle enjoyed the element of surprise, and information was usually shared at her discretion.

With Andrew hovering by his side, and Bibi flying overhead, it was obvious they weren't here to take in the sights, but Colin wisely decided to temper his need-to-be-in-charge attitude. Nonetheless, he couldn't resist asking, "Please, Isabelle. Answer one thing, and I'll wait for the recap. Did you see Charlie?"

She nodded but didn't elaborate.

He bit his tongue and followed meekly behind mother and son as they shouldered past the crowds toward Café Imperial, a favored local haunt within walking distance. The tantalizing aroma of freshly baked bread, roasted coffee beans, along with eggs and sausage reminded Colin he hadn't eaten since last night. He could use something hearty to hold him until dinner.

After placing their orders, the waitress poured tea and coffee in their respective cups. Isabelle took her time adding cream and a lump of sugar to her black tea, and even longer stirring the mixture. Colin wanted to strangle her. She thanked the waitress for the chocolate-filled croissants and full English breakfasts for Alain and Colin. As he wolfed down his food, he watched Isabelle daintily tear off a piece of the flaky treat and pop it in her mouth. She sighed with genuine pleasure as she savored each bite, chewing and swallowing with purposeful ease, as if she had all the time in the world. Colin's plate was empty when Isabelle sipped the last of her tea and dabbed the corners of her mouth with a linen napkin.

"For pity's sake," Alain snapped, dropping his utensils on the white china with a clatter. "Can't you see we're dying here?"

Lowering her napkin, Isabelle gave her son a piercing look. "I'm afraid I bring bad tidings, and I didn't want to ruin your appetite."

"Tell us," Colin pleaded from his side of the table.

"Charlie is convinced the child is yours, Colin. Not Drake's."

Colin was on his feet in an instant. "She's lying."

Isabelle lifted her hand in reproach. "Sit down and listen before you go off half-cocked."

"Please, *chaton*," Alain urged through tight lips.

"Charlie's crazy," Colin maintained as he sank back on his chair. "I haven't slept with anyone since I met you."

Alain faced Isabelle rather than meet Colin's earnest gaze.

"Maman, did she back up her assertion in a credible way?"

"Charlie alleges she and Colin had breakup sex, and this pregnancy is the result. She's almost nine weeks pregnant."

Colin was hurled back to the night in late May when they'd had unprotected sex after a tearful goodbye. He'd met her for dinner and hadn't been prepared for anything more than a civilized conversation between old friends. Sex had been the last thing on his mind, but they'd started reminiscing, and after the second bottle of wine, their brains shut down and raging hormones took over. Even if he'd thought to carry a condom, they were too far gone to use it. Could something so random and forgettable generate another life? Shaking his head in denial, he said, "I don't believe it. This has to be another one of Drake's maneuvers."

"Did you sleep with her on the night in question?" Alain asked in a soft voice.

Colin's heart sank. The disappointment on Alain's face was unmistakable, but he couldn't lie. "Yes."

"So, it's possible the child *is* yours."

Colin shrugged helplessly. "We won't know without a paternity test."

"You should insist on it before you negotiate with Drake," Isabelle counseled.

"I'm rescuing her regardless," Colin said. "It doesn't matter if it's my kid or Drake's. I'm not leaving her with him."

"I agree," Isabelle said. "But asking for proof is the next logical step. Both set of parents—yours and hers—will want to know if she's carrying your heir."

"What if Drake refuses?" Alain asked.

"It's in his best interest to prove the child is Colin's," Isabelle said practically.

"I dunno," Colin remarked grimly. "It might raise the stakes, but you didn't see the look of satisfaction on his face when he bragged about bedding Charlie. He'll see this as another failure rather than a triumph."

"True," Isabelle granted. "But enormous wealth should soothe his wounded ego."

"I don't trust him," Alain said. "Especially if the child isn't his. He'll milk this for all its worth, and when the cow dries up, he'll demand more. People like Drake are never satisfied. He may end up killing Charlie and her baby out of spite."

"Speaking of dying," Isabelle noted. "The girl needs medical attention. She's not well, and Drake is relying on his grandmother instead of a professional."

"What's wrong with her?" Colin asked.

"Terrible morning sickness. She's too thin and there comes a point when only an IV will work to restore her electrolytes. Who knows what this is doing to the fetus?"

"God."

"This isn't your fault, Colin," Alain said.

"You know I put her in harm's way when we took off on our vacay, and if I did knock her up, intentionally or not, this is on me. I have to rescue her."

"You and what army?" Isabelle asked mockingly.

"Sheath your claws," Alain scolded. "We can figure this out without resorting to cruelty."

"You seem rather calm, considering your position as royal consort is in jeopardy."

"What are you talking about?" Colin said frigidly. "Alain is still my fiancé."

"I hate to point out the obvious, but they'll force you to marry Charlie to make sure the child isn't born a bastard."

"Because a bastard can't claim the throne," Colin said bitterly. "Fuck my life."

Alain stood and threw his credit card on the table. "I need to go for a walk. Let's meet at our hotel in an hour to formulate a plan."

"*D'accord,*" Isabelle said, reaching for his card.

"May I tag along?" Colin asked.

Alain nodded.

Colin swallowed hard. He was certain Alain would tell him to fuck off, but his response, however lukewarm, was a million times better. With fingers intertwined, they walked out of the restaurant and silently headed toward Charles Bridge.

The cobblestone bridge named after King Charles IV, who commissioned the structure, crossed the river Vitava to Prague Castle in old town. It was mainly a tourist attraction and only used by pedestrians. Impressive statuary and ornate lampposts lined both sides of the bridge, but Colin was too miserable to sightsee. Alain, too, seemed wrapped in his own thoughts, and Colin was tempted to probe, but like Isabelle, Alain wouldn't comment until he was good and ready.

Midway over the river, Alain paused and drew Colin toward the balustrade. With their arms resting on the concrete, they watched barges hauling products in and out of the city, and squat tourist boats filled to bursting with visitors from all over the world.

Frustrated and tired of waiting, Colin blurted, "I'm sorry."

"I know," Alain said without reproach. "You had no idea a quick tumble would have such far-reaching consequences."

"She could be lying," Colin said, although he realized the stupidity of his statement. "Then again, why would she?"

"Indeed. For weeks Charlie's been under the impression she's back in your good graces. If this was some devious plot on her part, it would have played out differently."

"How do you figure?"

"She would have informed her parents the moment she realized she was pregnant and let them iron out the details. Instead, she made a concerted effort to win you back. I believe she genuinely loves you and hoped the reunion would happen organically. Drake was a complication none of us could foresee."

"Let's kill the motherfucker and be done with it," Colin said imperially. "No one will press charges when they find out what he did to Granny and what he's trying to do with Charlie."

"If it were only so simple," Alain said. "We have to catch him off guard, for one thing, and Charlie will still be pregnant whether Drake lives or dies."

"This is beyond fucked!"

"Especially when I've already had somewhat of a preview."

"What are you talking about, Alain?"

"Remember the premonition I had when we first met?"

"The one which made you faint?"

He nodded.

"You said you didn't remember much."

"I remember a lot of blood and a dead child."

"No," Colin whispered. "Do you think it was Charlie?"

"Who else could it be, *chaton*? I'm incapable of getting pregnant, and your body will only accommodate a child with medical intervention. It has to be her."

"Will she die?"

"I honestly don't know."

"Shit."

"I'm hoping we can circumnavigate the tragedy by getting her to a hospital. If she has a healthy pregnancy, it stands to reason she'll have a successful delivery."

"What about us?"

"There is no us if you marry Charlie."

"No."

Colin threw himself in Alain's arms and shook. There was no way he'd accept this outcome. After finally receiving his parents' blessing on their engagement, and with Isabelle on board with the plan, he couldn't allow a surprise pregnancy to upend his life.

"I won't marry her."

His defiant words broke on a sob, and he fell apart in the middle of the most trafficked landmark in Prague. Alain protected them from prying eyes with an invisibility shield and drew him closer, hoping the physical contact would ease some of the pain.

They silently watched the boats meander down the river like this was another ordinary day when, in fact, it was the worst day of his life. The wonderful future he'd planned with Alain by his side was falling apart, and there was nothing he could do to make a difference.

Chapter Seven

DRAKE LIFTED CHARLIE off the floor, where she'd been lying since he sent a telepathic zap her way. She looked out of it, and he wondered if maybe he'd gone too far. There would be no satisfaction if his precious hostage died before money exchanged hands. Carrying her back to bed, he propped her against a stack of pillows and lightly slapped her face, relieved as a spark of recognition flooded her eyes, followed immediately by a glimmer of fear. Charlie shrank away from his touch.

"Don't tell me you're buying into Isabelle's bullshit," Drake said, determined to keep up the Colin charade. Impotent anger had led to a misguided slip the other day, and now he was paying the price. If he wanted a cooperative Charlie, he'd have to convince her she'd imagined their entire exchange. "She's a senile bitch who's got a personal vendetta against my family."

Unconvinced, Charlie said, "I'm not sure who she is, but the woman insisted you aren't Colin. Now I'm wondering the same thing. You've been acting weird for weeks, and I swear you looked different..."

"Me?" Drake challenged. "Sorry if I haven't been myself lately, but this is on you, not me. It's hard to feel romantic, or be inspired to put my best foot forward, when the woman you love reeks of vomit. I guess I'm following your lead."

"I'm not doing this on purpose," Charlie whined. "You honestly think I'm enjoying myself? I want to look good for you, but it's hard when I feel like crap. And I wish you'd stop shaming me."

Drake put on his best face—Colin's finest good looks—and attempted to placate Charlie. "I apologize for being a dick, but I'm new to this, as well. I have no idea how to deal with a pregnant woman. One minute we're humping like rabbits, and then you shove me away like I have the plague. If I've been a little testy it's because I'm also adjusting to our new situation."

"I guess it's been a little crazy around here."

"No shit," he replied. "How about we start over? I'll be more supportive if you try to pull it together. You're dehydrated and probably hallucinating."

"You think it's all in my head?"

"If you're not getting basic nutrients, there's no telling how it'll affect your brain cells. And what about the baby? You need to force yourself to eat or suffer the consequences."

"Perhaps we should see a real doctor?"

"Will you feel better if I set up an appointment?"

"Don't send me to another midwife," Charlie insisted. "Maura is nice, but she hasn't been able to stop the morning sickness with herbs. I need real medicine."

"I'll see what I can do," Drake said, dripping with concern. "In the meantime, will you promise to get these crazy ideas out of your head? I'm Colin, your one true love, not some imagined bogeyman."

With glittering eyes, Charlie nodded. "That's more like it. The Colin I know would never hurt me."

"I'm under a lot of pressure," Drake added. "There's been stuff on the internet about Granny I need to check out. I think she might be dying."

"Oh my God," Charlie exclaimed. "No wonder you've been acting so strange. Shouldn't we go back to Sendorra immediately?"

"I'm going to call home and feel them out."

"Good idea. They'll be worried about the dowager, so our escapade might not be a priority," Charlie reasoned. "Let them know we're safe."

"I will," Drake assured her. "Meanwhile, I'd like you to try to eat something."

"I promise."

Drake added a mild sleeping potion to the herb tea, and he watched with satisfaction when Charlie managed to keep it down with a few slices of a pear and a wedge of cheese. After she dozed off, he called Maura.

"Get over here as soon as possible."

"Is Charlie okay?"

"Isabelle Simon paid me a visit."

"Blessed Goddess."

"We'll need more than your Goddess to stay ahead of the game."

"I'll be there shortly."

While he waited for his grandmother, Drake worked out a tentative plan, but it meant traveling, and he wasn't sure Charlie could handle a long car ride. He browsed through his contacts and smiled when he spied a familiar name. Dr. Raoul Davies, a charismatic blend of Latino good looks and upper-crust British mannerisms was an acquaintance who'd become a fast friend over the years. A talented plastic surgeon, Raoul had opened a clinic in Drake's hometown, where his patients, who came from the upper echelon of society, could recuperate after their procedures. The man's professional credentials were impeccable, but his moral compass was dodgy at best, and nonexistent when a request for opioids crossed over the legal limit. Somehow, he managed to stay under the police radar, an inestimable talent Drake found particularly useful.

Born in Sonora, Mexico, Raoul Gonzales had escaped the predictable fate—drugs, imprisonment, and early death—which had befallen a large number of his childhood friends. His mother had snared a clueless Brit tourist, married him in a rushed ceremony, and escaped with her ten-year-old son, leaving poverty and violence behind. Raoul's biological father had long since died of an overdose, so there were no impediments to keep the new family from moving to London.

Determined to raise a law-abiding son, they dropped Gonzales the minute the adoption papers were finalized and steered him toward a career in medicine. What his mother and new father hadn't realized was a decade within close proximity to one of the most powerful drug trafficking organizations in the world was more than enough time to warp the purest of hearts. Young Raoul had already assimilated the Sonoran mindset, and skirting the law was a game he enjoyed playing while he took great pains to conform to the rigorous standards set forth by his mentors. When finances had become an issue while he was still in college, he took matters into his own hands and picked up the phone. All he needed was a name to reconnect with his nefarious past—easily obtainable via social media—and the pipeline flowed with illicit drugs.

Drake wasn't sure he could convince Raoul to pay a house call, but he might consent to monitoring Charlie in Bruges if the price was right. As predicted, the good doctor refused to fly to Prague, but he made arrangements for a private charter to transport Drake and Charlie to his clinic on the outskirts of town. Drake's reluctance to job out anything, which would deplete his ill-gotten stash, was quickly snuffed out after he listened to Raoul's detailed arrangements. The man was a pro and familiar with subterfuge. Moreover, he could be counted on to take Charlie's rants with a grain of salt.

By the time Maura arrived, Drake had packed his and Charlie's belongings and arranged for a taxi to drive them to the airport.

"Are you sure you can trust this man?" Maura asked. "I'd hate to see this blow up in your face if he learns you're dealing with royal coffers."

"Oh, please. Raoul is a millionaire many times over. He doesn't need the money or the drama."

"Then why is he helping you?"

"We've had a symbiotic relationship for years. I recommend his services to anyone who asks, and he gives me a small commission."

"May I accompany you?"

Drake gave it some thought but declined her offer. "No. I want you to stay in the area and be my decoy. If they see you wandering around the city, they'll never suspect Charlie and I are gone."

"Who's with Isabelle?"

"Her son and Colin."

She narrowed her eyes. "Can I kill them and be done with it?"

Drake looked dubious. "Wait until I'm safely installed at the clinic before you do anything. I'm worried you might not be a match for three powerful witches."

"Colin's powers aren't fully developed, and I'm sure I can handle Alain. It's Isabelle who might pose a threat."

"Might?" Drake jeered. "Put your affairs in order if you're going to make an attempt on her life."

"You have such a low opinion of me," Maura said haughtily. "Must I remind you that I've been a practicing witch long before you were born? Who taught you how to cast your first spell? Wasn't it me who gave you all the advantages by helping you perfect your craft? You wouldn't have come this far in life if not for me."

Drake shook his head in resignation. "Have it your way, Granny. Do what you want, and I wish you good luck."

"Luck has nothing to do with it."

"Our coven has been trying to get rid of Isabelle for decades," Drake reminded her. "What makes you think it'll be different this time?"

"She's older and I've been tracking her for so long I can predict her movements."

"Don't underestimate her, Granny. There's nothing predictable about Isabelle. In fact, the key to her longevity has been her capricious and volatile behavior. No one has been able to keep up with the mood swings, and I sincerely doubt you'll succeed."

"We'll see," Maura said grimly.

"I've cleared my tab with the property manager, so there shouldn't be any money issues going forward."

"Thank you."

"Are you going to check into a hotel?" Drake asked.

"The less I reveal, the better. They can't squeeze out information you don't have."

"Will you at least keep your fucking phone close at hand? You're never around when I call, which defeats the whole purpose of a mobile phone."

"So you've said," Maura replied irritably.

"Because you don't listen," Drake snapped.

"I promise to stay in contact."

"Okay," Drake said, reining in the irritation. "Any suggestions on how to get Charlie to the plane without a major meltdown?"

"Tell her you're going home."

"And give her more of your special tea onboard?"

"Now you're talking sense."

"Would you mind getting her up and dressed for the trip?"

"So, I *am* good for something after all."

"Don't be melodramatic, Granny. Watching your saggy behind is my way of showing I care."

"You're an insolent piece of work."

"Thanks to you."

It didn't take Maura long to get Charlie ready. Granted, she was half out of it and looked nothing like the woman he'd seduced back in June, but she was standing on her own two feet and didn't stink. Her T-shirt appeared two sizes too small against her swollen breasts, and the baby bump was distinctly visible.

"You look good," Drake lied. "It's hard to tell how much your stomach has grown in a prone position."

She rubbed her tummy protectively. "I'm showing?"

Drake nodded.

"The first thing I'm doing after we're settled is going on a shopping spree," Charlie said with more enthusiasm than he'd seen in weeks. "All my clothes are tight."

"I'm sure it can be arranged."

"Did you tell them I'm pregnant?"

"Actually, I didn't," Drake admitted. "It seems Granny has taken a turn for the worst, and they don't expect her to live through the night."

"I'm so sorry, Colin. Maybe we shouldn't stay at the palace tonight."

"Good girl," Drake said condescendingly. "You're starting to read my mind."

"What did I say?"

"Now's not the time to waltz in and announce the pregnancy. I want it to be a happy occasion, not overshadowed by Granny's tragedy."

"I understand," Charlie said. "Did you make other arrangements?"

"Yes. We'll be staying at a friend's private clinic outside Bruges. This way they can keep a good eye on you and the baby while we wait for news."

"A real doctor will take over my care?" Charlie glanced at Maura looking contrite. "You've been kind, but I think it's time for an obstetrician to step in."

"No offense taken, my dear. I served my purpose here in Prague."

Charlie impulsively hugged her goodbye. "Does Colin have your contact information? I'm sure my parents will want to thank you for your services."

"Colin has already paid me."

"They'll want to give you something extra," Charlie said. "You've been so helpful."

Maura didn't even flinch, soaking up the undeserved praise. "Colin knows how to reach me."

"Come on," Drake said impatiently. "The cab's already downstairs."

Chapter Eight

THE ROAR OF revving engines followed by an abrupt change in air pressure wrenched Charlie out of her drug-induced slumber. When she opened her eyes to look around, nothing seemed familiar except for Colin, who was buckled into the seat beside hers. She tried swallowing to relieve the tightness in her ears, but she was too dehydrated to dredge up an ounce of spit. She tapped his arm. "May I have some water?"

Wordlessly, he handed her the bottle in his hand.

She drank greedily, grateful for the cool liquid and the instant relief as her ears *popped*. She handed back the empty bottle and took in her surroundings. "This isn't your plane."

"How'd you guess?"

"I don't see your royal insignia anywhere," she commented. "Who owns it?"

"A friend. Are you feeling better?"

"The nausea is gone, but I can barely keep my eyes open. How long is the flight?"

"A couple of hours," he said. "You've got time to take another nap."

"Why am I so tired?"

"Pregnant much?"

She hit him playfully on the arm. "Where are you taking me?"

"I already told you," Drake clipped. "There's a clinic outside Bruges run by the owner of this plane. He's a famous plastic surgeon with rich patients who expect royal treatment whenever they're 'indisposed.' Pickup is usually part of his service, be it by limo or private jet."

"La-di-da," Charlie exclaimed, twirling her little finger. "How's a plastic surgeon going to help with my morning sickness?"

"He's a qualified physician, Charlie. Pregnancy is nothing compared to the kind of work he does. I'm sure he'll figure out what you need until we can go home," he lied smoothly.

"Why not go straight to Sendorra?"

"No one will be in the right frame of mind to deal with our issues."

"Maybe your parents, but mine will be so glad to see me they won't give a shit about etiquette. Have the pilot take us to Navarre. Once they learn I'm carrying your heir, they'll overlook my summer escapade."

"Perhaps."

"You don't sound confident."

"Parents are unpredictable, babe. Especially in a crisis. It's best not to assume anything."

"So?"

"Let's stick to my original plan. We'll lie low in Bruges until the coast is clear."

"I think you're being overly dramatic, but I'm too tired to argue. Wake me up before we land so I can make myself presentable."

"No problem."

Drake was glad he'd thought to spike the bottled water with some of Maura's sleeping potion. He'd been assured the herbs wouldn't harm the fetus, but they would keep Charlie fogged up enough to avoid more questions. He needed her to remain compliant, and the less she suspected the better.

If Raoul learned the true nature of their visit, he would send Drake and his precious cargo packing. Turning a blind eye to illegal drugs was one thing, but blackmail and kidnapping raised the stakes to a much higher level. Drake was certain his buddy wouldn't jeopardize his career by aiding and abetting such a heinous crime.

Drake's decision to barter Charlie and her unborn child was a work in progress. Things were happening so fast he was simply reacting, but when Isabelle showed up at his apartment, he realized his survival was at stake, and it was time to formulate a viable plan. Leaving Charlie behind would have been the right thing to do, and might buy him some time, but he was too selfish to give her up. Why should he get stiffed after all the effort he'd put into this charade? The dowager's death had been an unfortunate complication, although to be fair, she was older than dirt and already on friendly terms with the grim reaper before he even showed up. Giving her the fatal nudge saved the royals from dealing with a senior on the verge of dementia. They should thank him for being merciful instead of chasing him down like some rabid animal

A few minutes before landing, he elbowed Charlie awake.

Blinking in confusion, she looked around in alarm. "What's happening?"

Dammit, Drake thought irritably. Did the stupid potion quit working already?

"I already told you, babe. We're on a private plane, and we'll be at our destination shortly. Do you need to use the restroom to freshen up?"

She nodded and unbuckled. "Come with me?"

Drake signaled for the flight attendant. "Would you help the princess, please?"

"Of course."

If Charlie had invited him to partake in the mile-high club, he might have accompanied her, but he'd sooner fuck a blow-up doll than touch her in this condition. Pregnant women were disgusting.

The waiting limousine was fit for royalty, and Drake sensed a shift in Charlie's attitude. If Raoul catered to this level of rich and famous, one could only assume he'd be the best in his field. Drake had never been to the clinic, but he had no doubt it would be equally impressive. Thankfully, it met his and Charlie's expectations, and when Raoul waltzed in and kissed her hand, turning on his swoony charm, she was won over.

He listened to her heartbeat and took her blood pressure, frowning when he was done.

"You look worried," Charlie commented.

"Your blood pressure is too high for someone so young."

"She's pregnant," Drake interjected.

"That explains some of it; on the other hand, it's even more worrisome," Raoul stressed. "We need to get your levels back to normal. Bed rest and a proper diet will help. Is the nausea still tormenting you?"

"How'd you know I've been sick?"

"Rapid heart rate and poor skin elasticity are a dead giveaway. Let's see if I can find the perfect combination of supplements to turn things around. Has anyone done an ultrasound yet?"

"No," Charlie replied. "You're the first doctor who's examined me."

Raoul glared at Drake.

"It's complicated," Drake replied stiffly.

"You'll have to enlighten me later. Right now, I have to attend to my patient."

Drake watched them whisk Charlie away, and he breathed a sigh of relief. He wasn't looking forward to Raoul's lecture, but he was glad to be rid of the responsibility of caring for a woman who no longer held his interest in any way but monetary. Whatever romantic feelings he'd harbored originally had been shattered by her betrayal. Granted, she had no idea she was cheating, but Drake was infuriated for having been duped by an ordinary human no less. It would be the last time he let his cock do the thinking. From here on it was each man for himself, and he was at the top of the food chain.

He was scrolling through his phone when the door opened, and an irritated Raoul stormed in.

"What are you playing at, Drake?"

"What do you mean?"

"She keeps calling you by another name. Are you the man I know, or have I been dealing with an impersonator all these years?"

Drake rolled his eyes. "Don't buy into any of her shit. I've heard pregnant women get stupid at some point. Lately, Charlie's been saying the oddest things."

Raoul didn't look convinced.

"Let it go, Raoul."

"Are the cops after you?"

Drake shook his head. "It's her family."

"Did you kidnap the girl?"

"Not really," Drake hedged. "Is she going to be okay? Nausea has been plaguing her from the beginning."

"Nausea and vomiting are a normal part of pregnancy," Raoul explained. "Charlie has a condition called hyperemesis gravidarum."

"Is it contagious?" Drake asked with a grimace.

"Don't be ridiculous. She's reacting poorly to the changes in hormonal levels, and her symptoms—severe nausea, vomiting, weight loss, rapid heart rate, and dehydration—are in keeping with her condition. If left untreated, miscarriage is a possibility. Why did you wait so long to get medical attention?"

Drake sighed. "It's complicated, buddy. Just fix her."

"You keep saying that, but it does me no good. Is she here against her will?"

"No."

"I know you're hiding something," Raoul grumbled. "You've got the familiar cagey look."

"Says the man who routinely skirts the letter of the law," Drake drawled.

"Dealing drugs is one thing," Raoul said. "Kidnapping is reprehensible, and furthermore, it's punishable by death. I want nothing to do with this scheme of yours."

"I only need you for the short term."

"As soon as Charlie is fit to travel, I want you both gone. We'll start an IV line to get her fluids regulated. In the meantime, find a hotel or somewhere else to stay. You're not welcome here."

"Your selective conscience is annoying, Raoul. Go ahead and play the dutiful doctor if you must. In the meantime, I will find a suitable hotel. Tell Charlie I'll be back to visit later in the afternoon."

Raoul didn't bother to reply, and Drake watched him walk away with purposeful strides. Did the guy honestly think Drake would seek him out if he wasn't engaged in something illegal? Their entire relationship had been built on drug trafficking in one form or another. Granted, Raoul wasn't an actual player, but he'd set up the connections, and looked the other way, if one of his patients needed a fix. This censorious attitude was tiresome. Drake had approached him hoping for an ally, and it wasn't working according to plan. It seemed the goddess was conspiring against him for some reason. He was due for a break, but at the moment, he was fresh out of ideas.

Calling in a few favors, he checked into the Dukes Palace, a five-star hotel in the center of Bruges. It was affordable, with the industry discount, and the first thing he did was set up an appointment for a full-body massage. With a few knowing winks, and the usual money exchange, Sandrine showed up at his door an hour later, promising a happy ending. A pleasant way to pass the time, a soothing massage took his mind off his current dilemma, until his phone rang around five in the afternoon. It was Raoul.

"You need to get your ass over here."

"What happened?"

"The ultrasound revealed something surprising."

Drake scoffed. "Is she going to lay a golden goose?"

"No, you bastard; she's expecting twins."

Drake rolled over and reached for his wallet on the nightstand. He shoved a handful of euros at Sandrine and signaled for her to get dressed and go. She'd served her purpose, and now he had more important things to deal with that didn't involve his dick.

The goddess had obviously listened to him bad-mouthing her earlier and decided to make things right. With this new information, Drake could buy his freedom at double the asking price. There was no way in hell the royals would jeopardize the babies by playing hard ball. Not only could Drake squeeze out of this tight jam, he'd do it in style. The future was suddenly much brighter.

He showered and changed into something stylish and hired a limo to take him back to Raoul's clinic. There was no longer any need to weigh costs when he had just won the jackpot. At the clinic, he went straight to Charlie's room and embraced her enthusiastically.

"I heard the news from Raoul."

She cocked her head quizzically. "You're happy? I was sure you'd be pissed."

"Why would I be angry?"

"Because this has turned into a high-risk pregnancy, and I'll require round-the-clock care."

"Yes, but the principality will be secured, and our parents will be over the moon."

"I've never felt more like a brood mare."

"Get over it," Drake snapped. "You only have one job, and I'm counting on you to do it well."

"I'll do my best, but I can't control my body."

"Follow doctor's orders to the letter, and it'll be a step in the right direction."

"He wants me to have complete bed rest until I'm stable," she protested. "It could be days."

"Or weeks."

"Don't even go there, Colin. I want to go home."

"In due time."

Chapter Nine

ALAIN TWITCHED IN his sleep, flailing at the incubus wrapping icy tendrils around his feet. He kicked to free himself, striking Colin in the thigh, who protested with a loud grunt.

He sat up abruptly, caught in the muddled space between nightmare and reality. Alain furrowed his brow as he continued to wrestle with an invisible force, and he looked down at Colin who peered up at him in concern.

"Did you just hit me?"

"I'm not sure." Alain blinked, slowly coming to his senses. He was in a comfortable bed in a hotel suite fit for a king, not a dank hospital corridor with blood coating the gray linoleum. He didn't want to alarm Colin with a macabre retelling of a cloudy vision, so he threw off the covers and grabbed the robe he'd tossed on the footstool by the bed. Shaking uncontrollably, he exited the bedroom in search of a stiff drink. Fortunately, their suite was fully stocked, and he'd already poured a generous portion of whiskey into a tumbler by the time Colin staggered out and joined him on the sofa.

The ornate fireplace didn't require magic to get it going, simply a switch, and Alain found it easily. Now the fake logs covering the gas vents were brightly lit, casting warm shadows into the dark room. The only other illumination came from the pin lights directly over the wet bar in the corner.

Colin snuggled up beside him, sheltering them both under the heavy duvet he'd dragged along when he exited their warm bed. Despite the fire and Alain's body heat, gooseflesh covered his bare limbs.

"Have a sip of my drink," Alain suggested. "You're shaking."

"You would be too if someone kicked you awake," Colin muttered irritably.

"Sorry."

"You freaked the shit out of me, Alain. What's going on?"

"Nightmare."

Alain took another swallow, waiting for the booze to melt the cold ball of fear that had settled in the pit of his stomach. He was rarely frightened. Growing up under Isabelle's watchful eye, he'd been tutored on every element of witchcraft, and learning how to defend himself was second nature. But no one had prepared him for the mind-shattering loss of confidence that had settled on him after finding Colin's lifeless body. Yes, he'd managed to revive him, but Drake was still out in the universe plotting their demise. This was no ordinary enemy, and even his dreams were being influenced by the sick fuck.

He recalled the macabre vision he'd unknowingly conjured up when his relationship with Colin was only a few hours old. At the time it had no meaning, but now it was much more sinister. Could the dead body on the bed be Charlie's? Would Drake kill her if she no longer served a purpose? It made no sense. He could parlay her safety to his advantage, turn this into a financial windfall if nothing else. Getting rid of her would be like closing a bank account before draining the funds.

"Tell me about your dream," Colin prompted. "You'll feel better once you talk about it."

"It's the recurring one from long ago."

"The bloody hospital scene?"

Alain nodded.

"You're not the only one plagued by visions. I've often wondered who was on the bed. Is this a self-fulfilling prophesy, Alain? Maybe my line is meant to die out with me. Why else would we both have premonitions about childbirth?"

Anything was possible, Alain thought, especially given the circumstances. He took another swallow and continued to ruminate over Colin's question. A few weeks ago, he would have dismissed the notion as preposterous. Now, he wasn't so sure. Prior to falling in love, his life had been steeped in methodical research. As a man of science, he refused to rely on ancient spells to try to solve life's mysteries. Making any assumption based on his sixth sense was inconceivable.

But a lot had changed since he'd opened his heart to Colin. Should he stop fighting his natural instincts and let elemental powers guide him on this treacherous journey? Using intellect and logic against a sociopathic warlock had been a mistake. Another misstep and he might lose it all, and yet...a successful rescue meant the end of his and Colin's dreams. When Charlie was safely back home, her family would insist she and Colin marry immediately.

It had taken weeks for Alain to realize his feelings for Colin went beyond sex. Once he admitted he was in love, and committed to a future by his side, he was wholly invested. There was nothing and no one who could dissuade him, but it seemed fate had other plans. Their road to happiness had been derailed by a drunken farewell.

He could be a selfish bastard and stay out of the negotiations. Leave the royal family to deal with Drake and let the chips fall where they may. Although, if he got lucky, they would fuck it up, and maybe Charlie would disappear forever. His gut clenched at the idea he'd entertain such a horrible scenario. Alain's entire career was based on helping mankind. Finding cures for stubborn diseases had been his life's work—garnering a Nobel Prize for finding the perfect combination of drugs to prevent Alzheimer's—and to even contemplate someone's death for his own selfish gain went against his moral code.

But falling in love was making him crazy, as Isabelle had pointed out on several occasions, and, beyond insanity, was a jealousy he couldn't contain. For the first time in his life, he was as territorial as a guard dog. Oh, but he was putting up a great front. Acting like the responsible partner in this sudden melodrama was easy, a question of putting his best foot forward, but Alain knew Isabelle wasn't fooled. She could tell he was wrestling with his darker side, knowing he had the power to put an end to all of this conflict if he just gave in for a minute. Charlie would disappear in a puff of smoke, and people would assume it was Drake's fault. Did he have the stomach for it? Was his and Colin's happiness worth a lifetime of regret? Squashing his conscience would more than likely have consequences, but he could sense the voices from the underworld shrieking in protest. *Don't be a pussy*, they taunted. *You have the ability to end this. Colin doesn't love her. He's yours! Destroy the mother and there will be no more impediments.* But what about the innocent child, Alain argued with himself. It didn't ask to be created and shouldn't suffer the consequences.

Alain shook his head like a horse fending off flies, hoping to banish the dark thoughts, but the taunting only grew louder.

Colin slid a hand up his thigh. "Let's go back to bed," he whispered. "I can fix whatever is ailing you."

Alain didn't think he was in the mood, but when he looked into Colin's earnest face, he realized sex was the perfect antidote. Desire flared between them, and the powerful connection that had drawn them from the first thrummed to life. Alain pushed Colin down on the sofa and landed on him hungrily. Without hesitation, Colin wrapped his limbs around Alain's torso and opened his mouth to receive a kiss so savage he'd whimpered in surprise.

Normally a tender and considerate lover, Alain was intent on leaving his mark tonight. He wanted to plunge into Colin and obliterate all thoughts of Charlotte and duty. Picking up on his mood, Colin tore off Alain's robe and tossed it to the side. When they were both naked, he lifted his pelvis and thrust against Alain's rigid cock, grinding their erections together in a feverish need to get closer.

"Fuck me," he whispered urgently.

"Not yet," Alain rasped. He repositioned, scooting down so his mouth was at Colin's core, and cradled between Colin's furry thighs, Alain consumed him with gusto. It was a frenzied feeding the likes of which he'd never experienced, as if his existence rested on his ability to bring Colin to new heights with his marauding tongue and delving fingers. The ethereal beauty underneath his touch was slowly coming apart in the most primal way, and Alain rejoiced in each moan, gasp, and convulsive shudder as he lay waste to his lover.

With the resilience of youth on his side, Colin rebounded after his first orgasm, rising to the next onslaught with impassioned pleas to "fuck me already."

Alain laughed and, lifting him by the arms, pulled him toward the bedroom, where they crash-landed on the wide bed. His mouth and hands roamed over the smooth skin lightly dusted with golden curls as soft as the underbelly of a kitten. And Colin purred with each pass of Alain's warm palm as he kneaded and stroked, ignoring the engorged cock straining against his taut belly.

"Are you ever going to fuck me, 'cause if you're having second thoughts, I'll be happy to take over," Colin teased.

"Not a chance," Alain rumbled. "Unlike you, I'm only going to get one go at this, and I'm holding out until I'm ready to burst."

"A little magic can give you another boner if you want to go multiple rounds."

"There's no fun in that," Alain said. "Now stuff the commentary and let me do my thing."

Seconds bled into minutes, and as they kissed each other breathless, Alain slowly rotated until he found himself on the receiving end of Colin's hungry mouth. He'd pushed Alain's thighs apart, leaving him open and exposed, and feasted on him like it was his last supper. The novice was turning him inside out, and Alain reveled in the experience. Always in control, he gladly gave it up to be at the receiving end of Colin's feverish lovemaking.

Before he spent, Alain gently pushed Colin away, and they wiggled around until Colin was on his back with Alain settled in-between his sturdy thighs.

"You ready for me, *chaton*?"

"Always," Colin affirmed.

Alain slid into the warmth with practiced ease, sighing with pleasure as his lover canted his hips to match his push with a corresponding shove. Thoughts of Charlie were obliterated with their rising passion, and when they crested as one, it was more restorative—and satisfying—than an optimistic vision.

They were lying in bed when Alain's phone beeped, announcing an incoming text. It was marked Unknown Caller, and Alain wondered if it was from Drake. They'd exchanged phone numbers before he and Colin left for the Seychelles, and although Drake's phone had undoubtedly been replaced, and his number changed, Alain's remained the same.

He clicked on the message and saw one word— *jumeau*—and an attachment. His heart sank when he opened the image. The grainy ultrasound showed two babies facing each other with thumbs in their mouths. The French word for male twins, meant he was looking at Sendorra's future ruler. One of these little darlings would take Colin's place someday if Alain could put aside his personal feelings and do what was expected.

"Who is it?" Colin asked sleepily.

Alain was torn between right and wrong. Revealing this monumental news would surely tip the scales in Charlie's favor, and therein lay his dilemma. He loved Colin to the marrow of his bones and would have laid down his life for him, but was he willing to hand him over to Charlie and walk away from his dream without a fight? There was no way he could keep this information to himself indefinitely. Colin or his parents would learn the truth, and if they realized he'd known all along, would they ever forgive him? Could he forgive himself?

"Some random," Alain muttered. "I deleted the text."

"They probably got your number off your website," Colin said. "You should take it down and just leave your business contacts."

"I'll attend to it in the morning."

Chapter Ten

DRAKE WINCED WHEN Charlie squeezed his hand in a death grip after seeing the twins on the computer screen.

"Jesus," he griped, pulling his hand back. "Do you mind?"

"No wonder I'm so sick."

"I suppose this is par for the course?" Drake glanced at Raoul. "Double the trouble?"

"Multiple births can be problematic," he confirmed.

"Are the babies healthy?" Charlie asked.

"Your boys appear to be in excellent health."

Turning to Drake, Charlie beamed. "Can you believe we're having twin boys? Your fathers will be ecstatic."

"Let's not get side-tracked." Facing Raoul, Drake demanded, "Do you know if the babies are in good health? Charlie hasn't been eating well, and although they may look fine, there's no telling if this lack of nutrition has affected their growth."

"Without examining the amniotic fluid, I can't say for certain if they are genetically sound."

"How does the test work?"

"We insert a fine hollow needle through her abdominal wall and withdraw fluid from the amniotic sac."

"Hell no!" Charlie exclaimed. "You're not poking a needle into my belly."

"It's relatively painless," Raoul assured her. "And it's the only way to know for sure if there are issues you'll be facing in the future."

"And if there's a problem?" Charlie asked. "I'm not getting rid of them."

"There's no point speculating when the test results could come back normal."

Charlie crossed her arms over her bump protectively. "I won't let you do it."

"First of all, I wouldn't," Raoul assured her. "Even though it's a fairly routine procedure, there's a degree of delicacy involved, and since I'm a plastic surgeon and have only performed one amniocentesis, years ago during my residency, I wouldn't feel comfortable attempting it. If you decide to go ahead, we'll call in a specialist."

"Charlie, this isn't your decision," Drake pointed out. "There's a lot at stake, and I have a say in this as well."

"No, you don't," Charlie said emphatically. "You're not my husband."

Drake narrowed his eyes. "I'm your husband in every way that counts."

She shook her head and waved her left hand in his face. "Last time I checked, you didn't put a ring on it. Whatever we have is not legally binding. You can't *make* me do anything."

Insulted by her defiance, Drake lashed out cruelly. "Perhaps I've been waiting for you to grow up before tying the knot. Has it even occurred to you I might be having second thoughts? You've been acting like a party girl on a bender since we got back together, and lately I've been dealing with nothing but sickness. Frankly, I'm tired of being your nursemaid."

Charlie's wounded gasp and brimming eyes left Drake with a satisfying boner, and he was certain she would start to see things his way rather than trying to assert herself. "Do the procedure and let's see what we're facing before any decisions are made."

"But Colin—"

He whirled around and left the room before she said another word. She could exercise her rights and refuse the amniocentesis, but hopefully Raoul would talk her into it. Better the devil they knew and all that rot. If there was anything wrong with either of the brats, his bargaining power would be severely reduced, but if they were healthy, Drake would be set for life. *If* he managed to pull off the exchange without getting caught or killed. Should one of the witches get their hands on him, justice would be swift, and probably painful. The royals might abide by the letter of the law and leave his fate in the hands of the high courts, but Isabelle and her coven wouldn't be so merciful. The key to success was staying out of harm's way.

Pulling his phone out of his back pocket, he pressed Maura's contact information and waited impatiently for her to pick up. After six rings, she answered with a breathless hello. Taking a huge lungful of air, she exclaimed, "You always call at the most inopportune time."

"Why? Were you having sex?"

Maura sniffed in outrage. "I almost tripped to reach the phone in time. My death would have been on your conscience, not that you even have one."

Drake's mocking laugh was loud and unapologetic. "Get a grip, Granny. I was just joking."

"Save it for someone else. What's so damned important?"

"What could be more important than our current dilemma?"

"I've been trying to outwit Isabelle's familiar."

"Excuse me?"

"The damned owl has been following me all morning."

"Aren't you supposed to be keeping a low profile?"

"I have to eat," she protested. "And you did tell me to be your decoy, so what does it matter if I'm out and about?"

"Kill the motherfucker next time you see him!"

"Easier said than done, dear boy. Why are you nastier than normal?"

"Stop changing the subject, Granny. Did the familiar see you entering the apartment building?"

"I'm not sure."

"I'll take that as a yes."

"I wish you'd give me a little more credit. I've survived for decades on my own."

"Let's face it, Granny. You're old and your reaction time is rusty as fuck. I'm worried Isabelle will find you and whisk you off to parts unknown to try to get more information on Charlie."

"Since you didn't share your whereabouts, it'll do her no good."

"Do you have a backup plan in case they show up at your place?"

"Stop fretting and tell me what's going on with you and that poor girl."

"Why do you refer to Charlie as the poor girl? She's not in any danger."

"She wasn't part of our plan, Drake. You let your hormones get in the way, and now things are a sorry mess. Like it or not, she's our responsibility, and we need to get her through this pregnancy in good health. I have no quarrel with her and wish you'd take her back to her parents."

"She's expecting twins," he blurted. "How's that for complications?"

"Dear Lord."

"He had nothing to do with it. I guess Colin has superpowers we didn't know about."

"He did have a twin who died in utero," Maura explained. "I'm not surprised he sired a set. Now you *must* take her back home. She'll need medical attention."

"We're at a clinic, Granny. How do you think we found out she's carrying two for the price of one?"

"What are your plans?"

"Dunno yet."

"Take my advice for once and send her back where she came from. With her safe return, the royal family might give you a pass."

"I'm disappointed in you," Drake said. "You were the one who started this, and now that it's gone off the rails, you can't take the heat. Find your spinal cord or shut the fuck up and let me take charge. They want us both dead, and bringing Charlie back sooner rather than later won't change the outcome."

"I'm sure I can talk Isabelle into a peaceful and fair exchange," Maura said haltingly. "Our lives for Charlie's."

"No."

Drake disconnected and shut off the phone. He knew she'd bombard him with callbacks or texts, and he didn't want to deal with any of it. He went in search of breakfast and spent an hour by himself enjoying a full English in Raoul's dining room. Like everything else about this clinic, it was run by the best chefs and could have been lifted from the pages of any fine dining publication. There were a few other guests who must have been family members of patients who'd recently undergone surgery, but the patients themselves were nowhere in sight. Which was just as well. He'd lose his appetite if some mummified thing walked in dragging an IV pole behind them.

Returning to the examining room, he was pleased to see a stranger dressed in a lab coat swabbing Charlie's belly with some kind of disinfectant. There was a syringe filled with clear fluid on the metal tray close at hand. Charlie was crying softly and didn't bother to look up when he walked in. Her gaze was fixed on Raoul who was sitting by her side clasping her hands.

"How soon before we know anything definite?" Drake asked the stranger who was packing up and getting ready to leave.

"We'll have some answers for you in the next few days."

"Days?" Drake interjected. "Can't we put a rush on it?"

"It takes time to analyze the fluid. There are hundreds of genetic abnormalities and speed won't change the outcome, but we might overlook something if we cut corners. Let us do our job properly."

Drake decided to drop it. The guy seemed pretty adamant, and getting into a losing argument in front of an audience wasn't his style. He could feel Raoul's disapproving glare and knew Charlie was still angry. Why waste his energy on a verbal tussle he had no chance of winning? If they had to wait a few days for the results, so be it. The delay would give him more time to plan his next move. With victory on his mind, Drake left the room in search of a computer.

ISABELLE WAS ALREADY seated when Alain walked into the dining room by himself. Colin had insisted another hour of sleep was more important than breakfast, and he'd shoved him away after Alain made several attempts to get him out of bed. In the end, it worked out for the best. Alain wanted to speak to his mother in private, and unexpectedly found himself with the perfect opportunity.

"Where's Colin?" Isabelle asked, glancing over his shoulder.

"In bed."

"Does he think he's on a vacation?" she asked irritably. "We have work to do."

"This is more important," Alain said grimly. He pushed his phone in her direction with the text message from Drake already opened.

She glanced at it and a frown appeared between her artfully drawn eyebrows. Handing back the phone she asked, "Does Colin know?"

Alain shook his head.

Isabelle took up her fork and knife and cut into her omelet. At a loss for words, Alain fussed with his coffee, adding sugar and cream and stirring mindlessly.

Growing impatient with his dithering, Isabelle admonished. "Spit it out, Alain."

He sighed loudly. "Why don't you just tell me what's on your mind?"

"Because this has to be your idea. I will not bear the brunt of your anger if anything goes wrong."

"I'm having a hard time coming to terms with my feelings."

"So, you'd rather the heartless bitch be the bad guy?"

"No," Alain said, drawing out the word. "I'm hoping you'll come up with a good suggestion. Some middle ground that doesn't involve death or deception."

"It's not possible in this case," Isabelle concluded. "You can only have Colin if you're willing to ignore your conscience."

"I'm not killing Charlie and the twins to keep my relationship intact."

"You won't have to lift a finger, Alain. Drake will do it for you."

"I don't understand."

"Stay out of the negotiations. The royals will fuck it up somehow, and Drake will lose his mind. Like a wounded animal, he'll turn on the ones closest to him. In this case it'll be Charlie and the twins. I can assure you things will not go as planned, and they'll be collateral damage."

"Is that how you do it?" Alain asked derisively. "Play the waiting game until your enemies are so freaked out they'll gnaw off their own legs to stay away from your destructive reach? Don't you ever stop to think about repercussions?"

"Sometimes it's not possible to get the job done without leaving a bloody trail in your wake."

"I'm not capable of such a cold-blooded decision."

Isabelle dropped her utensils and leaned forward jabbing her finger in Alain's direction. "For the record, I'm only here because you asked for my help. You and Colin were doomed from the start. Twins will definitely tip the scales in Charlie's favor. The royals will negotiate with the devil—better known as Drake—to get her back and marry them off straight away. Which leaves you holding your pecker and wishing you had a uterus. Give up this ridiculous fantasy, and go back to your science experiments. They were far more rewarding. In time, you'll set your sights on someone suitable. Colin is not your soul mate, no matter what you might think."

"I thought you liked him?"

"What's not to like," she acknowledged softly. "He's more than the sum of his parts, but your relationship can't possibly work because of the succession. He has responsibilities he can't shirk no matter how much he loves you. Be the better man and walk away."

"I promised the royals I would find Drake to avenge the dowager, and that's what I intend to do."

"This was before we learned the truth. Once they realize Charlie is carrying Colin's children, you'll become a footnote in this drama, an expendable partner who has served his purpose with honor, but one who is no longer a viable player. Staying in the vicinity will only confuse the boy. He needs to focus on his duty, and unfortunately it involves Charlie and his future offspring."

"Your heart is as cold as the coffee," Alain said, pushing his cup away. "I should have known you wouldn't provide any support."

"You're asking for the impossible," Isabelle maintained. "I have no way of helping you without killing a few people, and Colin will never forgive us if anything happens to Charlie."

"You're right," Alain agreed. "He won't. I'm going to break the bad news. I don't want him to hear about the twins from Drake or anyone else. He deserves better."

"What will you tell him?"

"Everything," Alain said. "Our engagement is over, and he needs to start negotiating with Drake for a peaceful resolution. I'm going home."

Isabelle looked dubious. "You can walk away without a backward glance?"

"It's the only sensible thing to do."

"Of course," she replied. "You've always been the voice of reason. How could I have ever imagined you'd be willing to cross the line for the love of your life?"

Alain stared into the depths of her purple irises and tried to understand what was happening here. Was she daring him to run amuck, and do what his heart desired, and to hell with the consequences? Was this her way of sanctioning a kill without actually saying the words? Going against the coven, and taking back what was rightfully his, might start a war, but he'd have the ultimate prize. Namely Colin and the future they'd planned. Could he actually pull this off without destroying the children or their mother? But if he succeeded in saving them, where would it leave him? Would Charlie agree to be Colin's wife in name only while Alain warmed his bed? Is that how he envisioned his life? A Nobel Prize winner reduced to the status of concubine because he didn't have the stones to walk away? Or perhaps he'd rather be known as the homewrecker who pushed the principality into a constitutional crisis after urging Colin to divorce Charlie so they could marry. His reputation would be destroyed along with his self-respect.

And what about the children? They would be the ones who suffered the most. Dejected, Alain strode toward the front desk and arranged for a ride to the airport. He scribbled a hasty note to Colin and returned to the dining room to ask Isabelle to pack his belongings and send them to Biarritz. A faceoff with Colin would only delay the inevitable, and Alain wasn't in the right frame of mind. He was torn apart with indecision, and for a man who never wavered, it was killing him.

As he expected, Isabelle warned him Colin would be more vulnerable without Alain by his side, but he argued, pointing out that Charlie should be their main focus and the vendetta could wait. The warlock would be on his best behavior if he wanted things to go smoothly. Besides, Alain maintained, she was present to watch Colin's back. What could possibly go wrong?

Chapter Eleven

HANGING AROUND IN case of trouble wasn't what Andrew envisioned when asked to keep an eye on his twin. Where was the action he'd been promised? Things had moved at lightning speed right after the dowager's murder and Colin's near-death experience, but everything had come to a grinding halt. Diplomacy and indecision were turning this adventure into a tedious game of wait and see. How Bibi could do this for so long was beyond him, but then again, she was an owl—designed to sit motionless for hours at a time.

He should have been off raising hell with his preternatural gang of spirits and assorted undead, but Isabelle had warned him, silently communicating in her creepy fashion, to lie low and take his cue from her familiar. If he wanted to be a part of this cat and mouse game they were playing with Drake and his dodgy grandmother, he had to find the patience required for the job.

For as long as he could remember, Andrew had kept an eye on Colin, but he'd been more on call than anything else. It hadn't been necessary to stick to him like a proverbial second skin. He'd show up whenever Colin was at a low point and required a shoulder to cry on or a listening ear. Now Colin had a boyfriend, and Andrew's role had changed somewhat. He was forbidden to materialize at will, especially when the new couple were in bed. Colin had repeatedly stressed voyeurism wasn't part of the deal. As if he cared to watch two guys doing the nasty. Andrew had always preferred the soft curves of a woman.

Before the pregnancy wreaked havoc on her good looks, Charlie had been the embodiment of the perfect woman, one Andrew would have happily called his wife—if he'd been alive. She was fun-loving, kind, a bit of a daredevil, and had a killer body. Her parents had been grooming her for years to be Colin's future bride, but somewhere in the mysterious workings of the mind and heart, paths had diverged, and she and Colin had grown tired of each other. There was nothing Andrew could do or say to convince his twin she was the perfect choice. Instead, he had to step back, grit his teeth, and stuff the commentaries to keep the peace.

When they broke up, Colin had moved on to Alain, a surprising choice in Andrew's opinion, but his views on love and romance were of little consequence as his experience was purely cerebral.

Nonetheless, he had to admire Charlie for her creativity. Upon realizing she was pregnant, she'd taken matters into her own hands. Unfortunately, she'd backed the wrong horse, hitching her wagon to Drake, thinking he was Colin. Andrew couldn't figure out how she could possibly mistake the two. Physical appearance notwithstanding, wouldn't they be different in bed? Or were they interchangeable between the sheets as well? Hell, he had no idea.

All he could do was pick up clues as they were randomly dropped. So far, he hadn't gleaned any new information, but Alain was acting strange upon leaving the suite this morning, and Andrew decided to follow him to the dining room. Bibi was perched on the wooden shelf above the clerestory windows strategically placed to brighten the large room, and Isabelle didn't even glance in their direction when he silently materialized.

So, when he learned Charlie was carrying twins, and they were definitely Colin's, and Alain hadn't bothered mentioning this new information to his betrothed, Andrew was deeply disturbed. What in the ever-loving fuck? The twins were his nephews, the future heirs of Sendorra, and he wasn't about to let them suffer his fate and spend the rest of eternity wandering around aimlessly. The people in charge needed to get cracking and bring them and their mother safely home.

He flitted away and appeared at the foot of Colin's bed. It was dark and his twin was snoring softly. Andrew willed the curtains apart, and light streamed into the suite, finally rousing Colin, who sat up, golden locks sticking up in wild spikes. He was naked and sported an assortment of hickeys and beard burn. Somebody had a good time last night. Maybe it would put him in the right frame of mind to receive this newsflash.

"What in the hell are you doing here?"

Or not.

"Answer me!"

We need to talk.

"Can't this wait?"

No.

"What's so damned important?"

Charlie.

Colin flopped back down and covered his face with a pillow. "Go away."

There's a new development that requires your attention.

"Wait until Alain gets back."

He's not coming back.

"What are you talking about?"

He left the hotel.

Colin hurled a pillow across the room, and it passed right through Andrew.

Hey!

Fully engaged now, Colin sat up, pushed aside the bedding, grabbed his robe, and shrugged it on.

"You're lying, Andrew. Alain is downstairs having breakfast with Isabelle. He should be back any minute, and if I were you, I'd make myself scarce."

I've just come from the dining room, and I can tell you with absolute certainty your boyfriend is on his way to the airport. He's having a moment and needs to be alone.

"Bull!"

Listen to me, Colin. Something has happened, and I believe you're completely in the dark.

"I can see you're just dying to tell me—go ahead."

Charlie's pregnant.

"That's already been established."

You are the father.

"Allegedly."

She's expecting twin boys.

The snarky comeback died on Colin's tongue. "How do you know?"

I heard the entire conversation between Isabelle and Alain preceding his sudden departure.

"Perhaps you misunderstood."

I am dead, Colin, not unhinged. Apparently, Drake, or whomever, sent an image to Alain's phone last night, and he showed it to Isabelle.

"He got a text last night, but he said it was an unknown caller."

And you believed him?

"Why wouldn't I? He's the most honest person I know. I would never question Alain's integrity."

Then why did he leave?

"Maybe he went to town to explore. We still don't know where Drake and Charlie are holed up."

Call him.

"I will!"

Andrew watched Colin make the call and wasn't surprised when Alain didn't pick up, and Colin voiced a savage epithet before disconnecting.

Told you.

"This means nothing, Andrew. I'll find him or Isabelle and get some answers."

You do that and while you're at it, find out if they know where Drake is hiding out? I need to recon before you guys show up.

"You've done more than enough for now."

Hostile much?

"Admit it! You've never liked Alain or his mother."

I like him well enough, but Charlie was always my first choice.

"Who brought me back to life, brother? If Alain and Isabelle weren't in my life, I'd be as dead as you."

I've no quarrel with either of them, but if you hadn't broken up with Charlie, this wouldn't be an issue.

"So, now you're convinced this is all my fault?"

It wasn't my dick shooting out twins.

"Fuck you."

I'll come back when you're willing to listen to my advice.

"Stay away from us," Colin warned. "I've had enough of your meddling."

Watching your back is my job.

"Distorting the truth isn't my idea of support. You're trying to break us up, so I'm free to marry Charlie."

Haven't you already come to this conclusion on your own? Marrying her, I mean? You know a bastard can't assume the throne. And why would you do this to someone you've known and loved your entire life? Weighing the years you spent with Charlie against the few months you've had with Alain should be a no-brainer. You have a duty to your country as well as the woman you used to love.

"Don't you dare lecture me," Colin snarled as he hastily pulled up his pants and shrugged on a shirt. He went to the bathroom to brush his teeth and tame his unruly locks, all the while radiating actual flames like sparklers on Bastille Day. Andrew had to remind himself he was dealing with a newly awakened witch who hadn't quite harnessed his skills and could burn down the hotel if he didn't get himself under control.

I'm going.

"It's about fucking time."

I'll be back when I have more news.

"Don't bother. Alain and I will take care of this."

What'll you do?

Colin raised both hands in Andrew's direction, looking fiercely determined to bring him down with a bolt of lightning, but he aimed above his head instead. The gold leaf plaster cornice crackled and split, falling to the floor with a horrid crash.

You can't kill me, Colin.

"Dammit, Andrew! If you don't shut up and leave me alone, I'll do something stupid."

With a heavy heart, Andrew realized Colin had chosen Alain over him and was beyond reason. It was the first time anything had come between them, and reminding his twin he'd already done something foolish months ago—getting drunk and impregnating his ex-girlfriend— might lead to a permanent estrangement.

I said I'm going. Quit the pyrotechnics or you'll set off the overhead sprinklers.

"Get out of here!" Colin screamed.

Andrew materialized in the dining room to find Isabelle and Bibi had taken off to parts unknown. Alain was nowhere in sight. Great. His expectations for a successful mission were sinking by the minute, but the notion of abandoning his post as familiar hadn't crossed his mind. He would see this through until Charlie was safely back where she belonged—in Colin's arms—and then he'd reevaluate his stance with regard to his twin.

With renewed determination, Andrew inspected every square inch of the hotel in search of Isabelle and Bibi only to come up short. At the beginning of their journey, they'd made a contingency plan by which they could track each other in case they were ever separated, and he employed it then. Concentrating, he attempted to pinpoint Bibi's whereabouts telepathically. The spires of Old Town Prague came into view, and he flitted off in that direction.

He found them in the gloomy apartment with Isabelle facing down a fellow witch who had to be Maura, Drake's grandmother. Fury radiated off Isabelle while her opponent tried to ward her off with an ineffectual spell which only made Isabelle angrier. Darkness descended in the enclosed space, and the stink of burning feathers became overpowering. Bibi retreated to the corner of the room with a loud squawk, flapping her singed wings and mewling in pain.

"How dare you touch my familiar," Isabelle hissed, curling her hands into fists. She was inches away from Maura and spitting mad. They were probably the same age, but Maura's gray hair, pallid complexion, and trembling lower lip made her look like a crone while Isabelle exuded confidence and good health.

Fear notwithstanding, Maura challenged, "Keep your owl in check, or I'll finish the job and have her for dinner."

Isabelle slapped her, and Maura's head rocked back. Without taking her eyes off Isabelle, she lifted a gnarled hand to her cheek and wolfishly bared yellowing teeth. "You'll pay for this."

"Oh please," Isabelle jeered. "You're no match for me."

The loud screech and soft thud from the fallen owl stripped the last of Isabelle's self-control, and she pounced on Maura and wrestled her to the ground. With a knee on the woman's ample chest and bloodred fingernails digging into the saggy skin around Maura's throat, Isabelle took her eyes off Maura for a second to check on Bibi. Seeing her beloved familiar lying on the floor like roadkill was a bitter pill to swallow. The owl appeared lifeless, but then she twitched spasmodically and slowly tottered to life on singed talons. Half her body was denuded, and the flesh scorched while the remaining feathers were charred beyond recognition. Bibi was the worse for wear but still alive.

Isabelle glared at Maura and asked in a steely voice. "Where has your cowardly grandson taken the princess?"

"I don't know," Maura replied in a shrill voice.

"Would you tell me if you knew?"

"Probably not."

Isabelle's nails dug in deeper, drawing blood this time and a loud protest from Maura.

"Let me go," she demanded. "I can't tell you what I don't know."

"Where's your phone?" Isabelle asked.

"In my pocket," Maura said, digging it out from the deep folds of her dress and handing it over. "You'll see his caller ID and location are blocked."

Isabelle glanced at the old-school flip phone and jeered. "Not all of us are techtards, my dear. I can assure you I'll have my answer within the hour."

"Wait," Maura said, trying to snatch the phone back. "You can't have my phone."

Isabelle pocketed the phone and squeezed a little tighter. Maura slapped at Isabelle's hand and writhed, doing her best to escape. Andrew recalled Isabelle bragging about her level of fitness with regular visits to her gym to lift free weights and participate in whatever defense class was the current rage. Lately it had been Krav Maga, but she was also schooled in kickboxing and judo. Now it was paying off. The woman was a lot stronger than most people her age.

"Help me," Maura cried, flailing ineffectually. Her cries for help grew more and more feeble.

Isabelle grimaced. "I wanted you to suffer, especially after you attacked Bibi, but I can't waste any more time."

Andrew witnessed Isabelle even the score with cold-blooded determination. She pressed her thumb on Maura's forehead, and it went through her skull as if it were made of clay. Maura's eyes rolled back in her head, and her mouth twisted in a rictus of pain while Isabelle dug deeper, smiling with grim satisfaction. When Isabelle deemed her enemy was well and truly vanquished, she pulled back her bloody hand and wiped it on Maura's dress.

"You idiotic cow," she muttered. "I should have done this years ago, but I listened to my council and waited until the time was right. They say revenge is best served cold, but I have to disagree. There's nothing better than winning in the heat of battle. Isn't that right, Bibi?"

The approval was weak, but heartfelt, and Isabelle rose, picked up her wounded warrior, and left the apartment.

On her way out, she remembered Andrew. "Come on, ghost. We have to get this phone to an IT guy."

Whatever doubts Andrew may have had with regard to Isabelle were quickly erased by her formidable display of strength and resilience. He was certain they'd have Charlie's location within twenty-four hours.

Chapter Twelve

ALAIN'S COLDLY PENNED missive informing him Charlie was expecting twins, followed by a lame apology for keeping the news under wraps, felt like a punch in the gut. It was worse because Alain had taken off to "think about their future" instead of facing the unknown with Colin by his side. The note also confirmed Andrew's unwelcome news, and Colin's anger and subsequent side effect—an instinctive desire to lash out—were difficult to restrain. With a pounding heart and speeding pulse, he gathered up the last vestiges of his self-control and stomped on a childish need to retaliate. Why harm innocent people with a raging fire when it was Alain who deserved the brunt of his anger? Colin was affronted and bitterly disappointed in Alain's cowardly behavior, but he had to get past this and rescue Charlie. There would be time in the future to settle his differences with Alain. No one jilted him on short fucking notice! As far as Colin was concerned, their engagement wasn't over until they had a chance to sit down like adults and hash it out.

He ordered a rental car and went back to the suite to pack his belongings. Alain's toiletries still sat on the bathroom counter, and he swiped them off the marble with a frustrated cry, watching the bottles of expensive face cream, hair products, and aftershave burst into a million fragments. With tears pouring down his cheeks, he crammed his few belongings into a carryall and headed back downstairs, only to come face-to-face with Isabelle and her party of two. Bibi was a pitiful facsimile of her old self, and Andrew appeared shaken.

"What the hell happened to her?" he asked Isabelle, pointing at the owl who drooped in her arms.

Dude…don't provoke her. She just destroyed Drake's granny and isn't in the right frame of mind.

"Neither am I," Colin said through clenched teeth. "Answer my question, Isabelle. What's going on?"

"Maura had the nerve to attack my familiar. I couldn't let it pass, especially after she's plotted to destroy your family. She got what she deserved."

"You killed her?"

"Executed is more apt."

"Did you find Charlie and Drake?"

"The IT guy I hired is working on their location as we speak."

"I'm sure there's a reason you've involved someone new, but I don't have time to listen. Text me the information once you have it."

"Where are you going?"

"On a witch hunt."

"By yourself?"

"If your dipshit son hadn't abandoned me, when I needed him most, I wouldn't be alone. As such, I have to take my chances with my familiar. Coming, Andrew?"

I thought you wanted nothing to do with me.

"Anything said in anger shouldn't be held against me."

Apology accepted, for whatever it's worth.

"Don't expect me to grovel."

As if.

"I'm not sure this is a good idea," Isabelle cautioned after listening to their exchange. "You're no match for Drake."

"Charlie needs rescuing, and I'm the only one who's got the balls to do it."

"Don't you dare speak to me in that tone," Isabelle huffed. "I've ended someone's life on your account."

"Killing Maura had more to do with you and the Simon Coven than me. I'm not as powerful as you in all things magical, but I can smell bullshit a mile away."

Isabelle gasped at his audacity.

Colin raised an eyebrow. "What? You think I should be more grateful? Maybe if you had Charlie by your side and Drake's body buried in some landfill, I'd be impressed, but a dead witch who was simply following orders from her psycho grandson isn't the grand prize. And just so we're clear," Colin continued. "You may think you know what I'm capable of, but you haven't seen me in action. Alain will attest to my magical skills—if you can find him. You might want to check under his bed. That's usually where a fraidy-cat will lie in wait until the boogie man leaves the premises."

"Alain is no coward," Isabelle rejoined frigidly. "He did what was best, given the circumstances."

"For him, maybe."

"No, this was for you. He evaluated the entire situation and bowed out so you're free to marry Charlie. It was the right thing to do."

Colin scoffed. "It doesn't take a genius to figure out whose side you're on."

"Once your bruises subside, you'll acknowledge his sacrifice."

"We didn't have a physical altercation," Colin clarified.

"I'm talking about your wounded ego."

Snap

Colin could feel the heat coursing through his nerve endings, but his anger should be directed at Alain, not his mother. Isabelle, for all her snide remarks, was the high priestess of her coven, and she'd walked this earth long before Colin was born. Her powers were astonishing, and he had no wish to get on her bad side. On the other hand, there was no need for her continued involvement if Alain was no longer in the picture.

Drawing on the last of his reserves, Colin took a deep breath and, in a more respectful tone, suggested she go back to France. "I think it's best if you and I part ways. Since Alain has unofficially broken our engagement, my safety is no longer any concern of yours. Thank you for all you've done so far, but my family and I will handle this going forward."

"I'm not sure I agree."

"You have no say," Colin reminded her. "Please text me the minute you have a location."

"Of course."

Colin picked up his carryall and headed toward the hotel portico. He could feel Isabelle's gaze on him the entire time and wondered if he was making another colossal mistake. Facing down Drake on his own was like going to war with a handgun instead of the necessary arsenal to back him up. Despite her loyalty to Alain, and tacit approval of his departure, Isabelle was an ally in this fight against Drake. Pushing her away was a knee-jerk reaction to Alain's surprisingly bad behavior and short-sighted on his part. He walked back inside the hotel.

"I'm sorry for taking out my anger on you, Isabelle. Alain and I have unfinished business, but I won't let it detract from the problem at hand. Any help you might offer would be welcome."

She smiled at him and bobbed her head. "A wise decision, Colin. I accept your apology and will accompany you on your quest to find Charlie. However, I need twenty-four hours to nurse Bibi. Once she's able to fly again, I'll meet you on the outskirts of Bruges."

"Won't it take longer for her feathers to grow back?"

"Our combined magic will speed up the process. She'll be fit to travel by tomorrow."

"Bruges, you say?"

"Yes. I just got a text from my guy. Drake's last call to Maura was from a hotel in downtown Bruges. I'm assuming Charlie is with him."

Colin nodded. "He won't let her out of his sight. I'll cancel my car and take a commercial flight. Let's have the concierge recommend a hotel, and I'll make a reservation for adjoining rooms."

"Promise you'll wait until I arrive before you contact him."

Colin paused. Hurrying to his destination and then sitting around to wait for Isabelle wasn't his first choice. He'd never been the patient sort, and inactivity would get him to thinking about Alain and all that could have been. "I'll try but I can't promise."

"At least you're honest," Isabelle conceded. "Leave word for me if you decide to explore, but for heaven's sake, do not attempt to confront Drake on your own."

"Okay."

She headed toward the elevator and he went back to the front desk to make new arrangements.

ALAIN'S PHONE HAD been blowing up with text after text from Colin, and after deliberating for a few minutes, he shut it down. The note he'd left for him at the front desk, explaining why he had to get away, should have been sufficient, but as usual, his young prince wouldn't accept it at face value. Alain knew running away was an immature solution hardly fitting their status, and yet, he was also cognizant of his weakness when it came to Colin. He was eloquently persuasive, an expert negotiator who would use any means available to achieve his goal, and Alain usually succumbed, allowing his heart to dictate his actions rather than relying on his mental acumen, which was a far more reliable tool when it came to hard choices. It was a hell of a thing to realize he had no idea what direction to take in a previously successful and well-managed life.

Perhaps Isabelle would convince Colin to see reason. She wasn't romantically invested, and hard facts presented in the light of day, without the lingering scent of shared orgasms, might penetrate Colin's thick skull. Alain was mentally exhausted and decisions made under duress were rarely sound. Putting distance between them would allow him to collect his thoughts and look at the big picture without being distracted by verbal tussles or influenced by emotions. He had faith in his mother's abilities to ensure Colin stayed safe until he could rejoin the party.

The plane ride home was uneventful, and he breathed a sigh of relief when Merlin greeted him at the front door with a brush against his legs. He didn't have luggage to contend with, having left on the spur of the moment, so he picked up the big cat, and scratched behind his ears. Alain undressed and dove into bed with Merlin who perched on a pillow by his head purring contentedly.

Unfortunately, his troubles followed him while he slept. Tossing and turning fretfully, he awoke bathed in sweat and shaking with anxiety. Once again, the sight and smell of fresh blood permeated his senses, and his analytical mind, the one that dug and dug until it found a solution, couldn't let this vision go unanswered any longer. He would use magic to get to the bottom of it, and if he fainted again, he'd get up and start over. Alain had shoved his elemental skills aside in favor of scientific research and reason, and it was time to get back to basics.

A refreshing shower and a pot of freshly brewed coffee revived him, and he powered on his desktop and started a list, something he normally would do at the beginning of any project. Bullet points helped him organize his thoughts, and if he could employ the same techniques that won him the Nobel Prize, instead of taking off in all directions, he might come up with some answers.

He spent an hour at his desk, refilling his coffee cup several times, and when he was done, he reviewed his notes.

<u>Facts as known:</u>

Late May—Colin breaks up with Charlie, but impulsive sex turns into a pregnancy.

Early June—Alain and Colin hook up.

Late June—Alain and Colin escape to the Seychelles. Ask Drake to remain as a decoy.

Also in late June—Charlie finds out she's pregnant. Rather than pick up the phone and tell Colin, she travels to Biarritz to attempt a reconciliation. She succeeds but it isn't Colin who is back in her life. Drake takes over Colin's role in every way.

July—Charlie is firmly ensconced in the imposter's bed. Drake decides he wants her and the throne for himself, then kills the dowager when she starts to get suspicious. Colin returns to confront him and is almost killed. Drake leaves the area with Charlie.

August—The fugitives (Drake and Maura) hide out in Prague with Charlie.

Early September—Location ascertained and breached. Drake on the run again.

Also September—Twins are confirmed by ultrasound. A ransom negotiation is expected but hasn't materialized yet.

<u>Still unknown</u>:

Location of hideout.

Charlie's state of mind and physical condition.

Will Colin marry her before childbirth to confirm legitimacy?

What will Drake do once money changes hands?

Who died in the vision?

Alain pushed away from his desk, disappointed when nothing jumped out immediately. There were still more questions than answers, and he wasn't any closer to finding a solution. Frustrated, he retired to the living room. The last cup of coffee felt like acid in his stomach, and he was painfully aware a meal of sorts would be beneficial, but he was too wired from the caffeine to stop now.

Eager to recreate the atmosphere the first time he conjured up the gory hospital scene, Alain set fresh logs on the grate and started a fire. He then poured himself a brandy and took a few sips, mindful of his roiling gut. The liquor would hopefully counteract the stimulant so he could attain the proper state of mind to delve into the future.

Pulling Merlin on his lap, he stared into the leaping flames and chanted the necessary words. Perhaps this time, a clearer picture would emerge, and if not, he would keep trying until he got some answers.

Chapter Thirteen

AFTER THE LAST confrontation with Drake, which nearly killed him, Colin was mindful of the danger and agreed to Isabelle's request to lie low until she joined him in Bruges. It was a testament to his personal growth that he didn't go charging off to rescue Charlie, even if he managed to discover her location on his own. Although he hungered for revenge and was anxious for Charlie's safety, and the twins by extension, he was more realistic this time around. At the hotel, he left word for Isabelle in case she arrived while he was gone.

Andrew urged him to put on a disguise before he stepped outside. Still considered an eligible bachelor, he was a paparazzi favorite, and any Prince Colin sighting usually meant a financial reward for the photographer. He didn't begrudge anyone an honest day's work, but having his face splashed on the internet might alert Drake, and the element of surprise would be gone. He had ordered his bodyguards to remain in Sendorra, and they'd protested, knowing they would get holy hell from his fathers, but to Colin's way of thinking, an entourage would only slow him down. Nonetheless, it made him vulnerable to a surprise attack, so he gave in to his familiar's good advice and spent an hour working on a disguise. A store in the hotel lobby supplied the basics, and he grabbed a bottle of temporary hair dye to change his familiar blond locks into an edgier shade of deep purple. In addition, a couple of paste-on tattoos, clip-on earrings, skinny jeans, and shit-kicking boots completed the transformation.

He'd never been to Bruges before, and the charming medieval town was a good distraction for several hours. With Andrew by his side, he walked through the maze of narrow cobblestone streets and alleys, sampled the local beer, and bought a Belgian waffle to munch while taking a relaxing boat ride on one of many canals to view perfectly preserved buildings from a different angle. To work off some of his nervous energy, he climbed the Belfry of Bruges, an ancient bell tower in the center of town, which served as an observation post. Three hundred sixty-six narrow steps later, he stood on the observation deck and soaked in the view. Afterward, he rewarded himself with another beer and people-watched until it grew dark. On his way back to the hotel, he popped into a chocolate shop, one of hundreds in the area, and bought a sizeable chunk of fudge. If he couldn't have sex tonight, he'd have the next best thing.

According to the front desk, Isabelle hadn't arrived yet, and he forced down his disappointment and went upstairs for a quick shower to wash out the hair dye before plunging into the huge claw-foot tub for a nice long soak. On the spur of the moment, he called Alain. When it went straight to voice mail, he left a long message informing him of the latest developments, including his location, and making it crystal clear he would not be dumped in such a lame-ass way.

"If you don't have the balls to face me and tell me it's over, then consider yourself engaged and off the market until further notice. Touch anyone, and I swear to God I will gut you, but not before I turn your hookup into a eunuch."

And on that sour note, Colin dried off and dressed for dinner. Just as he was knotting his tie, there was a knock on the door. He yanked it open and sighed with relief when Isabelle, looking refreshed, shouldered her way past.

"I have news," she said, preempting his barrage of questions.

"Spill."

"The last call Drake made to Maura was from a private clinic about forty minutes outside town. Upon further examination, I found out it belongs to an accomplished plastic surgeon who uses it to house his pre– and post-op patients. I'm not sure what his involvement is, but I doubt he's part of this scam. Drake must have called in a favor and is using the clinic as a safe house."

"What's your plan?"

"We'll reconnoiter after dinner."

"We?"

"You and Andrew, Bibi and I."

"Thank God," Colin said gratefully. "How is the poor thing?"

"Bibi is making a good recovery. I was able to apply a magic poultice, which resulted in a new growth of feathers so she can take flight. They're fragile but at least she's mobile."

"Shouldn't she rest for a few more days?"

Isabelle shook her head. "She won't be grounded, even if I insist. Bibi would rather die than give up her position as my familiar."

"That's harsh."

"Injuries come with the job. Someone is bound to get hurt during this manhunt, and if you can't accept it, you may as well go home. Let me handle Drake."

"Hell no," Colin protested. "For Granny's sake and for Charlie and the twins, I have to strike the death blow. Don't deprive me of the satisfaction."

"Have you ever killed anyone, Colin?"

"No."

"You'll probably choke at the last minute."

He gave her a disdainful look. "Don't assume anything about me."

"Then I'll be your wingman, just in case."

"Thank you. Are you hungry?" Colin asked.

"I could eat."

The conversation over the excellent three-course meal was congenial, and Colin steered clear of any mention of Alain. Following his lead, Isabelle refrained from giving any unwanted relationship advice. They were like combatants in the heat of battle, putting aside their differences to ensure a successful mission.

"How will we get to the clinic without being spotted?" Colin asked over coffee and a slice of cherry tart.

"We'll fly."

Colin raised both eyebrows. "You know I can't fly."

"I'll carry you."

"You can?"

"Of course," she said dismissively. "I told you there's much to learn. Your powers are unharnessed, but I'm certain I can unleash them in due course. For now, you're coming along for the ride."

"Will I be able to astral travel on my own someday?"

"I don't see why not."

"Don't I have to have some special gene?"

"You already have it."

"And how do you know this?"

She shrugged. "The same way I know you haven't given up on Alain."

"Isabelle…"

"Not now, Colin. There will be time in the future to return to this discussion."

"Can I please say one thing and I won't bring it up again?"

She indicated her approval with a nod and Colin continued. "All my life I've been searching for something or someone to complete me. Despite the many advantages I've had by dint of birth, there's been a hollow feeling deep inside, like something was missing. At first, I thought it was my dead brother, and I grieved for him. My life would be different had Andrew lived, but then I met Alain, and he filled the void, slotting into the vacancy like a missing puzzle piece I didn't know was lost. I'm happiest when we're together, at peace with myself and my role as future ruler. I suppose you think I'm being melodramatic, but I don't see how I can go on with only half a heart. Alain is my soulmate, Isabelle. This situation with Charlie was unexpected, and I'm aware of my obligations, but I won't give up Alain without a fight. I love him too much."

"You can't expect a man of his caliber to be a second-string player. If he can't be your legitimate consort, he'd rather be nothing at all."

"Let's agree to disagree for now," Colin acquiesced.

"You're delaying the inevitable and making things harder on both of you. An amputation is usually the best way to get rid of an infection."

"I'm not some gangrenous tissue," Colin fumed. "Alain and I are destined to be together."

She picked up her wine glass and took a healthy swallow. "I'm too jaded to believe love conquers all. Everyone is replaceable to a degree. You might not be in love with Charlie, but children will be the glue to make a loveless marriage stick."

Colin squeezed his eyes shut. "I can't talk about this right now."

"Agreed," Isabelle said gently. "I'd like to leave at midnight."

"What should I wear?"

"Comfortable, warm clothing. And shoes you can run in."

"What about weapons?"

"The only one you'll need is courage."

A chill went through Colin, and he tried to think of Charlie's relief upon being rescued, instead of dwelling on what might go wrong. In his hotel room, Colin leafed through magazines and turned on the TV for background noise. He was tired and knew he'd benefit from a nap, so he set his phone alarm for eleven o'clock, to make sure he was ready when Isabelle knocked. He slept, albeit fitfully, and he was already dressed and ready to go before the alarm went off.

Isabelle was punctual, and she looked like a fashionable ninja in her black track suit, athletic shoes, and gloves. Her hair was pulled back into a low chignon and held in place by a thick, black headband, which also protected her ears. Bibi quivered on her shoulder, and although Isabelle was paler than usual, he couldn't sense any fear. Her grasp was firm when she reached for his hand and instructed him to think of Charlie.

Colin obeyed without a word and the hotel room faded away. Frigid winds buffeted his face, and he sucked in a sharp breath, surprised they were underway with no warning. Flying through space was as exhilarating as zip-lining, but as mind-numbingly frightening as bungee jumping, an extreme sport he and Alain had attempted when they were vacationing in the Seychelles. He took his eyes off Isabelle and made the mistake of looking down. His stomach heaved at the sight of city lights blinking in the distance, and he felt a rising sense of panic as realization hit. The only thing keeping him from certain death was Isabelle's strong grip.

"Eyes on me," she ordered, picking up on his growing agitation.

Colin's gaze veered upward, and he didn't take his eyes off Isabelle as they sped across the sky like a comet. One day, he would look back on the unique experience and marvel, but right then, he hoped she wouldn't drop him.

Their landing wasn't quite as smooth as the takeoff, and Colin found himself at the bottom of the pile with Isabelle and Bibi sprawled on his back. They were inside a linen closet, and he burst into nervous giggles while Andrew looked on in concern.

Are you okay?

"I will be as soon as you guys get off my back."

Isabelle slowly got to her feet, and Colin flipped over and sat up gingerly. Bibi swayed like a drunk, and Isabelle reached to steady her.

"Goodness," she exclaimed.

Colin grinned. "The most fun I've had in forever."

Isabelle removed her headband and smoothed back her hair. "Once you got over the yips."

"It was frightening at first," Colin admitted. "But now that I know how much fun can be had, I'll pester you until I can solo."

Isabelle tutted disapprovingly. "Have you always been so impatient?"

Yes.

She gave Andrew a pitying glance. "How do you put up with him?"

No choice.

"I won't be bullied," Isabelle clarified. "You'll learn at my pace and no sooner."

"Bummer," Colin muttered. "Can we go?"

"Follow me."

Isabelle opened the door, and they left the room in single file. Colin expected to walk into a hospital setting, but it looked like an elegant hotel with thick carpeting, brocade wallpaper, and strategically placed wall fixtures resembling old fashioned gas lighting. Perhaps somewhere in the building there was a section where the doctor could perform procedures he deemed necessary, or maybe they'd landed in the wrong place?

He tugged on Isabelle's jacket and whispered, "Are you sure this is the clinic?"

She glared at him, with her arresting amethyst eyes, and he let go. "Sorry."

Silently, they made their way up the corridor, sticking to the shadows in case someone showed up unexpectedly. The end of the hall opened into a marbled foyer with two elevators. There was no nurse's station or anyone present to give them directions.

In the elevator, Colin's hand hovered over the control panel, and he glanced at Isabelle.

"Up or down?"

"Up."

"You sure?"

"Up," she stressed angrily.

He bit back a sassy remark and complied. When the elevator slid open, they were on another floor, an exact replica of the one they'd left behind. Isabelle led the way once again, and this time she stopped at a door, and the ornate crystal knob spun on its own, allowing them entry.

Colin could barely make out a body in the dim room, but whoever was in charge had left the light on in the bathroom, and it shone a path to the hospital bed. Charlie was surrounded by soft pillows and an IV pole with lifesaving fluids dripping slowly down the clear tubing. She was asleep, and most importantly, alone. Colin moved closer and looked at his childhood friend. The vivacious beauty who'd been the center of his universe had changed since he last saw her four months ago. Even in repose, he could tell Charlie wasn't herself. Her perpetual tan was gone, and her pale skin was flaky in spots. Even her hair had lost its luster and dark roots were overtaking the blonde highlights she hadn't touched up in months. Charlie had always been fastidious about her appearance, and it hurt to see her in this condition. He couldn't imagine what she'd been through and would continue to endure until the twins were born. He clasped her cold hand and gave it a gentle squeeze.

Her eyelids flickered and when she opened her eyes, they widened in alarm. He probably looked like an assassin, dressed in unadulterated black, with a knitted cap covering his hair. He'd expected some confusion on Charlie's part, but he didn't anticipate her next move. She opened her mouth and let out a blood curdling scream.

Chapter Fourteen

COLIN CLAMPED A hand over her mouth, which made matters worse, and she grew more agitated, whining and clawing at him to escape.

"Dammit, Charlie," he said roughly. "Stop it!"

She froze at his command.

He yanked off his knit cap, and his hair tumbled down, catching the light from the open bathroom. It shone brightly, changing his overall appearance in an instant.

Charlie whimpered.

"If I take my hand away, will you promise not to scream?"

She nodded.

He let her go and took a step back.

Her eyes darted around the room, flickering between him and Isabelle, pausing briefly on Bibi. Charlie looked thoroughly confused. "What's she doing here, and why are you dressed like a thug?"

Before he could reply, there was a sound outside the door, and Isabelle threw an invisibility shield over their small group. A nurse walked in a second later and hurried toward the bed. "Are you all right? I heard a scream."

Charlie looked to Colin for an explanation and let out a soft moan when she didn't see him.

The nurse asked, "Are you in pain?"

She shook her head.

The nurse checked the IV line to make sure it was in place and attached a blood pressure cuff. While it indicated the numbers, she listened to Charlie's heartbeat. When the machine clicked and the cuff deflated, the nurse glanced at the reading. "It's a little high, but nothing to worry about. Did you have a nightmare?"

"I...don't know," Charlie stuttered.

"I'd give you something to sleep, but we save the drugs for emergencies. It's not good for the twins. Would you like a cup of chamomile tea or hot chocolate?"

"No, thanks. I'll try to get back to sleep on my own."

"Good girl." The nurse helped Charlie get settled, and after checking the IV line one last time, she said, "Ring if you need me."

"I will."

As soon as the door closed, Colin and Isabelle were visible again.

Charlie broke into tears.

"Please don't cry," Colin said gently. "There's an explanation for all of this."

She buried her face in her hands and sobbed. "I think I'm going crazy," she said in between hitching breaths.

"Listen to me," Colin begged. "You're not seeing things or losing your mind. I'll explain it all, but we need to get you out of here first."

"I've been asking you for months to take me home."

Colin sighed. "It wasn't me."

She howled.

"Isabelle, can't you do anything to calm her down?"

Charlie lifted her tear-stained face. "If she touches me, I'll scream again."

"She's a friend."

"Leave me alone," Charlie begged. "When I wake up it'll be better."

Colin glanced at Isabelle and she muttered a curse in French and then chanted something in a language he didn't understand. All of a sudden, the room was quiet, and Charlie was asleep.

"Thank fuck."

"Can you lift her?" Isabelle asked.

"Of course."

He pulled the needle out of Charlie's vein and pressed his thumb over the spot of blood seeping through the pinprick. Without realizing it, Colin was using magic to stop the bleeding. Later Isabelle would point it out, but right then, he was working on instinct. Charlie was heavier than he'd expected, and his eyes automatically went to her obvious baby bump. Could the twins make such a difference already? They were probably no bigger than a potato at this point, but the additional weight was noticeable. He prayed Charlie wasn't part of Alain's vision. This might be his only chance to provide the requisite heirs, and he had to make certain nothing went wrong.

"Are we flying out of here?" he asked Isabelle.

"I can't take both of you."

"Take her," he said, thrusting Charlie into Isabelle's arms. "I'll meet you back at the hotel."

"How do you plan on getting away, Colin?"

"By cab. If anyone stops me on my way out, I'll pretend I'm Drake. He's not the only one who can play mind games."

The door slammed open, and Drake walked into the room. "Did you think I'd leave her unguarded?"

Oh, shit.

Andrew did his best to create a diversion, circling Drake like a whirling dervish, but the warlock was impervious to his machinations. With a sweeping gesture and a muttered incantation, Drake sent Andrew careening across the room.

"Stay in your lane, ghost. Come closer and your brother will pay the price."

"Leave him alone," Colin ordered Andrew. "I'll handle this."

"Now," Drake continued lazily. "Where were we?"

"My parents are willing to negotiate Charlie's release," Colin informed him coldly. "Not that you deserve anything, but she's an innocent party and shouldn't suffer any more than she already has."

Ignoring Colin, Drake addressed Isabelle. "Hand her over or you both die."

Isabelle sneered. "Have you checked in with your gran lately?"

"Last I heard she was fine."

"You're obviously behind on the news. Don't threaten me, or you'll end up like her."

Drake narrowed his eyes. "Did you hurt her?"

Isabelle inched closer to Colin and passed the still sleeping girl into his arms. "She got what she deserved."

It took Drake a second to connect the dots, and he struck back with a viciousness Isabelle didn't anticipate. It would have been a fatal blow, except Bibi shielded her mistress and caught the worst of it. The avian warrior's tiny frame, already pummeled from her altercation with Maura, wasn't strong enough to withstand Drake's fiery arrow. With one final triumphant screech, Bibi collapsed in a heap of smoking feathers. Isabelle cried out in anger and raised both hands in Drake's direction to retaliate, but he was too quick. He cast a binding spell around her, locking her magic in place. She screamed in frustration as she tried to break loose.

"How's that for quick reflexes?" Drake asked with a diabolical smile plastered on his face. "You're a washed-up witch who should have stepped down years ago. I'll put you out of your misery after Colin hands over what's rightfully mine."

"Like hell I will," Colin challenged. "You won't see a dime if you kill anyone else in this room."

Isabelle's aura was darkening by the second, and Colin wondered how long it would take her to break the invisible ties holding her in place. Maybe Drake had a point and Isabelle was no match for the younger warlock who was intent on bringing her down.

Colin sent her a subliminal message, hoping she would receive it. *Go, if you can break away. I'll talk him down until you come back with help. He needs me to negotiate the ransom.*

Isabelle didn't even twitch, but Colin heard her distinctive voice in his head. *I underestimated him. I'm sorry.*

You'll get him next time. Get out of here.

Thank you.

"Hey," Colin called out to distract Drake. "Let's take this down a notch and negotiate like civilized humans. If money is your end game, you'll get it."

"Except now I want my revenge," Drake maintained. "You should have stayed dead, but here you are messing with a perfectly constructed plan."

"Our parents won't negotiate unless there's proof of life."

"Then I'll wait," Drake replied. "Once the money exchanges hands, I'll stop your fucking heart. Alain won't be around to save your ass this time."

A light flashed and Isabelle disappeared, leaving a wisp of smoke behind.

"Fucking bitch," Drake raged. Whirling on Colin, he lunged and yanked Charlie out of his arms. She woke up and when she saw Colin and his doppelganger within a few feet of each other, she let out a piercing scream.

A lot of people poured into the room this time—nurses, orderlies, and security guards brandishing weapons.

Charlie struggled to get away from Drake, raking nails across his cheek in an attempt to break free. He dropped her unceremoniously, and she landed on the hard floor with a jarring thud. Clutching her belly, she whimpered and waited for the next blow to land, but Colin and the nurses ran forward to help. He got down on his haunches and lifted her into a sitting position. "Are you hurt?"

"Shook up more than anything."

"Get away from my fiancé," Drake barked.

"She's not your fiancé," Colin argued.

"What on earth is going on in here?" Raoul asked as he crossed the threshold. "This is a medical facility, not a boxing ring. You people have no regard for my patients. I've received multiple complaints, and it's barely five in the morning."

Colin stood and reached for the doctor's hand. "I apologize for the ruckus. I'm Prince Colin of Sendorra, and I'd like to take Charlie home."

Raoul took a deep breath and zeroed in on Drake. "Care to explain?"

"He's a con artist, Raoul. Does he look like a fucking prince to you?"

"I'm the heir apparent of Sendorra," Colin asserted. "There's a reason for my attire."

Drake snorted. "He's an imposter who wants to cash in on the action. Don't let him fool you."

Raoul grimaced and queried Charlie. "Can you tell me what's going on?"

"My lower back hurts."

Raoul got into doctor mode immediately and insisted they clear the premises. Only key personnel were allowed to remain by Charlie's side, but Colin caught a glimpse of blood on her nightgown and held back.

"I'd like to stay by her side," Colin pleaded. "If it's okay with Charlie."

"I'm not going anywhere unless he goes," Drake countered.

"Only one of you can stay," Raoul stated. "Who do you want, Charlie?"

Charlie looked at the two men standing at the foot of the bed and pointed at Colin. "I want him."

"Get out, Drake."

"You're making a mistake, Raoul."

"We'll talk about this later."

Drake fumed and tried to shoulder his way to Charlie's side, but security was closing the space between him and the bed. Colin watched and waited, expecting Drake to retaliate with magic, but he surprised everyone by following Raoul's orders, although his parting shot was chilling.

"You may have won this round, but the battle isn't over," he warned. "I don't have to be in your presence to make your life miserable or destroy those fucking twins. Think before you act, or you won't live long enough to regret it."

He left without another word.

Chapter Fifteen

WHEN ISABELLE MATERIALIZED and crumpled to the floor in Alain's library, he thought he was having another vision. There had been so many since coming home, but his mother was no illusion. She was, however, nothing like the confident woman he'd last seen in Bruges. Her normally elegant attire had been replaced by a black tracksuit, unrelieved by any suggestion of color, and, lifting her gently, he could tell by her pallid complexion and enlarged pupils she'd had some kind of shock. She melted into his arms and broke into harsh sobs. This was more astounding than anything else.

"What is it, Maman?"

"Drake." She tried to elaborate but the words never came.

Terror combined with a heavy dose of guilt flooded through Alain's system upon hearing the name of his nemesis. He put an arm around Isabelle's trembling shoulders and slowly led her to the sofa where she sank down gracelessly. When he tried to pull away, her icy fingers clutched at his hands to keep him close.

"Stay," she begged, chest heaving with ragged breaths.

"I'm not going anywhere, but I think you could use a stiff drink."

"Make it a double."

He rushed to the sideboard and filled two crystal tumblers with single malt whiskey. She downed hers in two swallows and, without further prompting, recounted the events of the last twenty-four hours.

"So...let me get this straight," Alain clipped. "You left Colin unprotected?"

"I had no choice," Isabelle lamented. "After Drake killed my darling Bibi, he froze me in a binding spell, and I couldn't attack him even if I wanted. I would have flayed him alive for what he did to Bibi, but I couldn't get through his shield. Colin urged me to leave if I could manage it—he knew I'd bring help."

"Drake's spellcasting must be weak if you were able to escape."

"Drake never expected me to abandon Colin, so he focused his attention elsewhere. I managed to get away, with some difficulty, and my powers are completely drained as a result."

"Did Drake hurt Colin?"

"Only verbally. He's holding his own for now, but I'm not sure how long he can last without our help."

"What else have you done, Maman?"

"I killed Maura."

"For Christ's sake," he admonished.

A tear trickled down the furrows of Isabelle's cheek, and he couldn't help feeling sorry for her, despite the storm raging in his gut.

"We have to stop Drake once and for all," Alain insisted. "How soon can you get going?"

"I'm going to need a few days to recuperate."

"We don't have the luxury of time," Alain seethed, finally releasing his pent-up anger. "I'll go by myself."

"You're no match for Drake, Alain. He's more powerful than I realized."

"Colin and his familiar will back me up," Alain assured her. "You know the inherent power of three is irrefutable. We will take him down."

"I can't lose you."

"If Colin dies, there's no point in living," Alain declared. "I've gone around and around with my questions, seeking answers from your goddess, and even dabbling in dark magic to try to look into the future—"

"And?" Isabelle cut him off.

"There were no ready solutions, only a blinding need to remain by his side come what may."

Isabelle sighed in resignation. "I'm not going to fight you on this anymore. Colin continues to surprise me with his courage and sense of duty. He's far greater than the sum of his parts and worthy of your love."

"You have it the other way around," Alain said. "I don't deserve his love or loyalty, after leaving him in the lurch, but I hope to redeem myself in the next few hours. He deserves a man who's willing to stand by him and face the unknown with grit and determination. I hope I'm not too late."

"Let's look at a map so I can give you the exact location of the clinic."

Now that a decision had been made, Isabelle rallied, and they put their heads together to come up with a plan. Alain would have loved to astral travel to speed things up, but he hadn't done it in years and couldn't take a chance at failing or depleting his powers if he managed the journey. He hired a private plane instead and landed in Bruges in under two hours.

His rental car, a sturdy Mercedes Benz SUV, was costly, but he'd chosen a larger vehicle to have the necessary room to transport Charlie if they succeeded in getting her away from Drake. Alain had no idea if she was in any condition to travel, but lowering the backseats would convert the area into a bed if she needed to lie down.

It was late morning by the time he arrived at the clinic, and he walked in the front door and demanded to see the director. His credentials had gained him entry to loftier establishments, and the guy in charge probably had no idea he was connected to Colin or Charlie. From what he'd gleaned from Isabelle, Drake wasn't exactly forthcoming, and it was doubtful he'd had time to warn anyone Alain de Gris might show up.

Dr. Raoul Davies greeted him with wary politeness. Alain sensed a caginess about the fellow, but he couldn't put his finger on the reason why. Was he actually a party to this outrageous kidnapping? Or complicit by default? If he'd offered Drake his clinic as refuge, then he surely had to have some part in this scheme. Alain decided it was best to view him as the enemy until he established the doctor's motives.

"What can I do for you?" Dr. Davies asked after inviting Alain to join him for some refreshments.

"I happened to be in the area, and the Andorran Royal Family asked me to check in on their only daughter, Princess Charlotte. I understand she's recuperating here for some reason. Did she have cosmetic surgery?"

The doctor's smile froze in place as the words sank in. "The royal family?"

"Didn't you know Charlotte was a princess?"

"I wasn't aware of her status."

Dropping all pretenses, Alain leaned forward and confronted the man. "Are you suggesting you didn't know your buddy has been impersonating my fiancé, Prince Colin of Sendorra? Drake tricked Charlie into believing he was Colin and kidnapped her when he was discovered. Now he's demanding a ransom for her release. I would think long and hard before you answer my question, Davies. It might make a difference in your sentencing."

"How dare you accuse me of anything? I've done nothing wrong."

"You're harboring a criminal, which makes you an accessory to the crime."

The look on the doctor's face spoke volumes. "I wasn't aware Charlie had been kidnapped. As for the impersonation...it explains a lot. She's been calling Drake by Colin's name ever since they arrived. I attributed the confusion to her condition. She was severely dehydrated and malnourished. It never occurred to me she was being duped. I've met Prince Colin and the resemblance to Drake is certainly uncanny. It's no wonder he was able to pull this off."

"Is Colin safe?"

The doctor looked puzzled. "Why wouldn't he be?"

"Because Drake despises him and has sworn to bring down the entire family. He's already killed the dowager."

The doctor was on his feet in an instant. "I left them upstairs unattended."

"Let's go," Alain said. They hurried out of the room, and Alain prayed he'd find Colin in good condition. He'd never forgive himself if anything happened to him while he'd been trying to find answers. For the umpteenth time since Isabelle's return, he'd berated himself for running away.

Colin was sitting by the bed holding Charlie's hand when Alain walked in. In an instant, he was by Alain's side, and the relief on his face gutted Alain. It took every ounce of self-control to keep his emotions in check. They embraced and held each other for a few seconds. "I'm sorry," Alain whispered.

"You should be," Colin muttered.

"Are you okay?"

"I am now."

"Where's Drake?"

"We haven't seen him since he walked out of here."

"When was this?"

"Earlier," Colin said vaguely. "I've lost all track of time. He threatened to destroy the twins."

"We won't let him anywhere close."

"He said it could happen from afar, Alain. Charlie's been bleeding since he left."

Alain looked at Doctor Davies. "Is this true?"

"She's been spotting on and off since she arrived. We've called in a specialist who deals with high risk pregnancies. They are monitoring her closely and suspect she's bleeding more on account of her fall. The uterus is intact, and there are no contractions."

"We need to get her out of here," Alain said. "Is she well enough to travel?"

"I would wait until the bleeding stops altogether." A female doctor walked in and introduced herself. "I'm Doctor Angela Whittaker, Charlie's current attending."

Alain stretched out his hand. "Alain de Gris."

"It's an honor to meet you," she replied. "Congratulations on the well-deserved Nobel."

"Thank you."

"Do you think she'll carry the twins to full term?" Colin asked.

"Multiple births are always high risk."

"Can't you give us any guarantees?"

"I'm afraid not. We need to keep an eye on her for the next twenty-four hours to see how this plays out."

"Will you let me know if she's in trouble?"

Dr. Whittaker looked at Charlie who continued to sleep. "I'll share anything as long as the princess agrees."

"Aren't there drugs you can administer to prevent miscarriage?"

"They're usually given when a woman goes into premature labor. Three to four weeks before a due date is acceptable, but not this early in her pregnancy. She's barely into her second trimester. The outcome of this current bleeding event is unpredictable."

"It's so frustrating," Colin said bitterly.

"I wish I had better news."

"Do you know anything about male pregnancies?"

Doctor Whittaker's eyebrows rose in surprise. "As a matter of fact I do."

"Can the twins be transferred to a viable uterus, if necessary?"

Alain opened his mouth to protest, but the determined look on Colin's face shut him down.

"Finding anyone willing and able to surrogate in a pinch is highly improbable," Dr. Whittaker explained.

"I'm intersex," Colin stated. "And the children's father. Get me ready just in case."

"No," Alain objected forcefully. "Absolutely not."

Colin gave him a withering glance. "It's my body and my decision."

"Jesus Christ, Colin. Your fathers will hit the roof."

"They have no say."

"You're not in charge yet," Alain reminded him. "They can and will forbid you to attempt something so risky."

"I'm just taking necessary precautions, Alain. Charlie may pull through this crisis like a champ, but my offer remains on the table. It's better to be prepared for any eventuality."

"Are you fucking serious right now?" Alain demanded. "I can't believe you'd even suggest such a thing."

"It's the least I can do," Colin maintained. "Why shouldn't I pay for my mistake? I'm prepared to lend my body in the event it's required."

Alain felt like throwing up, but he recognized the determined look on Colin's face and knew there was nothing he could say to change his mind.

"This will certainly make a difference going forward," Dr. Whittaker said thoughtfully.

"Can it be done?" Colin asked.

"Normally it takes months to prepare a uterus for implantation. We'll have to give you double doses of hormones, and you'll be miserable."

Colin shrugged. "Do whatever it takes to make this work."

"You're already assuming Charlie will miscarry," Alain said frigidly.

Colin whirled on him. "I'm simply taking precautions, and I'd appreciate a show of support."

Alain felt like an asshole, but he couldn't allow this to happen. "*Chaton*, please reconsider."

Colin's mouth flattened into a hard line, and his blue eyes glinted like diamonds. "Go ahead and leave if you can't deal with it."

"I'm not going anywhere."

"Then shut the fuck up."

"Colin?"

All eyes veered toward Charlie, who blinked awake. "What's going on?"

Colin rushed to her side while Dr. Whittaker checked her vital signs. "How are you feeling?"

"A little sore. Who's that?" she asked, pointing in Alain's direction.

"Alain."

"The boyfriend?"

Alain dipped his head in acknowledgement. "Actually, I'm Colin's fiancé."

Chapter Sixteen

"WHAT A DICK move," Colin observed as they walked down the hallway toward the elevator.

Alain gave him a side-eye. "I was merely reminding her of my role in this soap opera."

"It was juvenile."

"I suppose it was," Alain admitted with a shrug. "You bring out my inner brat."

"Don't make this about me," Colin said harshly. "Pulling the territorial card on the heels of your desertion is insulting. The man I fell in love with was conflicted about the rightness of our relationship, but he remained steadfast once he committed. You've been blowing hot and cold since you learned I fathered the twins."

"Why are you using the past tense?" Alain asked. "Have you fallen out of love so quickly?"

"No, you moron! I'm fucking pissed at you and worried about Charlie's health."

"Is that why you didn't bother to consult me before you offered to be a human incubator? You've made your feelings on male pregnancy clear from the very beginning. What's changed?"

"I'm responsible for this entire fiasco and should bear the brunt of it. Carrying the twins is a last resort, and I hope to God it isn't necessary, but I'm not going to let them die if there's a chance I can save them."

"I don't approve of your altruistic decision, but I'll stand by you if it comes to pass."

"See," Colin said in bewilderment. "You're doing it again."

"What?"

"Fucking with my head," Colin explained. "I was certain you'd give me an ultimatum if I went through with this, but now you're telling me you'll support me no matter what."

Alain lowered his gaze, and when he lifted it to respond, his amber eyes sparkled with emotion. "I regret my sudden departure, and you have every right to be furious, but don't ever question my love. It's visceral and therein lies the problem. This new development with Charlie is unsettling. I'm used to being in charge, and always coming out ahead, but this situation is out of my control, and messing with my conscience. I was hoping the distance might give me a fresh perspective. My timing could have been better, and I'll admit it would have saved a lot of confusion if I'd been forthcoming, but I was ashamed to voice my true feelings."

"I don't understand."

"I resent Charlie and everything she has to offer. The children I can't give you were created on the fly and have nothing to do with love and commitment."

"You should have said something," Colin said gently. "You were so stoic I didn't think you cared one way or the other."

"Oh, I care all right," Alain asserted. "Too damned much if you want to know the truth. The idea of sharing you is awakening the warlock I put to rest years ago. I refuse to give you up, but dark magic shouldn't be the solution."

"I'm on your side for whatever it's worth."

"Then we'll figure out a way—together. In the meantime, we have to address the immediate problem of Drake. We're sitting ducks if we can't figure out the best way to shut him down."

Colin snorted. "I was there when he almost killed Isabelle. How is she faring by the way?"

"Shaken," Alain admitted. "She underestimated the bastard and feels like she let you down by leaving."

"Andrew seems to be of the same mind. He's disappeared."

"How odd."

"Right? At least Isabelle is out of harm's way," Colin said. "Bibi's death was horrible, but she saved your mother's life. You should have been there, Alain. I've never been so terrified."

"If anything had happened to you, I'm not sure I would have survived."

"Still standing," Colin said grimly.

"What do I have to do to redeem myself?"

"Kill Drake, for starters."

"I'm working on a battle plan."

"Stop thinking and start acting. Drake has left a swath of destruction we never anticipated. At this rate, he'll destroy all of us before you formulate your strategy. Sometimes you just need to work off instinct."

"Point taken."

"Good," Colin said. "Let's see if the asshole left a message with Doctor Davies. Maybe he can provide some insight into Drake's madness."

Instead of answers, they found more destruction. Drake had taken out his anger and frustration on his buddy, who'd betrayed him by advocating for Charlie. The acrid stench of blood and loosened bowels permeated the doctor's office, and Alain quickly got into healer mode, using witchcraft to stop the bleeding while Colin ran to get help.

Drake had literally gutted Raoul, and it took a team of surgeons to scoop up his intestines and put them back in place. The chances of surviving the brutal attack were infinitesimal, but he was in a medically induced coma and holding his own for the moment. The rest was in the hands of fate.

Alain and Colin were exhausted and could have used a hot shower, room service, and a few hours of sleep, but they didn't dare leave Charlie unprotected. There was no telling if Drake would circle back to try to spirit her away during the confusion.

Colin was napping on a recliner by Charlie's bed, and Alain slept fitfully on the cot they'd set up for him on the other side of the room. It wasn't until the morning shift came in to check Charlie's vitals that Colin noticed the message on his phone.

The money exchange has to proceed. You may have won this round, but the fight isn't over. Check her sheets if you don't believe me.

The hair-raising text prompted Colin to send for the obstetrician who confirmed the bleeding continued, but the twins' vital signs were within normal limits.

"I'd love to get the hell out of here," Colin muttered. "At least I can control the situation back home and have guards posted around the clock. There's nothing to prevent Drake from turning up here and wreaking more havoc."

"He seems to be doing enough damage from afar," Alain pointed out.

"Can't you put up wards and whatnot if we transport Charlie back to the castle?"

"Yes. We'll have a lot more control in Sendorra."

"Let's go home, Alain."

"Excuse me," Dr. Whittaker interrupted. "If you still intend to attempt a fetal transfer, we need to start your treatments immediately."

"Seriously?"

"I'm afraid so."

"Can I hire you to come along for the ride and monitor us in Sendorra?"

"Surely you can find someone in your own country."

"I want you."

Dr. Whittaker gave an embarrassed laugh. "Do you have any idea how much I make on an hourly basis?"

"I have deep pockets," Colin said. "Money is the least of our worries."

She studied him for a few minutes, probably checking her schedule in her head and weighing the pros and cons. To Colin's relief, she asked "How soon did you want to leave?"

"Is an hour enough time to get ready?"

"I'll need at least two more hours."

"Fine."

"Colin?" Charlie called out.

"Hey," he said, moving closer to the bed. He grabbed Charlie's hand and gave her a reassuring squeeze. "I didn't realize you were awake."

"Are we going home?"

"Yes."

"Thank God. What about...Drake? Can he still hurt me?"

"You'll be safe with us. I'll explain everything once we're on the plane."

"My lower back is killing me," she complained.

Colin glanced at the doctor for answers.

"I can give her a mild sedative."

"Screw that," Charlie said. "I want something to knock me out for the duration. Wake me up when this nightmare is over."

"I'm sorry, but I can't administer narcotics in your condition."

"Have I mentioned how much I hate being pregnant?"

"You've had a rougher time than most," the doctor said soothingly.

"I'll make up something herbal to ease her discomfort," Alain offered.

"Thank you," Charlie said gratefully.

He nodded and walked out the door.

"Do his skills extend beyond research?" Dr. Whittaker asked.

"Alain is a believer in holistic medicine. He always travels with a bunch of herbs and whatnot."

"Handy."

Colin smiled, glad he didn't have to explain witchcraft at this juncture. He wondered if Alain had come to terms with Charlie yet. Probably not, but at least he was here. They'd have to work on finding a peaceful resolution to assuage his pride as well as his ethics. An idea took form in Colin's head, but he would keep it close to the cuff until it was fully fleshed out. There were too many variables at this point.

His fathers were front and center on his mind, and he wasn't looking forward to breaking the news about Charlie, the twins, Drake's malevolent plotting, and his decision. There would be an epic battle to win them over, but he was gearing up for the worst. It was his body, after all, and his life to do with as he pleased. They could take it or leave it, but it wouldn't change his mind. Ensuring the monarchy was his main objective and the best argument he could provide. Drake had no clue he was intersex, and all his efforts to derail Charlie would be for naught if the twins were no longer inside her body. They would be protected, and Charlie could walk away unscathed. It was a good plan, and he was going to lay it out in detail, get Alain to back him, and present a united front once his fathers got over the initial shock.

He didn't think Charlie would object. She was sick of being pregnant, and he hoped she would give her permission without any conditions. Colin was willing to let her co-parent, and she'd have a special title to go along with the job, but he couldn't marry her. Not if he wanted to keep Alain. There was absolutely no wiggle room when it came to this decision. Now he just had to pull it off.

Chapter Seventeen

COLIN THANKED THE efficient staff at Dr. Davies's clinic who, for reasons he didn't bother to examine, were well-versed in subterfuge. When he informed them it was life or death they leave the premises without tipping off Drake, they worked diligently to make it happen. He left a huge tip and a note for Dr. Davies to call him if he survived his ordeal. The latest news from the hospital was optimistic.

Dr. Whittaker insisted they call her Angela since she was now the official attending physician and their employee for the duration. A taxi dropped her off at the hangar reserved for noncommercial flights, and she looked like a different person in her leggings, fur-lined boots, and cable-knit sweater. Her hair was pulled back in a ponytail, and shearling earmuffs completed the picture of the efficient professional.

Charlie was settled in her makeshift bed, and once they were airborne, Colin drew Angela aside for a private conversation.

"I feel it's important you have some background on my family dynamics before we land. I have two fathers and one of them is also intersex. They fell in love at first sight, and Errol agreed to carry a child so the line of succession was secure. It was the only reason my grandparents gave their blessing to a same-sex union. From what I gathered, the pregnancy was uneventful except my twin died in utero for some reason. All my life I've wondered if he would have lived if we were conceived traditionally."

"One has nothing to do with the other," Angela assured him. "How old are you?"

"Twenty-one."

"There have been many advances in the last two decades. Nowadays, a male pregnancy is nothing like it was back in your father's time. The mortality rate has dropped exponentially."

"That's good news," Colin said. "Nonetheless, I'm apprehensive. Do you think I'll be okay?"

"You look healthy enough. I'll know more after we do some blood work. And speaking of testing," Angela continued, "I'm going to need access to a hospital and fully functioning laboratory. Charlie should be in a medical environment."

"There's a state-of-the-art hospital in Sendorra with an entire wing dedicated to intersex pregnancy, due to my father's experience. You won't lack for anything by way of equipment."

"Always reassuring. Where will I stay?"

"I can offer you a palatial suite, or if you'd rather be close to Charlie, we can set up nice quarters for you at the hospital."

"As much as I'd love to live in a palace, I'd be more comfortable within easy reach of my patient in case of an emergency."

"I'll make the arrangements."

"Thank you."

"You're welcome," Colin replied. "How many weeks before my uterus is prepped?"

"If we're aggressive with the hormones, it shouldn't take more than three weeks."

"Too long," Colin worried.

"I disagree," Angela said. "Conventional therapy can take up to eight weeks."

"How will I feel?"

"I could lie and tell you it'll be a breeze, but I won't insult you. The sudden influx of hormones will mimic pregnancy. You'll have nausea, acne, headaches, and I predict your libido will disappear."

"Sounds like a blast." Colin exhaled and gave her a sheepish smile. "At least I'm getting a head start and won't have to carry for nine months."

"Four months tops. In any case, we may not even need your uterus. Charlie might recover, and this will be a nonissue. Can you explain why this trip feels like a diaspora? Who are we running from?"

Colin grimaced. He'd mistakenly assumed Angela would be oblivious to their surreptitious departure, but she was astute as well as competent. She might change her mind, if he revealed they were under attack by a powerful warlock, and witchcraft played a huge role in his and Alain's life, but keeping silent about their predicament would be doing her a disservice and might put her in danger.

"Charlie was kidnapped several months ago, and the asshole behind the attack is my cousin, Drake. He's a ruthless psychopath who decided to inhabit my life. Since he happens to look like me—the resemblance is startling— it was relatively easy. Charlie was a victim of his switch and bait. All this time she believed we were together."

"My God!" Angela exclaimed. "That's reprehensible."

"He's a sick fuck, and now that his plan is unraveling, he's determined to kill all of us. Drake was instrumental in the death of my grandmother, the Dowager Princess Alexandra, and he's tried to kill me on more than one occasion. We caught a lucky break when we found out he was hiding in Bruges, but poor Dr. Davies has paid the price."

"What happened to him?"

"Drake lost his mind when the doctor listened to Charlie instead of siding with him. He left the man for dead, but we were able to get him to the hospital in time. He might pull through."

"Thank goodness," Angela commiserated. "Do you think this mad man will try to follow us?"

"For sure, but I'm confident I can keep you and Charlie safe in Sendorra. It's my home turf and I have many more resources at my fingertips. Try not to worry."

"The only thing I worry about is my patient. I'll leave the rest in your hands."

"We should have some sort of code, so you'll know it's me you're dealing with, and not Drake. He's arrogant enough to impersonate me again, and I don't want you drawn into his twisted game."

"What do you suggest?"

"Do you have a nickname?"

"Jellybean."

Colin barked out a laugh. "Seriously?"

"My older brothers baptized me at a young age and it stuck."

"Who else knows about it?"

"Only family members."

"Okay," Colin nodded. "I'll address you by your nickname whenever I visit Charlie. If you hear any other greeting, be on guard. Drake might figure out a way to get past security, but you can be Charlie's next line of defense."

"Should I carry a weapon?"

"Do you know how to use a gun?"

"I come from a hunting family," she informed him. "I can also gut and dress a deer in under an hour if necessary."

"Your skills might come in handy."

She smiled affably. "How about a dagger or pepper spray?"

"Whatever you're comfortable with is fine with me. I'll let security know you'll be carrying so they don't flip out."

"Carrying a gun in my line of work seems counterintuitive. I think I'll stick with pepper spray for now. It might buy a few more minutes."

"It's your call, Angela. I hope I haven't scared you shitless."

"Growing up with three brothers and their friends has taught me how to stand up to bullies."

"Drake is in a separate class altogether," Colin warned. "Don't make the mistake of underestimating him."

"I won't."

"Ask if you need anything. There's food and drinks onboard."

"Thank you, your highness."

Colin nodded and returned to his seat beside Alain.

"Did you pump her for information?" he asked tersely.

"Yes, and I also warned her to be on the lookout for Drake."

"I thought so," Alain replied. He sighed and clutched Colin's hand. "Is there anything I can say or do to dissuade you from acting on this crazy impulse?"

"It's not an impulse, Alain. This is the perfect solution to our personal Rubik's Cube."

"Go ahead and convince me this isn't the worst idea you've ever had."

Colin knew he'd only have one chance to get his point across, and he had to use reason when presenting his case. His cerebral lover wouldn't be swayed by emotion or histrionics. Colin had tried in the past and it never worked on Alain.

"Put aside your fears for my safety and think of the big picture. If Charlie lets me shoulder the responsibility of carrying the twins, my obligation to marry her disappears. No one but her immediate family, and mine, knows she's pregnant. Her parents can walk away from this disaster with their honor intact."

"What if she says no?"

"If Drake continues his subliminal attacks, she may have no choice. I doubt she'll want to hang on to this pregnancy if her life, or the twins, are at risk."

"She's been groomed to be your wife from a young age," Alain argued. "Do you honestly believe she'll give you up without a fight?"

"Once she realizes what we're up against, she'll give in to my request."

"You seem pretty sure she'll be amenable."

"The girl I knew and loved isn't selfish. Our breakup was amicable. We both realized we were wrong for each other. I can't blame her for rushing to Biarritz to attempt a reconciliation when she found out she was pregnant. It was self-preservation—not malice. She hoped we'd fall in love again. Any other princess would have forced me into a loveless marriage, but Charlie's not vindictive or petty. I give her major points for keeping her parents out of the loop."

"She won my admiration a while back for trying to work it out on her own, but I'm sorry she fell into the wrong hands. Nobody deserves Drake, least of all Charlie."

Colin sighed with relief when he noted the shift in Alain's attitude.

"Do I have the okay to proceed with my plan?"

"What did you have in mind?"

"Convince my parents."

"It won't be easy, *chaton*."

"Nothing worthwhile is ever easy, but I know how to handle those two. I've had years of practice."

"And you're a tenacious shit who usually gets his way."

"Guilty as charged."

"Isabelle has had a change of heart and won't stand in our way."

"As if she could stop me."

"Well, she was under the illusion we'd fall in step with her plan."

Colin snorted.

"Don't get cocky. Having her on our side is always a good thing."

"If you say so."

THERE WERE MANY advantages to being a royal, but today Colin was especially grateful. His fathers were waiting on the tarmac with a team of royal guards, an ambulance to take Charlie and Angela to the hospital, and enough security around the perimeter of the airport to keep out the curious. Complete privacy was guaranteed, and Colin breathed easily for the first time in days.

In the limo on the way back to the palace, Colin voiced his appreciation.

"Thank you for keeping our arrival on the down low. I was hoping Charlie's parents wouldn't be here."

Prince Sebastian looked grim. "We thought it would be best for now."

"Your father and I wanted an update before bringing her parents into the discussion," the Duke of Maitland explained. As always, Errol was a reliable buffer for Prince Sebastian's oftentimes autocratic behavior.

"I don't even know where to begin," Colin said.

"Will you allow me to lay it out chronologically?" Alain asked.

"Please do," Colin expressed with relief. "You're much better at it than I'll ever be."

Instead of briefing the royals in the war room, they retired to the library, a friendlier environment that brought the tension down several notches. Over a light lunch, Colin listened while Alain explained, sparing none of the gory details; however, he did leave out the new information on the pregnancy.

"I thought he'd be stopped by now," Prince Sebastian said in disgust.

"He's a wily bastard," Errol commented.

"And batshit crazy," Colin added. "The guy has managed to slip out of our grasp on several occasions."

"What's going on with Charlie?" Prince Sebastian demanded.

"Do you want the good news first or shall I start with the bad?" Colin asked.

Chapter Eighteen

CLOAKED IN AN invisibility shield, Drake drove back to the clinic later in the day to check on Charlie. When he learned she was gone and Raoul might recover, he lost all control and unleashed his fury on the inanimate. Setting off the overhead sprinklers and damaging the plumbing system, he left the entire clinic in a stinking quagmire of backed-up sewage and ruined furnishings. Driving away, with gleeful satisfaction, Drake thought of the people responsible for destroying his plans, and his buoyant mood plummeted.

His failure to keep Charlie hostage, or walk away with the fortune he'd envisioned, filled him with white-hot rage, and his hatred for Colin coalesced into a burning desire to bring him down, regardless of the cost. Alain and Isabelle were high on his kill list, but it was Colin who'd engineered the escape, and he'd be the first to die. Drake had come too far to give up now, and moreover, he refused to be bested by a boy who'd never appreciated his good fortune. He'd begged Drake to impersonate him, and now Colin wanted to yank it all away. Fuck him and his pissant boyfriend, Alain. They wanted to be together so badly Drake would make sure they died in each other's arms.

Taking stock of his finances, Drake realized he was close to broke. He'd been counting on the ransom to bail him out, and now he didn't have enough to pay for the hotel or the car he'd rented. He'd have to leave the area in a hurry, certain the authorities had received detailed descriptions from Raoul's staff, and besides, there was nothing he could do to Charlie from another country. If he wanted to continue his subliminal attacks on her and the brats, she had to be within striking distance.

Without Maura to keep him in check, Drake descended into the darkest corners of his psyche. He reverted to old habits, relying on street smarts to keep him ahead of the law. He dumped his car and jacked another, heading south toward Sendorra, which lay between France and Spain. It would take him days to get there, but flying was out of the question due to airport security, which probably had his name on a Most Wanted fugitive list, and traveling by train was just as risky as it was uncomfortable. He was better off driving, changing vehicles as often as possible to keep the police off his trail. As he drove, his mood alternated between steely determination and feverish agitation.

He decided to use women as a distraction. Charm and good looks, along with cunning and a dose of magic, had paved the way for his sexual conquests in the past, and it was no different now. To his mind, finding solace in a warm body was better than brooding over his failures. One of his hookups, a dark-haired beauty named Yesenia, reminded him of Charlie before she got pregnant, and he persuaded her to go on the road trip. If things didn't pan out, or she got too clingy, he'd dump her well before arriving in Sendorra. Predictably, Yesenia lost her appeal after a few days, and they both agreed it was time to catch a train back to Belgium.

Nearly a week passed before he arrived on the outskirts of the small principality he'd never seen before. Biarritz had been the royal headquarters during the summer months he'd subsumed Colin's place in the royal hierarchy. He'd lost sight of the original plan because it had been such a heady experience. Only meant to be temporary, a stopgap so Colin and Alain could get away without parental interference, power and privilege had destroyed whatever conscience Drake possessed, and greed had influenced all his decisions going forward.

None of his generation had ever been invited to the imperial palace in Sendorra. It was one of the many reasons Maura harbored an abiding grudge against the late dowager. Her younger sister was so much in love with her husband, the former ruler Prince Emile, she never challenged his wishes to keep witchcraft and her magical siblings as far away as possible. It was no wonder the entire clan embraced the envious resentment that trickled down from mother to daughter to Drake.

Snow had fallen early this year, and the locals were gearing up for the season. Sendorra was a winter lover's paradise and usually drew skiing enthusiasts from different parts of the world. In a pricey outfit he'd managed to purloin at a ski shop a few towns over, Drake tramped the snow-covered streets of the small Alpine village. One more tourist wouldn't turn heads, even if his picture had been posted in public places. He looked nothing like the blue-eyed manager who'd posed for his last employer's official headshot. With green contact lenses, a full beard dyed in the same dark auburn he'd chosen for his hair, Drake looked like any other rich dude in search of fun.

Rather than stick out as a loner, Drake joined a small group of men and women heading toward the ski lifts. As usual, women gravitated toward him in droves. They spent some time on the easier slopes, but Drake, having been raised in a Northern climate, was an avid skier and showed off his skills with aplomb. After successfully conquering the more difficult slopes, and winning the admiration of his companions, his spirits lifted as he basked in the praise. They ended up at a popular bar after the long day, and he casually brought up the subject of the royal family to see if he could get more information.

There was none.

Any news was deliberately withheld, and the citizens of Sendorra weren't in the least bit concerned. Colin had always been reluctant to share information regarding his private life. Habitually envious, Drake resented Colin's down-to-earth attitude. He thought back on the meager wardrobe he'd had to replenish when he stepped into the role of prince. The shopping sprees had been a delicious perk, and soaking up the attention wherever he went was another bonus he'd enjoyed. He didn't understand how anyone born with so much could turn their back on such bounty.

Drake was relieved when one of the girls invited him back to her room. It would save him the expense of finding lodgings, and he planned to milk the connection for all its worth. The premier five-star hotel, located in the center of town, was lit up like a Christmas tree. It was Sendorra's pride and joy, home to the international casino that was a chief source of revenue for the principality. Drake's heartrate picked up when he spied the familiar green felt tables and spinning roulette wheels. With magic at his fingertips, he didn't have to be a card shark. He mainly had to keep his greedy impulses under control. Once the establishment grew suspicious of his "lucky streak" they'd find a way to escort him off the premises. It was better to win a little each day instead of seeking the big jackpot. The money would augment his dwindling income, and casino monitors would ignore him. Hanging around the casino would also give him more opportunities to find out where the royals had taken Charlie. He had to find her before he could resume his torture. Once Colin realized he was unstoppable, they'd pay the ransom, and Drake could begin his killing spree in style.

IN ANOTHER DIMENSION, home to preternatural creatures of every kind, Andrew watched Drake. He kept his distance after finding out the hard way the warlock not only felt his presence, he could see him. It made spying difficult but not impossible. Ghostly Bibi was by his side, no longer a blackened wreck. Her beautiful white feathers were restored, and she gleamed like one of the angels floating around their vast space. How they'd managed to find each other was a mystery they'd never solve, but it was comforting to have her by his side once again, and communication seemed better in this unnatural state.

"Drake is up to no good," Andrew mused. "I can see the wheels spinning in his Machiavellian brain, and I'm worried about our charges."

"I'd like to peck his eyes out," Bibi replied.

"Can you do it in ghostly form?"

"I could practice on a field mouse."

"Report back afterward. I'd like to know what weapons we'll have on hand when we attack."

"Later," she said, flying off into the unknown.

Andrew watched her go with grim determination. They were both reeling from their misadventure at Drake's hand. All his non-life he'd protected Colin, and Bibi had been Isabelle's familiar for decades. To fail at such a spectacular level was humbling, and the need to redeem their honor was uppermost in their minds.

He was sickened by Drake's smarmy moves on an innocent woman who'd casually offered her body—and hotel room—for the night. Andrew was appalled by her lack of judgement. Didn't she realize Drake was a cold-blooded psychopath? They'd just met for heaven's sake. Andrew wasn't a prude, but he did have his standards. He grimaced as they stripped, then left the room in a hurry to wander up and down the hallway while they jumped each other's bones.

Bibi was back with a speck of blood on her beak.

"You must have been successful," Andrew chortled.

"I got it done, but I left one good eye so the poor creature could continue to forage."

"Good of you for being magnanimous."

"Hurting innocents is not in my job description," Bibi stated primly. "Why are you wandering the halls like a ghost?"

"Pun intended?"

She beat her wings and swayed, making clacking noises meant to mimic laughter. She was having way too much fun in her new role.

"They're doing the nasty."

"Say no more."

They left, certain the sex would go on most of the night. In the morning, they'd return to take up their posts. In the meantime, looking in on Charlie was a good idea. He'd stuck around in Bruges long enough to know they'd spirited her away in a Lear jet, and she was in a private room at the local hospital. Andrew was convinced Drake would make another attempt to destroy the twins before they saw the light of day. Well, it wasn't going to happen on his watch. Neither of those babies was going to die in utero. Andrew had resigned himself to his fate long since, but he wanted his nephews to enjoy many years on earth before shedding their mortal coils.

The hospital was quiet, and Charlie seemed to be doing better than the last time Andrew had seen her. She was sleeping peacefully and the machines monitoring her vitals showed normal numbers. There was no one in the room, so the chance of bumping into Colin before he was ready to face him, could be postponed. He was sure his brother was holed up somewhere in the palace with Alain. He hovered over Charlie and stared at the baby bump when it moved slightly. Curious, he snuck a peak under her taut belly to check on his nephews. They were floating happily in their amniotic sac, sucking peacefully on their thumbs. He wondered what their personalities would be like. Was one of them going to resemble Colin and the other Charlie? He and his twin were nothing alike so perhaps these two would follow in their footsteps. He couldn't wait to meet them.

He decided to hang around until morning and was glad for his decision when a young female doctor walked in with Colin bringing up the rear. He'd caught a glimpse of her in Bruges before he booked, but now he was able to get the full measure of the woman. She appeared competent, and Charlie smiled when she woke up and saw her standing by the bed.

"Good morning," the doctor said cheerily. "How are you feeling today?"

"I feel good," Charlie replied. "May I have some breakfast?"

"Of course. We'll make it a light one to see if you can keep it down."

Colin perched on the edge of the bed. "You look and sound a lot better."

"Thanks," Charlie replied. "Getting away from Drake has done wonders for my disposition. He must have been poisoning me or something."

Andrew bobbed his head in agreement. If she only knew.

"I'll come back later to check on you again," Colin said. "Try to get some rest."

"Shouldn't we talk about the future?" Charlie asked. "We have to make some decisions."

"There's no rush."

Andrew could sense Colin evading, and he wondered what was going on. He couldn't ask without showing himself, but curiosity had always been his downfall, and he followed Colin at a distance. It was hell staying away, but his pride wouldn't let him surface until he had some kind of solution.

As soon as he left the hospital premises, he saw Drake walking hand in hand with his new girl. They were headed his way, and Andrew quickly backtracked toward the room he'd just left. Charlie was eating a bowl of oatmeal with gusto, chatting with the doctor between bites. She seemed fine, so Andrew flitted back outdoors to check on Drake again. He was sitting on a bench, with his arm draped around the girl's shoulder, but he wasn't looking at her. His gaze was fixed on a window four floors above ground. Without looking, Andrew was sure it was Charlie's room. Drake's aura, only visible to Andrew, was growing darker and darker. Soon a black cloud enveloped him, and the dark energy unleashed a noxious wave that reeked of death and decay. What the fuck was he doing?

Andrew returned to the hospital room in time to watch Charlie clutch her belly and cry out. The monitors beeped alarmingly, and the doctor checked Charlie's vitals, trying to determine what had happened so suddenly. Andrew looked under the hood, or in this case, Charlie's belly, to check on his nephews, and they were being tossed about like sailors on a dingy during a storm. Once outside the fragile cocoon, Andrew observed Charlie thrashing and moaning. Angela kept telling her to calm down. It was just a cramp, she said, a reaction to her first solid meal in a while, but Andrew knew better. It was Drake fucking with all of them.

Charlie settled and allowed the doctor to examine her internally. After Angela was done and had removed her gloves, she frowned in confusion. "Everything feels normal. I'm not sure what caused the cramps."

"Maybe I should forego solids for now," Charlie said. "I'm hungry, but I can't stand the aftermath."

"It seems like an extreme reaction to a tiny bowl of oatmeal," the doctor remarked.

"Let's stick to gelatin for today," Charlie grumbled. "We'll try eggs tomorrow."

Andrew left without waiting for the doctor's reply. He knew this incident had nothing to do with food. He saw Drake sitting on the same bench, smiling, the dark cloud escaping on a breeze, leaving nothing behind but sunshine and light. Andrew checked to make sure he hadn't imagined this, but the expression on Drake's face said it all—the warlock was gloating in satisfaction, like a big cat with his latest kill oozing entrails from his clenched jaw. Andrew shuddered and took off, chasing after Colin. Fuck his pride. He had to warn him Drake was close and gunning for revenge.

Chapter Nineteen

COLIN WAS ON the phone with Angela when Andrew took shape. The delight upon seeing his twin was quickly replaced with a wrinkled brow as his attention switched back to the call.

"Are you positive it wasn't indigestion?" he grilled.

He signaled for Andrew to stay put while he continued to question Angela.

"And no strangers have paid Charlie a visit?"

Her negative answer made him rake his fingers through his hair in frustration.

"Dammit. I'll be there shortly," Colin informed, adding, "We need to double up on my shots."

He disconnected and glared at Andrew.

"It's about fucking time you showed up! Where the hell have you been?"

After Drake killed Bibi, I was sort of lost and mopey. Fortunately, Bibi is back.

"Back where?" Colin asked, looking over Andrew's shoulder for any sign of the owl.

By my side in ghostly form.

"I'm sure Isabelle will be happy to hear the news," Colin huffed. "Let me remind you of your obligation as my familiar. You're supposed to give notice before taking bereavement leave."

Sorry.

"You should be. I could have used your support on several occasions. Are you ready to do battle?"

I have so much to tell you.

"Spill."

Andrew caught him up on Drake's whereabouts and mentioned he'd been seen outside the hospital with his current bimbo.

"How the fuck did he get into the country without my knowledge?" Colin ranted. "His image is plastered all over the place."

He's in disguise.

"I should have known."

You can't anticipate everything, brother.

"I can and I will."

Tell me.

As Colin laid out his plan, Andrew's image flickered in and out like a poor internet connection. In truth, he was probably having a moment of acute anxiety, and this was one way of manifesting his feelings.

You can't risk your life this way, bro. You're irreplaceable.

"Maybe, but I won't let anyone else die on my account."

Has Charlie agreed?

"I haven't talked to her yet, but I'm sure she'll consider it after I explain. Now that she's seen Drake for what he is, it'll be easier to convince her."

What's she getting out of the deal? Are you offering marriage?

"Marrying Charlie is my father's solution, not mine. You've got to remember we broke up in May. It was a mutual decision."

Until you fucked her. Talk about mixed messages.

"There's no need to be crass. Shit happens when you're drunk and start to reminisce."

I wouldn't know.

"And therein lies the problem."

Still. After what she's endured, it doesn't seem fair to wrench those twins away and leave her with nothing.

"Charlie will die if I don't intervene. And so will the twins. Don't you get it? Even if I double the ransom, Drake will continue these attacks and destroy them for no good reason other than he hates me and our entire family. Do you honestly think he'll live up to his end of the bargain?"

Probably not.

"There is no probably about this," Colin fumed.

Things will work out to your benefit if this plan of yours is successful.

"What do you mean?"

You'll get the requisite heir and spare without losing the man of your dreams. Sounds like a huge loss for Charlie and a big win for you.

"Are you being deliberately obtuse or what?"

Let's say I'm playing devil's advocate, so you're prepared to justify this decision to Charlie and the rest of the world, especially our fathers.

"I would think she'd jump on any chance to survive," Colin said resolutely. "I'm not going to lie and tell you I haven't thought of the benefits if we succeed. It'll be the perfect solution for Alain and me, *if* I can pull this off, but there are no guarantees. The swap might kill one or both twins, and I might not survive the procedure. It's not without risk, but nothing worthwhile is easy. I've had nightmares about male pregnancy since I first learned how it works, and how Da almost died during childbirth. Alain has had visions of blood and death in a hospital setting. It took a lot to convince Alain. I'm not going into this lightly, Andrew. To be honest, I'm terrified, but what alternatives do I have? At the moment, Drake appears to be invincible. Charlie and the twins don't have the luxury of time. We know this is an improbable solution, but it's the only one we've got."

Your argument should satisfy the naysayers.

"Are you going to back me up on this decision? I can't do this on my own, Andrew."

I'll support you in whatever way I can.

"Having you around is a huge benefit and all I can ask for at the moment."

There's other stuff I can do, but we can talk about it later. You need to clear this up with Charlie first.

"I'm not looking forward to revealing my magical lineage to Charlie. She's going to flip out."

She's probably experienced some form of magic from Drake and Maura.

"No doubt. It might actually help her to understand she wasn't imagining any of the strange things going on in her life."

I think she's resilient enough to cope.

"I hope you're right. Give me the info you have on Drake, so I can pass it on to security."

Alain joined him in the car on the way to the hospital, and Colin gave him a quick rundown on the latest.

"He's in town?"

"Yeah, he's staying at the casino hotel with some girl. I've given security all the particulars."

"Which'll do diddly once he realizes we're on to him."

"Feel free to jump in with a suggestion."

Alain reached for his hand and gave him a reassuring squeeze. "You're doing fine without my help."

"I'm doubling up on the hormone therapy as soon as Charlie gives the okay."

"Today?" Alain blanched.

"No time like the present."

"Your parents are still on the fence," Alain reminded him. "Don't you need some official document to approve your decision?"

"I just need to pick up the phone and tell them we're under attack again."

Alain shut his eyes and heaved in resignation. "I want to be present throughout each procedure."

"I should hope so, but at the moment, I need to sit down with Charlie and tell her what's happening. I'm certain it will go over better if you're not around."

Alain nodded. "You know her best."

"Thank you."

"Would you drop me off at the hotel first?"

"The casino?"

"Yes."

"No," Colin panicked. "You can't confront him on your own."

"Relax. I'm not going to approach him."

"Won't he sense your presence?"

"I was raised by a high priestess, Colin. A simple disguising spell will keep me safe."

"What if he smells you?"

Alain chuckled. "He's not a vampire or werewolf."

"Doesn't a warlock have olfactory senses that are above average?"

"Nothing I can't deal with. Please, try not to worry."

"Swear you won't engage."

"On my mother's life," Alain said calmly. "I'm just going to get the lay of the land."

"The limo will come back for you after it drops me off at the hospital."

"Sounds good."

They kissed goodbye at the hotel portico, and Colin worried his lower lip all the way to the hospital. He had so much on his plate right then, and he didn't need to add Alain's safety to the mix, but there was no convincing the man. They were both stubborn and opinionated. It was a small miracle they could agree on a sexual position without a long argument before stripping down and dirty. Colin wondered how long it would take for the hormones to start working their poison on his libido. Would his limp dick be instantaneous, or did he have a few days to stockpile orgasms? Shuddering in anticipation of what was to come, he pushed the negative out of his head and focused on the positive.

Charlie was awake when he arrived, and Angela was sitting by her bed reading something on an electronic device. They both raised their heads and smiled.

"How are you feeling?" he asked Charlie, bending to kiss her lightly on the top of her head.

"I'm better."

"You'll probably get sick again once I'm done talking to you."

"Would you like some privacy?" Angela asked.

"It's best you hear this so you know what we're up against."

Colin pulled up a chair and took a deep breath. He didn't know how far back he should start the story for it to make sense. Channeling Alain, he decided to lay it out sequentially. He started with his birth, and the magical connection he shared with his grandmother, and kept on talking until he was done. Neither woman interrupted, but Charlie's eyes grew wide while Angela slowly put her device aside and peered at him intently. Instead of stopping to allow them to ask questions, he jumped right into the present and Drake's subliminal attacks while offering his solution. Charlie's cheeks were shining by the time he finished his saga.

"Why didn't you ever share this, Colin? We were so close."

"I denied the magic for years, and my fear of male pregnancy seemed irrelevant to our situation."

Angela stood and got to ready to leave. "I think it's time for me to go. I'll ask my questions when you step outside."

Colin nodded. "Okay."

Charlie's tears hadn't abated, so he passed her a box of tissues and waited. It was a lot to take in at once, and he gave her as much time as she needed to come to grips with the situation.

Finally, her tears let up and she blew her nose. "Let me get this straight, Colin. The man who asked me to join him in Biarritz was Drake?"

"It was him from the minute you got the first text."

"The connection between us felt so genuine," Charlie whined in anguish. "The sex was beyond amazing, and you kept telling me how much you regretted our breakup. My pregnancy no longer seemed like the end of the world because you were in love with me again."

"It wasn't me," Colin said gently.

She buried her face in cupped hands and wailed. Colin didn't know what to say to make it better, but he got off the chair and perched on her side of the bed. Hugging her tightly, he offered her support while giving her time to grieve. Finally, she asked, "How could I have been so blind?"

"You wanted to believe things would work out. Drake beguiled you with his charm and smooth talk. It's what he does best. I can't blame you for falling under his spell. He's far more appealing than I'll ever be."

"But it's you I love," she entreated.

"Is it?" Colin asked. "We broke up for a reason, Charlie. You know our relationship had deteriorated beyond help. Our sex life was mediocre at best. The man you were crazy about wasn't me."

She pushed him away, anger overtaking the self-pity. "Maybe I should just marry Drake, and he'll stop trying to kill the twins and me. We were happy before you showed up."

"You don't mean that," Colin said. "And even if you were crazy enough to run away with Drake, I won't give up my kids."

"They're *partly* yours. I know my rights and you can't make an arbitrary decision to suit your purposes. They are my children, and this is my body."

Dude, you need to chill or rein in the royal card. She's not buying into your plan.

Colin cleared his throat. "You have every right as a mother to be territorial. I get it. But if we don't do something to stop Drake, the point will be moot. He'll kill you and the twins out of spite. Is that what you want?"

"Of course not, but I won't be dismissed because you've decided to take on the role of mother and father. Then what'll happen? You marry the scientist and live happily ever after with my children?" She crossed her arms over her chest and huffed. "I don't think so."

Colin sighed. "You'll have a royal title as co-parent."

"I should be your wife."

"No. Marriage between us was never an option after we broke up. Just the other day I was giving you major props for keeping your parents out of the loop until you informed me. It's not your fault you fell for Drake, but forcing me into a loveless marriage is a mistake. We'll never be happy, and I'll resent you until the day I die."

Charlie's eyes glittered, and her lower lip wobbled, but she held it together. "You can't expect an instant decision when I'm only learning about this today."

"Angela will start me on hormones while you're giving it some thought. Think back on the last year we were together. If you're honest, you'll admit our relationship was over long before we broke up. I'll give you anything you want—a title, your own palace, a monthly income, and shared custody. Anything in the world except marriage."

"You're offering me crumbs, Colin. I want a husband," she said. "I want you."

"Why risk your life for someone who doesn't love you in the way you deserve?"

She waved him off. "Go and don't come back until I'm ready to give you my answer."

"Timing is critical."

Charlie snorted. "So is my sanity."

"Do you think I'll have an answer by tomorrow?"

"OUT!"

Chapter Twenty

ALAIN'S ATTENTION WAS caught by the boisterous cheering coming from the roulette table. He approached cautiously, mindful of his promise to Colin. He didn't want to catch the warlock's attention, but he had to lay eyes on the man to make sure he was one and the same. Drake, still in his disguise as a sexy ginger, was unaware he'd been made. An attractive woman was by his side, chicly dressed in black, and they were openly affectionate after each win. His lucky streak continued for several more rounds, and casino monitors were busy keeping an eye on him as he raked in the chips. Alain could tip the casino off, but Drake would disappear and reappear in another disguise. Better the devil he knew...

He pondered his options. Isabelle would advocate a sneak attack, but Alain didn't have the stomach to kill anyone in cold blood. The act of taking a life, however much it was deserved, would leave a lasting impression, and Alain was certain it would change him forever. Despite the inner voice urging him to destroy Drake without warning, he couldn't do it. His ingrained distaste for violence and the darker aspects of magic transcended his need for revenge. Unless it was in the heat of battle, Alain couldn't and wouldn't mete out justice like some rogue vigilante.

Colin, on the other hand, had no such qualms. Perhaps it had to do with his royal lineage, but he didn't seem to have any problem making life and death decisions. He was born to rule, and the job came with a myriad of hard choices. Despite his age and inexperience, Colin had shown he was capable of any task, no matter how difficult. Everyone, including Alain's own mother, assumed Alain was the alpha in their relationship. He was older by more than a decade and had a string of successes in his field, including a Nobel Prize, whereas Colin only recently graduated from college and had never worked a day in his life.

His prince was compliant when it came to most of Alain's wishes, but he could be bullish if he didn't get his way. It was easy to forget one half of Colin's DNA was honed from sturdier stock. His other father, the Duke of Maitland, had been a commoner before becoming royal consort. Born in the Shetland Islands, and tossed out by his parents for being gay, the gruff Scott was hardworking, stalwart, and a celebrated sculptor in his own right; he was a no-nonsense sort who could see past all the royal trappings. He had no use for pretension, and he'd instilled this same quality in his only child.

There was much to love about Colin, and Alain had fallen hard, but it came with a price. One Alain had been willing to pay; however, they could lose it all if Colin insisted on going through with the fetus transfer. Despite Angela's reassurance, Alain was aware of the risks involved, and yet, Colin was determined to pursue this dangerous option. He was so sure it was the answer to all their problems he refused to listen to any of Alain's reasonable objections. Many things could go wrong—primarily a botched transfer, resulting in death to one or all of the participants, including donor and recipient. *If* it went according to plan, and the transfer *was* successful, with the babies carried to full term, then yes, Colin had come up with a brilliant solution and should be given a meritorious award. But Alain's scientific background kept churning up one dire scenario after another, and it was messing with his head.

All of this uncertainty could be easily avoided if Drake disappeared. Surely, there was someone in the coven who specialized in this sort of thing. Would jobbing out a murder absolve him of the sin? No. He'd be complicit regardless of who wielded the death blow. But Alain was getting desperate. Why hadn't the authorities succeeded in stopping the warlock? He'd almost murdered a man back in Bruges. Shouldn't Interpol be hot on his trail by now? Perhaps an anonymous phone call to the right people would be something Alain could do without suffering a pang of conscience. He decided to check on Raoul's progress before calling the authorities. He was out of his medically induced coma and doing better. They chatted for a few minutes, and Alain mentioned spotting Drake in Sendorra. Raoul said he'd inform the police.

Colin texted to tell him he was waiting in the limo outside the hotel. When Alain slid into the backseat, he noticed Colin's hair was disheveled, and he was worrying his lower lip bloody. It didn't take a genius or psychic to see his fiancé was having a bad day.

"What happened?" Alain queried, bracing for the tirade.

"Charlie didn't buy into my plan."

"Did you disclose the pros and cons?"

Colin gave him an icy look. "Give me some credit, will you? It all boils down to the marriage proposal. She's not happy relinquishing her role as consort."

"I see."

"We're fucked," Colin said harshly. "I thought she'd jump at the chance, but she's turning into a mama bear."

"Perhaps you're rushing her, Colin. She needs time to come to terms with this new information."

"We don't have time!" Colin yelled.

"Tone it down," Alain clipped. "I won't be subjected to your bad mood—I'm not in the best frame of mind either. If you want to act like a child, do it elsewhere."

Colin grimaced, as if he'd been slapped, and he reached for Alain's hand and slumped against him. "I'm sorry for taking it out on you."

Alain's anger receded instantly. "Forgiven."

Colin sighed and softly suggested, "Let's go back to the palace and spend the rest of the day sampling good food, vintage wines, and enjoying some raunchy sex. I had my first hormone shot today and Angela warned me the cumulative effect will alter my libido. We need to ride the sex train while it's still humming."

"Then what happens?"

"A long drought."

Alain grinned. "Lead the way, *chaton*."

They indulged in the wonderful interlude they both needed to reconnect. The last time they'd had great sex was the night before Alain abandoned Colin, and one traumatic event after another had left them with hardly any time to make love. The hours passed in a pleasant blur, and by the time they fell asleep in each other's arms, they were replete with their emotional connection lovingly restored.

The next morning, energized and ready to tackle whatever problems they encountered, they shared breakfast with Errol and Sebastian. Unwilling to shatter their postcoital glow, they steered the conversation away from Drake and Charlie, but the reprieve was short-lived. Sebastian started to probe the minute he took his last bite, asking question after question, which Colin answered truthfully. Not to be left out, Errol interjected, whenever clarification was necessary, and the relaxed atmosphere took a downward turn as the implications of Colin's decision hit home.

"I forbid you to proceed with this ridiculous idea," Prince Sebastian ordered. "I don't care what will happen to Charlie if Drake continues his vendetta. You are more important than anyone else involved."

"You don't mean that," Errol retorted. "Charlie's life is of equal value as are the lives of the twins."

Sebastian glared daggers at his husband. "Colin is the heir apparent. We are unable to produce another. Do the math."

"Charlie is carrying our grandchildren and should be protected at all cost," Errol reasoned. "Perhaps Colin's solution isn't so farfetched."

"It's out of the question," Prince Sebastian maintained.

On his feet, Colin bellowed, "Enough!"

All eyes were on him as he struggled for control. His fingertips were already glowing with the fiery power generated by strong emotion, and he clenched his fists to bank the flames. Although his fathers were now aware of the magic in his blood, they didn't need a demonstration. Nonetheless, he couldn't stand idly by while they decided his fate. Clearing his throat, Colin stated, "I am the future ruler and of legal age. As such, I have the right to make my own decisions. When I tell you this is our best option, you must realize I've looked at this problem from every angle and didn't come to this conclusion lightly."

"You have five minutes to convince me," Sebastian dared.

"Aye," Errol agreed. "Ye ken we have your best interest at heart, but you *are* of age, and I'm willing to listen with an open mind."

"Thank you, Da," Colin said, grateful for the support.

Errol nodded. "Proceed."

"Even if we are stupid enough to pay the ransom, Drake will continue to wreak havoc on Charlie and the twins because he's determined to destroy us. If she's no longer pregnant, his attacks will cease. It's the perfect solution."

"Go on," Prince Sebastian prompted.

"There are several possible scenarios that might play out with a fetal transfer. First, the transfer is a success. I leave the area with Alain and hide out somewhere secure until the twins are born. Second, one twin dies and I live, which still solves the problem of the heir. Third, both twins die and I survive. The crown is still secure, and we have more time to figure out the succession. Last, and least desirable, I die but the twins survive. My consort will act as regent until the twins are of age. The monarchy remains secure."

"You don't have a consort," Prince Sebastian reminded him.

"Yes, I do. We just need to make it official. Alain and I will marry in a quiet ceremony before the transfer."

"Hold on a second," Alain interjected. "You're not seriously suggesting I raise those boys without you by my side."

"I wouldn't trust them with anyone else."

"What about their mother?"

"Charlie has many good qualities, and I love her like family, but you're better educated, respected worldwide, and more mature. You would have no problem stepping into my shoes."

"Be that as it may," Alain blustered. "Raising your children and ruling in your stead is daunting."

Colin nodded. "This is not the desired outcome, but we have to prepare for any and all eventualities."

"Has Charlie agreed to this bizarre plan?" the prince inquired.

"Not yet," Colin admitted. "She's trying to come to terms with too much at once."

"I would object to relinquishing my rights if I were in her shoes," Errol said. "It's hard enough to have the children cut out of you, but to expect her to give up her place as consort is cruel and unfair."

"I don't want to marry her." Colin was emphatic. "I've said so from the beginning. As the biological mother, Charlie will have complete access to our children. She'll also be consulted on major decisions affecting her boys, have a title, and her own palace. In essence, we will co-parent."

"Marry her and be done with it," Prince Sebastian remarked. "She'll agree to anything if you make her consort. Once she's happy, you and Alain can resume your relationship."

"The marriage will be a sham," Colin objected. "Furthermore, Alain will never agree."

"I'm right here," Alain countered. "And I can speak for myself."

Colin gave an apologetic half smile and nodded for him to state his objections.

Turning toward Sebastian, Alain asked, "Are you honestly advocating an extramarital relationship?"

"I mean no disrespect, Alain, but we're in an impossible situation. Sometimes we have to make hard choices for the greater good."

"Your son's future and your monarchy are at odds," Alain reasoned. "Colin is trying to work around the antiquated clause in your constitution that has no place in modern society. Luckily, Charlie has provided the potential heirs to this throne, but it didn't happen with any kind of forethought or official sanction—"

"It was a drunken goodbye fuck," Colin informed them bluntly. "The breakup was a mutual decision—I didn't dump her. You have to stop acting like she is some pitiful virgin. Charlie and I were having sex for two years before we parted. My biggest regret is knocking her up by accident, but we live in an era of online hookups and people would just as soon fuck on their first date than get acquainted. You should be grateful I'm making an effort to legitimize these children who are technically not my responsibility."

"The onus is on you," Errol disagreed. "I don't care how it happened. They are your blood and you should do the honorable thing."

"I'm offering my life," Colin insisted. "Marrying Charlie is out of the question. If you can't deal with it, I suggest you go on vacation somewhere far away. Alain and I will take over from here."

Errol and Sebastian exchanged worried looks, and finally Sebastian said, "Let's table this discussion until we hear from Charlie. Her preferences will determine the outcome."

"My decision is not negotiable," Colin said tersely.

Before they could say another word, he left the dining room with Alain at his heels. In their quarters, Alain gathered him in his arms, and Colin dissolved into hot tears of frustration.

"They can't force you into an unwanted marriage," Alain soothed.

"I'm exhausted," Colin admitted. "Standing up to them is harder than anything I've ever done. Hell, I'd rather face Drake than see the disappointment on their faces."

"Did you mean it when you proposed we marry before the transfer?"

"Yes, but you have the option to walk away from this mess. It's a lot to ask, but I'll be forever grateful if you decide to marry me."

"I don't want your gratitude, Colin. I said yes to your marriage proposal a while back, but things have changed. There's one condition you have to meet before we proceed."

"Now what?"

"Should a medical crisis arise, and only one life can be saved, it has to be yours. This important stipulation must be included in our prenuptial contract."

Colin sagged against Alain wearily. "Whatever it takes."

Chapter Twenty-One

CHARLIE AND ANGELA were deep in conversation when the door swung open and Drake, disguised as Colin, walked into the room. Dressed in skinny jeans and a hoodie, there was nothing unusual about his appearance. He flashed a smile and winked at Charlie.

"What's up, princess?"

Charlie frowned. "Didn't I ask you to stay away until I called?"

The surprise registered for a nanosecond, but Drake quickly recovered. He stuck out his lower lip, looking to placate her with a wounded expression. "You know I'm lousy at taking orders, and I wanted to check on you."

"Nothing has changed since yesterday."

"Maybe I have," Drake lied.

"Oh? Is a marriage proposal back on the bargaining table?"

"I'm considering it."

"Your fathers must have insisted you do the honorable thing."

"You don't think much of me, do you?"

"Not after yesterday," Charlie grumbled. "Accident or not, these babies are yours, and they won't be the legitimate heirs unless you marry me."

Drake shrugged.

"Any untoward reactions to your shot?" Angela queried.

Drake had no idea who she was or what she was talking about, but a neutral answer seemed best. "I'm fine."

"No dizziness or nausea?"

"Sorry?"

The bossy slut was studying him like he was her latest science project. Drake wanted to shut her up with a spell leaving her tongue-tied, but she pulled out her phone and dialed something before he made his decision.

Angrily, he demanded, "Who did you call?"

"What's my name?" she asked, answering him with a question.

Drake scowled. "What are you playing at?"

Charlie watched their exchange, gazing between Colin, Angela, and the door. In a piercing voice, she said, "Answer the question, Colin."

Glancing at the doctor's name tag, he replied, "Dr. Whittaker."

"And my nickname?"

Drake took a few steps closer.

"Stay where you are," Angela ordered.

"Who the hell do you think you're talking to?"

"You're not Colin," Angela stated and reached into her pocket.

As soon as he saw the pepper spray, Drake dropped all pretenses, raised a hand in her direction, and mumbled an incantation. Angela's face twisted, her eyes rolled back in her head, and she collapsed like she'd been shot.

Charlie screamed and Drake clamped a hand over her mouth. "Shut up, bitch."

She squirmed, eyes wild with terror, and with one hand still over her mouth, Drake pawed at her hospital gown with his free hand, moving it aside so her belly was exposed. He dug into the ripe mound of flesh with jagged fingernails, enjoying the mounting hysteria as tears pooled in Charlie's expressive eyes.

"Thought you were safe?" Drake jeered. "I'll destroy you and your brats bit by bit. They'll leak out of your body in oozing, putrid chunks, and no one will be able to save them."

Charlie shook her head violently, causing Drake's hand to slip. "Why take your hatred out on me?" she rasped. "I never did anything but try to please you."

"You made a fool out of me."

"Not intentionally!" Charlie cried. "We're prepared to pay anything you ask. Just take the money and get out of here. You can have a good life somewhere far away."

Drake replied by digging in harder, drawing blood and a strangled cry. The trickle became a steady stream of bright red which looked obscene against the fecund backdrop. Charlie keened in desperation, and Drake lapped up her terror with diabolical glee. Half the fun of killing these babies was seeing the look of pure anguish in their mother's eyes.

Suddenly, the door burst open, and the dynamic changed in an instant when the real Colin and Alain appeared with a team of security in full combat gear. Bibi and Andrew hovered over the group, and the room filled with loud orders and confusion.

"Get away from her," Colin exploded, striking Drake with a fire ball which narrowly missed his heart.

The warlock tried to retaliate, but Colin was quicker, and he shot a fiery arrow this time, singeing the soft shell of Drake's ear. He hollered in outrage and then numbed the blistered flesh with a healing spell. Bibi picked this vulnerable moment to extract her revenge and she dive-bombed, digging her beak into Drake's left eye with a loud squelch. Drake flailed and tried to fend off the attack, but he was no match for the snowy owl who was intent on maiming him. She savaged the gelatinous orb while Drake roared in pain.

He'd used a lot of his power in the last thirty minutes, and trying to take down these people, including the ghostly familiars, on his dwindling strength was impossible. In a swirl of black smoke that blinded everyone in the room, Drake slipped out the door and down the four flights of stairs to the street. He didn't go back to the hotel as he suspected they'd have people posted at all the entrances. Cursing himself for poor planning, he threw an invincibility shield over his bruised and battered body and ran.

The fact that Colin and Charlie had a fail-safe didn't bode well. They were ahead of the deadly game Drake had started and seemed to be winning after each round. His chance to retaliate lessened with each failed attempt. Now he was minus financial resources and one eye. Without looking in the mirror, Drake knew the damn owl had struck a deadly blow. It irked him beyond measure, and his anger was quickly devolving into madness. Thoughts of money and escape no longer filled his thoughts. All he wanted to do was lay waste to the people who'd stood in his way.

He jump-started the first vacant car and drove out of town. Revenge would have to wait a few more days until he gathered his strength and worked out a better plan.

AFTER THE SMOKE cleared, the hospital room became a hub of activity as doctors and nurses poured in to help. Angela quickly recovered with no residual damage. Her collapse was determined to be an ordinary fainting spell, but Colin knew better. He'd seen Drake in action, and the damage he'd inflicted. Now everyone had a better understanding of the urgent need to transfer the twins into a safer environment.

The babies' vital signs were normal, but Charlie's blood pressure had spiked to dangerous levels, and her breathing was erratic. Although the stomach wounds weren't life-threatening, they looked ghastly, and Angela expertly cleaned and dressed them while Charlie looked the other way.

Colin barked out orders to the security team, charging them to find Drake and drag him back to Sendorra to face justice. Then he called his fathers to give them an update. Meanwhile, Alain stepped outside to touch base with Isabelle. He informed her there would be a wedding in the immediate future, and she'd better leave home at once if there was any hope of attending. After disconnecting, he paced the halls to give Colin and Charlie some privacy.

Angela had given Charlie a mild sedative that was safe for the babies, and badly needed to even out her vital signs, which were all over the place. Her equilibrium had been completely shattered by Drake's attack. Colin's previous warnings of Drake's intentions had been taken lightly, but after experiencing the hatred firsthand, Charlie was well and truly convinced her life and those of her children, were in jeopardy.

"I'm sorry I doubted you," Charlie said. "I thought you were using Drake as an excuse to avoid marriage."

Colin scrubbed his face with both hands. "Have you ever known me to lie when the truth is so blatantly obvious?"

She shrugged. "It's hard to let go of a childhood dream."

"To be sure, and if circumstances were different, and I wasn't in love with Alain, I wouldn't hesitate to marry you."

"How can you choose a stranger over me?" She started to cry again, and Colin pulled several tissues out of the box by her bed and handed them over.

"Thanks," she snuffled.

Colin watched her blow her nose and compose herself before he answered her question.

"Falling in love with Alain wasn't a conscious choice, Charlie. No one walks into a gay club looking for a husband. My life was complicated enough without adding one more challenge. The moment my feelings evolved into something deeper, I knew it would be a disaster because Alain isn't intersex, and I'm forbidden to carry a child. I tried to convince myself it was a sexual attraction that would fade in time. Neither of us realized the random hookup was a tiny seed that would eventually bloom into a lush garden. If I could change anything, I'd erase the night you and I had sex the last time we were together. It was a mistake, and I should have known better."

"But our mistake might provide you with the heirs you badly need."

"Yes, and I'll never call it a mistake again. I'm sorry I've disappointed you, but I hope you know there was no contest between you and Alain. You and I were over long before I met him. Let's do our best to safely bring these children into the world. They'll forever bind us like family.

You'll always have a place of honor in my life and the principality."

"Won't your subjects think less of me?"

"How could they when I'll give you the respect you deserve?"

"What if I meet someone and want to get married? Will I retain all the privileges accorded to your surrogate?"

"Naturally, we'd have to vet your choice, but if he passes muster, there shouldn't be a problem. He can move into your palace and join the family."

"I want it in writing," Charlie decided.

Colin heaved a sigh of relief. "You'll agree to the transfer?"

"After the contract is signed."

Colin reached for her and gratefully kissed the top of her hand. "Thank you."

"You're welcome."

"Let me find Alain and tell him."

"Make sure you warn him I'll rip his heart out if he hurts you."

Colin gave her a mock salute. "You bet."

He found Alain leaning on the wall just outside the door. His look was hopeful when he noticed Colin's wide grin. "Good news?"

"The best," Colin said, throwing himself at Alain and wrapping him in a tight embrace. "All systems go."

"Maman is on her way."

"For what?"

"To attend our wedding," Alain reminded him. "You didn't think I'd get married without her to bless our union."

"Speaking of approval," Colin said. "We need to sit down with my fathers and a lawyer. Charlie wants a contract before the transfer."

"Smart girl."

"You're both thinking ahead."

"Does she know what I want?"

Colin shook his head.

"She might object to my stipulations."

"Maybe she won't even notice," Colin said hopefully.

"Don't make the same mistake," Alain warned.

"What do you mean?"

"Holding back the truth is only asking for trouble. Charlie needs full disclosure."

"Do you know how hard it was to get her to agree?"

"I've been right here, *chaton*. Of course, I know it was an uphill battle, but I sure as hell don't want any issues if an emergency arises. We need clear guidelines for everyone."

"For fuck's sake."

"It's for my peace of mind."

"You're scaring me with the implications."

Alain kissed him softly. "Don't be frightened. I'm overly cautious and methodical."

"Sometimes I wish you weren't so damned sensible."

"You wouldn't love me if I was any different."

"Any news on Drake?" Colin asked, changing the subject.

Alain shook his head.

"I hope he's hurting."

"You and Bibi certainly did a number on him."

"Unfortunately, he lived to fight another day."

"Yes, but we're on our guard, and soon he won't be able to hurt the twins."

"I hope you're right."

Chapter Twenty-Two

DRAKE'S STOLEN VEHICLE was top-of-the-line with a superb communications system, which would serve him well since he'd left most of his belongings behind. Going by memory, he hooked his burner phone to the car's Bluetooth and called the Bradford Coven. He asked for the high priestess, and the call was rerouted to a person named Agnes. He vaguely remembered his granny mentioning someone by her name, but he hadn't met her in person. This put him at a disadvantage. If she had been Maura's protégée or friend, she'd have some background information on him and might be inclined to help, but a complete stranger would tell him to get lost.

Which is exactly what happened. Agnes's brusque greeting signaled his current standing with his Wiccan tribe. Like a warden dealing with a repeat offender, she informed Drake he'd been outcast in a unanimous vote, and expecting any kind of help was out of the question. He was a pariah, a shameful stain on their good reputation. When he argued his case and reminded Agnes it was Isabelle Simon who'd killed Maura, she placed the blame squarely on his shoulders for engineering the entire mess. Agnes warned him she'd alert the authorities if he continued to pester any of the other members.

Humiliated by her dismissal, Drake called his mother to elicit some sympathy, and see if she might rally the remaining Bradfords to go to bat for him. The call went straight to voice mail, which was in keeping with their history. She purported to love him but was never around when he needed her. His staunchest ally had been Granny Maura, but the decaying Simon witch had killed her behind his back. Well, he got his revenge by slaughtering her familiar, except the stupid owl had managed to retaliate when he least expected it. The farther he drove, the angrier he got, and the bitter taste of failure lodged in his throat like a fish bone. He needed something strong to wash it down, so he stopped at the next service station hoping for some high-octane relief.

Like many rest stops along well-traveled roads in Europe, this one offered more than gas. There was a self-service area, where one could load up on snacks or a simple hot meal, if so inclined. They also had a tiny shop with the usual kitschy souvenirs including bottles of booze in assorted sizes. Before leaving the vehicle, Drake stuck a screwdriver in his back pocket, the only serviceable weapon he could find in the glove compartment. He didn't plan to use it, but his powers were ebbing, due to overuse, and the hefty tool, which could serve as a shank, was a good backup. Drake was prepared for anything except for the gasps of horror when he walked into the shop. In his eagerness to drown his sorrows, he forgot he looked like the walking dead. He selected a large bottle of whiskey, paid in cash, and as he was hurrying out the door, a slim man dressed in hikers' gear stopped him and offered assistance.

"I can clean and bandage your eye until you see your doctor."

Drake studied the stranger with suspicion. "Why?"

"I'm a nurse."

"You don't look like one."

He shrugged. "I'm on vacation. Do you want my help or not?"

Was he a cop disguised as a nurse? Drake's instincts were off, and paranoia was now his default, but he allowed the guy to lead him to the restroom so they were out of the public eye. Instead of being grateful for this act of kindness, Drake was provoked to another level of anger at the pity emanating from the gentle man who was swabbing his face with a cleansing pad he'd pulled out of a first aid kit. How dare he look at him like he was a loser? Something dark and primordial gripped Drake as he reeled from the insult, and he pulled out the screwdriver, stabbing the guy in his neck. The pity in the stranger's eyes morphed into shock, and Drake felt a rush of gratification that was almost sexual in intensity. He left the guy in a heap, screwdriver still in place, and walked out the door.

Back in his car, Drake unscrewed the cap on the whiskey and took several long swallows. It burned all the way down, and the warm glow added to his sense of accomplishment. Maybe this was an omen, and his bad luck would start to change if he stopped acting like a victim. He put the car in gear and left the rest stop. About ten miles down the road, a traveler's lodge beckoned, and he decided to stop for the night. This time, he remembered the disguising spell to cover his bloody socket, and although it was a temporary fix, it served the purpose. He paid for his room in cash and beguiled the clerk into foregoing any form of ID. He wasn't sure how far the authorities in Sendorra and Belgium had extended the manhunt, and he didn't want to leave a paper trail. One meal was included in the price, and he requested a dinner tray be delivered as soon as possible.

He sat on his bed and waited until the food arrived and was devoured before he went to the bathroom to finally look in the mirror. All his life, Drake had relied on his good looks to open doors. Coupled with confident charm, and a touch of magic, there was nothing he couldn't obtain if he set his mind to the task. The destruction caused by Isabelle's familiar shook him to the core. He was hideous, a repulsive wreck with nothing to show for his sacrifice. Even his last act of violence had left a sour taste. Shattering the mirror with a balled-up fist, he sank to his knees like a supplicant and knew what he had to do. Calling upon the darker side of magic was a huge step, and one he'd avoided in the past. The deities populating the underworld were selfish and unforgiving if crossed. Once he accepted their sinister help, the deal would be irreversible. Drake's moral compass had long since blurred, but he'd never sunk this low. Maura would have stopped him in an instant, but he was out of options, and this seemed like his best choice.

He concentrated, turning his focus internally, and slowly the cold tiles of the bathroom floor faded as Drake, in a dreamy state of self-induced hypnosis, left his damaged body behind. He sank into the earth, past the hard crust to the mantle, and downward through the lithosphere until reaching the asthenosphere, where he hoped to emerge in the bowels of hell. According to a sultry Norwegian sorceress he'd bedded for a while, and Greek mythology, Tartarus was the place to find a malevolent deity who'd be willing to barter favors.

At a price.

Drake had passed the point of caring.

He'd give up anything to win this battle.

The caterwauling of the dammed and the blistering heat from eternal flames signaled his arrival, as did the sight of a one-eyed demon lumbering forward on hoofed feet. Drake should have been terrified by the sight of the nine-foot monster, but his psychotic brain only saw salvation.

The demon questioned him without moving his lips. "Have you come to strike a bargain?"

Drake nodded.

"You have many enemies, and they are powerful."

"More than you can handle?" Drake challenged.

"No."

"What'll it take?"

"A life."

"Mine?"

"You're too damaged."

"You want a couple of unsullied newborns?"

The demon's eye gleamed with avaricious delight. "Yes."

"Can you do something about my appearance?" Drake asked. "I can't stay under the radar looking like...you."

"Call upon me when you need a disguise."

Drake shook his head. "I don't need a disguising spell; I want something permanent."

"Which also comes with a price."

"Name it."

"In due time."

Drake made a moue of disgust. "Are we done here?"

In response to his arrogance, the demon transformed into an enormous serpent with greenish scales and bulging yellow eyes. Drake was rooted to the spot, unable to look away from the swaying head and forked tongue flicking in and out as it got closer and closer. Strings of saliva hung from the slimy organ quivering as it approached Drake's good eye.

"Please, don't," he begged

The forked tongue snapped against his temple, and Drake felt a stinging pain which matched the throbbing in his bloody socket. He whimpered and the serpent withdrew with a hiss and shifted back into the figure of a Cyclops.

"You can act like an asshole where you come from, but this is my realm, and you will show respect, or I'll crush the life out of you."

"Sorry," Drake offered immediately. "I'll do better next time."

The demon backhanded him with a loud grunt, and when Drake came to his senses, he was back on the cold bathroom floor. He stood on shaky legs and looked at his image in the mirror over the sink. The right side of his face was a mottled web of broken capillaries, and his ruined eye oozed a bloody trail of gore. The skin was split in a jagged line where the serpent had tapped him with his tongue. Had he only imagined the trip to hell? But…he bore the unmistakable marks of his encounter. What in the actual fuck just happened? Drake grabbed two bottles of vodka out of the minibar and downed them in a few gulps. They hardly made a dent, so he polished off the entire display, mixing different varieties of booze until he passed out.

He awoke at dawn the next day and staggered to the bathroom. Clutching the sink for balance, he looked in the mirror and gaped. His familiar features stared back at him, symmetrically perfect as usual. His damaged orb was restored, replaced with a functioning eye to match the other. The atmosphere in the bathroom grew frigid and Drake's body erupted in goose flesh. A harsh voice he thought he'd never hear again whispered in his ear.

"Like what you see?"

"God, yes."

"He had nothing to do with this transformation," the demon rebuked.

"Sorry."

"Get going, Drake. The world is passing you by while you stand here admiring yourself. I can just as easily turn you back into a gargoyle."

"I'm on it."

Drake showered, shaved, and donned the same tired outfit he'd worn when he left town. He reached for his wallet, which somehow felt thicker, and he broke into a smile when he saw it bulging with money he knew he didn't have yesterday. Dealing with the devil was certainly lucrative. He went to the dining room and helped himself to the expansive breakfast smorgasbord.

Brimming with good cheer after the delicious meal, Drake stopped at the front desk and paid cash for another night. He would go back to Sendorra today with a new disguising spell in place. Without much ado, he invoked his one-eyed deity, and the creature materialized almost instantly.

"What do you need?"

"I'm ready for my new look."

"Anything special?"

"Something completely different."

"Biker dude?"

Drake imagined the dark hair, amber colored eyes, full-on biker leathers and nodded. "Can you throw in a motorcycle while you're at it?"

"I can do anything, but let me remind you about the price."

Drake waved him off with a careless flip of his wrist. "I'm good for it."

The hefty Harley Davidson was the finishing touch Drake needed to add to the illusion of a badass biker. He was riding high on success when he was pulled over by a lone cop who ended up experiencing Drake's renewed power with a fatal heart attack.

Unrepentant, Drake continued his drive into town and headed for a local bar. He spent the first hour flirting with the bartender, and when he won her confidence with his generous tips, he pumped her for information on the royal family.

Something mysterious was going on, she confided. The normally transparent royals were being unusually reticent, and tradesmen, caterers, and florists were coming and going in a steady stream.

"Are they planning a wedding?" Drake asked.

She shrugged. "Who knows?"

"I thought the prince broke up with his girlfriend last summer."

"Maybe they got back together," she suggested.

"The prince is a switch-hitter," someone yelled out. "He's been mooning over some older guy for months."

"Is that right?" Drake pretended surprise. "Are they getting engaged or something?"

"Why are you so interested?" Ginny, the bartender asked. "Are you a reporter looking for a scoop?"

"What if I am? Will you be willing to help me?"

She narrowed her eyes. "How?"

"Sneak me into the palace in the disguise of a waiter."

"They have their own staff."

"What do you suggest?"

"So you *are* sniffing around for a photo op."

"Gotta make a living, hon. I'll split the revenue if you give me a hand."

She grinned. "Just a hand?"

Drake caught the tease and flirted right back. "Are you offering more?"

"A guy who looks like you shouldn't have to bargain."

"I'm a gentleman above all else."

"Aww...now I'm definitely interested. Let's get the hell out of here."

Ginny not only offered her body, she convinced Drake to give up the motel room and move in with her for the duration.

"You should be more careful," Drake pretended. "How do you know I won't slit your throat and run off with your hidden stash of tip money?"

"Because you're as sweet as an angel and fuck like a machine. I've never met anyone with your stamina."

"Then I'm your guy."

"Awesome."

"I'd like to visit the palace in the next few days. Do they have tours of the public rooms?"

She nodded. "I'm off the day after tomorrow. Can you wait until then?"

"If I'm sufficiently distracted."

She sat on him and wrapped her arms around his neck, grinding down on his cock as he arched to meet her.

"How's this for starters?"

Chapter Twenty-Three

IT HAD BEEN five days since the attack at the hospital, and Colin had been receiving hormone shots daily. So far, the only side effect he'd noticed was mild cramping. Born with a uterus but no ovaries, Colin had never given the life-sustaining organ a moment's thought. It was just there—like his heart, liver, and kidneys. Since receiving the shots to thicken the lining of his uterus to prepare for implantation, he'd become hyperaware of this extra organ. If the transfer was successful, he'd be nurturing his children until they were ready to greet the world.

At once terrifying and astonishing, this was a natural phenomenon most women agreed upon, but since Colin didn't have a biological mother or sister, and was never around pregnant women, he didn't realize his feelings were perfectly normal.

It was the Duke of Maitland who'd carried the twins after marrying Prince Sebastian, and his experience was entirely different from Colin's. He had the necessary ovaries to produce eggs that were fertilized with the prince's sperm in a laboratory setting. Five days after fertilization, two embryos had formed a fluid cavity resulting in the formation of fetal tissues and placenta. They were then implanted in Errol's uterus.

Charlie had already laid the groundwork. Now it was Colin's turn to take up the challenge and bring the twins safely into the world. His sole duty was to provide a healthy environment to allow them to mature. In the most basic sense, he was an incubator, and the months leading up to the birth would be a preview of fatherhood. His life would be irrevocably altered once he performed this selfless task.

After his initial reluctance, Alain was now firmly on board with Colin's decision and took a keen interest in the process. He consulted with Angela whenever Colin had a question he couldn't answer. In his own way, Alain was acting like an expectant father. Even though the twins were not of his blood, they belonged to the man he loved, and their well-being, and Colin's, took up every waking moment. The vacant place in his heart, normally reserved for children, was swelling in anticipation of a future he never dreamed possible.

Which is why he panicked with the latest news. Charlie wasn't doing well. She'd been through too much since discovering she was pregnant, and the upheavals were taking a toll. The bleeding had started again, and although it was in trickles, Angela was concerned. She advised they get on the transfer sooner rather than later. When Colin argued he wasn't ready, she stressed the unpredictability of Charlie's situation. No one could accurately guess if and when the spotting would turn into a life-threatening crisis. Anticipation was the key, and averting a disaster with careful planning was better than being caught unawares. If Drake somehow managed to get close enough to inflict more damage, they wouldn't stand a chance in preventing a miscarriage.

Under these mitigating circumstances, the royals agreed to speed up the wedding ceremony. As Alain stood beside Colin surveying the wedding venue, he recalled the days following their first hookup. He'd used his preternatural skills to try to get more background on his mysterious young man, but it was a fruitless experiment ending in an unexpected fainting spell. There were two things he took away from the unpleasant experience. One was a clear vision of a bloody hospital scene, which was slowly evolving and would become a self-fulfilling prophesy if they didn't act immediately.

The second thing he clearly remembered was a wedding scene. At the time, the participants of the ceremony had not been revealed, but a detailed picture of this chapel, with its artfully decorated interior—pine and holly wreaths, red velvet ribbons, and lit candles— brought his vision into clear focus. In less than twenty-four hours, the carved wooden pews would be filled with elegantly dressed men and women while organ music played Handel in the background.

They'd agreed to meet David, the late dowager's social secretary and event planner. He'd known Colin for years and loved him like a son. Sam, the palace chef, was David's husband, and there was no one better suited to plan the scaled-down event than the two men who served the principality with single-minded dedication. If things had gone according to plan, David would have come up with a spectacular wedding befitting the heir apparent, but he'd experienced Drake's machinations firsthand, and knew what the warlock was capable of doing.

The ceremony would be as simple as possible; however, Colin *was* the heir apparent. They couldn't keep it a secret without incurring public disapproval. David had cut a deal with the press, and for an exclusive interview and photo-op with the newlyweds, they would delay the announcement until the ceremony had been performed. This way, there was less opportunity for Drake to launch another attack.

Drake had been frighteningly active since fleeing the hospital with blood dripping down his face. He had left a swath of destruction along his route, a stolen car and a couple of dead bodies, but no one had yet to pinpoint his location. The stolen vehicle had been abandoned in a train station two towns over and the authorities had confirmed his identity by multiple fingerprints he didn't bother to wipe down. They were also clearly visible on the screwdriver he'd left on his hapless victim. The healthy young cop's sudden demise was questionable, but there was no doubt in Alain's mind who'd caused the fatal heart attack. The violence was escalating, instead of dissipating, and the CSIs were convinced they were dealing with a psychopath. Alain couldn't agree more. The Drake they'd first met last summer had degenerated into an irredeemable shell of a man, who would only stop when death claimed him.

Since Bibi's death, Isabelle had been plotting hundreds of ways to make Drake pay for his sins, but without her familiar, she was at a disadvantage. Astral travel was taxing on any able-bodied witch, and her age and extreme sorrow at Bibi's departure had sapped her last reserves. Even her talent for scrying, the ancient art of divination, was waning. She wasn't sure if it was her advancing years or PTSD causing her to lose concentration, but when she gazed into the mirror to try to find the warlock, she came up empty. All she could do was lay protective wards around the hospital, and Charlie's bed in particular. She'd also raised several around the palace, but the reality was they'd be ineffective if Drake set his mind to the task. Any warlock worth his salt would be able to break a protective ward with the right spell.

Alain, aware of his mother's sudden weakness, insisted they hire extra security. Highly skilled operatives were posted at strategic points of entry and exit in rotating twenty-four-hour shifts.

"I feel like we're living in a war zone," Colin complained when he noticed the increased security. "Is this necessary since we've put up the wards?"

"I'm afraid so," Alain replied. "We can't assume we're safe anywhere."

"This is taking prewedding jitters to new heights."

"I'm sorry, *chaton*."

Colin hooked his arm over Alain's. "It's not your fault. Will you accompany me to the hospital to get this last hurdle out of the way?"

"Of course."

Charlie's signature was still missing from the important document giving the doctor's permission to transfer the twins. Among the countless paragraphs of legalese were clearly defined protocols—Colin's life took priority over anyone else.

Worried about the upcoming meeting, Colin asked, "What does your sixth sense tell you about her reaction?"

"It's hard to say," Alain remarked. "She might insist on saving the twins first, but she could do the unexpected and acquiesce."

"A fight will only delay the inevitable."

"Of course, but once you explain I would become regent in the event of your death, and the twins would be raised under my care, she'll rethink her stance."

"I don't think she hates you."

"Hate is a strong word, and to be fair, Charlie doesn't know me well enough," Alain reminded him. "And there's the rub. If we were better acquainted, she might not object to my raising her children, but allowing a stranger to take charge won't sit well."

"So, saving my life first is the better option?"

"However painful," Alain said. "It might be the only choice for her."

"We'll soon find out."

DRAKE SAT OUTSIDE the palace gates in one of Ginny's short skirts, thigh-high boots, and oversized sweater. He "borrowed" the outfit as soon as she left for work and took a bus instead of using the motorcycle. The magenta-streaked blonde wig was a nice touch, and he easily passed for a pretty young girl.

He could feel the protective wards around the perimeter of the palace but didn't make any attempt to penetrate. Then he saw the black limousine streaking through the heavy iron gates. The royal banner fluttered on dual mounts attached to the front fenders, and he surmised Colin and Alain were on their way to visit Charlie.

Drake got back in the bus line, and after thirty minutes, he got off in front of the hospital, only to find the same protective wards, along with several gun-toting security guards watching all the entrances. Irritated, he had to figure out a way to get past the magical wards so he could make good on his promise to the demon. A miscarriage would be inevitable once Charlie laid eyes on him again, and if fear didn't work, he'd slice her open and pluck the twins out of her.

But first, he had to get past the wards. Without the family grimoire at his fingertips, or Maura a phone call away, Drake realized he'd waste precious time trying to decipher the correct pathway. It was a knotted maze of spells created to keep out danger—in other words, specifically designed for Drake. This must have been cast by the bitch, Isabelle.

He huffed in frustration and stood to go, but the one-eyed demon with fur-covered hindquarters materialized, blocking his way.

"Where do you think you're going?"

Drake hated the demon's ability to invade his thoughts so easily, but he supposed it was better than trying to decipher Greek or Latin or whatever ancient language they spoke in hell.

"Home to figure out the wards."

"Can't you do it here?"

Drake shook his head. "I need stuff."

"What exactly?"

"The usual—candles, crystal, incense, and salt. And the family grimoire. It's going to take me a day or two to figure this out."

"You can always ask me to break down the barriers," the demon taunted.

"I'm not racking up anymore debt. I can figure this out on my own."

"Don't take too long. Your first payment is due in a few days."

"You sound like a goddamn loan shark," Drake accused. "Give me some space."

"Two days," the demon replied and vanished.

Drake already regretted his decision to throw his lot in with the devil, but he knew there was no backing out. He was stuck as surely as he'd been with the usurers back home. There was nothing to do but procced with the plan.

On his way back to the apartment, he pulled out his burner phone and tried calling home again. His mother answered this time, and her apparent disgust almost made him disconnect, but he needed answers.

"It's me," he said, going for normal.

"What the hell do you want?"

Ditching the niceties, he asked, "Where's Granny's grimoire?"

"I don't have a clue."

"Can you find it for me?"

"Even if I could, you'd be the last person to get your hands on it."

"I had nothing to do with her death."

"I've been hearing otherwise," his mother said reprovingly. "Who are you, and what have you done with my son?"

"I'm right here, Mom. You're just seeing me without the blinders. Granny wanted me to have the book and take her place in the coven."

"Didn't they throw you out?"

"Can you get the grimoire and send it to me?"

"Where are you?"

He gave her Ginny's address and hoped he was doing the right thing. "Don't even think about giving this address to the authorities."

"I'm staying as far away from you as possible."

"What about the book."

"We'll see."

"Mom, come on. This is important."

"It's always life and death with you, Drake."

"Send the book, and I'll never bother you again."

"Famous last words."

"I swear on Granny's grave."

Chapter Twenty-Four

CHARLIE'S EYES WERE red and swollen when they walked in the room, and Colin couldn't help the pang of guilt upon seeing her unhappiness.

Kissing her on the cheek, he grasped her outstretched hand and held it tightly. "What's the matter?"

"I'm a little emo today."

"Is there anything we can do to help?" Alain asked gently.

She shook her head.

"Hey," Colin soothed. "You'll start feeling better once your body goes back to normal. Then you can go on vacation with your friends or something."

"Or something," she repeated gloomily. "You know how much I've hated being pregnant?

"You've said it often enough."

"A part of me will miss it even more."

Heart hammering, Colin asked, "Are you having second thoughts about the transfer?"

"I'm feeling guilty and inadequate," Charlie admitted. "What will people say about my decision? Won't they think less of a woman who gives away her children?"

"You aren't giving them away," Colin replied. "This decision will keep them safe. It's the right thing to do—you'll be a hero."

"Why couldn't I have kids without the drama?"

"Don't be so hard on yourself," Alain interjected. "Drake has caused most of your problems. I'm certain things would have gone more smoothly if you were involved with someone else."

"Like the actual father of my twins?"

Alain managed a weak smile.

Colin heard the resentment in her voice and was reminded how easily this plan could go pear-shaped. The fate of the principality, his and Alain's future, and the lives of the unborn children hung in the balance while Charlie wrestled with self-esteem. She seemed more concerned about public opinion than anything else. But Colin bit his tongue instead of taking the bait. They'd already had this conversation on numerous occasions, and they were running out of time.

"Angela thinks we should move on the transfer as soon as possible," Colin mentioned instead. "The agreement between us needs to be signed and routed through proper channels before the surgery can proceed."

"Leave the papers on the nightstand."

"I can't," Colin stated. "This has to be done today."

"What's the rush?"

"You're bleeding, Drake's still out there, and Alain and I are getting married in forty-eight hours. We'd like to schedule the transfer the day after the wedding. There's no time to waste."

Charlie's mood shifted as he enumerated the obstacles they were facing. Her coloring rose, fresh tears made an appearance, and the monitors beeped alarmingly, causing an influx of nurses and doctors.

"What's going on?" one of them asked while they checked Charlie's vitals.

"It's nothing," Alain assured them. "The princess is a little agitated."

"I'm fine," Charlie said irritably, wiping her tears away with a tissue. "Stop fussing."

"Would you like a glass of warm milk and a cookie?" one of the nurses asked. "You know I can't give you a sedative."

"How about a shot of vodka?"

"I'm sorry, princess."

"You can go on a bender the minute you've recovered from the procedure," Colin placated. "We'll even throw a party for your contribution to the principality."

"Stop trying to bribe me," Charlie said. "I'm not in a joking mood."

"Would you like to speak with a counselor?" Alain asked. "A neutral party might help address some of your doubts."

"I don't want a shrink."

"Then read the damn contract and sign it," Colin snapped. "I'll be outside with Alain if you need me."

"Fine," she huffed.

"Fine," Colin repeated on his way out.

Alain drew Colin into an embrace when they were alone. "You guys bring out the worst in each other."

"This is why we broke up," Colin agreed. "We're more like siblings than lovers."

"Well, you did grow up together."

"She was much more agreeable as a kid."

"There's a lot at stake," Alain reminded him. "Don't lose your patience."

"I'm doing my best, but she's not making it easy."

"I know."

"Why can't pregnant women have alcohol?" Colin asked.

"Huh? What's with the weird question?"

"I'll be in Charlie's shoes in a few days, and I'd like to know if I can drink or not."

"You can have a glass of wine once in a while," Alain advised. "It won't hurt the babies."

"Can I have one with each meal?"

"A lot of women do."

"Good, because cookies and warm milk won't provide any comfort during a meltdown."

"Stop comparing yourself to her," Alain scolded softly. "Your experience will be completely different."

Before Colin could respond, Alain's phone rang. He didn't recognize the number, so he let it go to voice mail.

"Who called?" Colin asked.

Alain retrieved the message and listened intently. He disconnected and frowned at Colin.

"Who was it?"

"The doctor in Bruges. Apparently, he's no longer in a coma and wanted to thank me for saving his life. He also asked about Charlie."

"Some good news for a change," Colin said. "Did you know he and Charlie were simpatico?"

"All I know is he's a plastic surgeon and didn't deserve to die."

"How did he get your number?"

"I gave him my card when we first met."

"Did he want to speak with Charlie?"

"Not sure. I'm calling him back," Alain said.

While Alain was on the phone, Colin ventured back into Charlie's room. She was reading the contract and lifted her gaze when he walked in.

"I'm not done."

"Do you mind if I sit and wait?"

She made a gesture for him to go ahead and continued to read.

Colin waited, preparing for the worst as she flipped page after page. He cringed at her shocked intake of breath.

"Colin?"

"Yeah?"

"Have you read this?" Charlie asked with an incredulous look on her face.

He nodded.

"You want me to sign my children's death warrant?"

"This is just a precaution, Charlie. I was asked to include it in the contract."

"What the hell is wrong with you? It's not fair to ask me to choose between you and my children."

Colin approached her bed. "A worst-case scenario has to be addressed. It's standard procedure."

"I won't give my consent. Wasn't the whole point of this transfer to make sure they survive? This document clearly states your life is more important than theirs will ever be!"

"I'm the heir apparent, Charlie. They can't replace me if I die in childbirth."

"They'll get two for the price of one," she said angrily. "If you die, and I'm sure you won't, our sons will succeed."

"And they'll be under the watchful eye of a regent until they're eighteen."

"I'll raise them."

Colin shook his head. "You can't. My husband will be their custodian until they are of age."

As reality sank in, Charlie's anger intensified, and she quickly tore the document in half. "Deal's off."

"Charlie, be reasonable."

She shook her head. "Get the fuck out of here."

Colin left the room before he said something he might regret and bumped into Alain who had just disconnected his call. He'd been walking down the hallway to rejoin him. Colin's temper, already on simmer, erupted in a flash of light, and sparks flew off him like frightened fireflies.

Gripping him by the arms. Alain shook him roughly. "What just happened?"

"She called it off because of your death clause."

"Your parents wanted the same reassurance," Alain argued.

"I told you it wouldn't fly."

"Now what?"

"We have them draw up another document, and my father can present it himself."

"Do you think it'll make a difference?"

"I dunno."

"Maybe Dr. Davies can talk some sense into her."

Colin looked confused. "Who?"

"The guy from Belgium," Alain explained patiently. "I invited him to the wedding."

"Why would you? We barely know him."

"He asked if he could come."

"Do you think this has to do with Charlie?"

"He seemed quite interested in her progress," Alain explained. "One more guest won't make a difference."

"What else did you talk about?"

"Drake."

"What about him?"

"He asked and I told him what he needed to know."

"Including the magic?"

"All of it."

"How did he react?"

"He insisted on coming to the wedding."

"Getting back to Charlie," Colin continued. "Do you have a plan B?"

"No."

"Perhaps Angela can be more persuasive," Colin suggested. "She'll lay it out in medical terms, so Charlie will realize the odds of anyone dying are pretty slim."

"We still need a contingency plan."

"What then?"

"Let me think about it," Alain replied.

Chapter Twenty-Five

RAOUL PUT DOWN his phone and absorbed Alain's information. Drake's strong ties to witchcraft didn't surprise him in the least. While many would scoff at the notion of magic, Raoul's childhood in predominantly Catholic Mexico had been filled with stories of *brujas* and *magos*. One couldn't believe in God without recognizing the fallen angels who ruled the underworld. It stood to reason Drake had landed on the wrong side of magic. It explained a lot about the guy's ability to inhabit other people's lives so seamlessly and his utter disregard for humanity in general.

Raoul was grateful to have survived the brutal attack, but whenever the nurse came in to change his colostomy bag, the smell assaulted his senses, and his appreciation for life was quickly replaced by a virulent rage that left him lightheaded from the adrenaline spike. And while it was a temporary situation, and they'd reconnect his plumbing eventually, it didn't make it any easier to bear. The unpleasant task was a daily reminder of Drake's treachory and Raoul's poor judgement. He'd gone out of his way for Drake on many occasions, and he didn't deserve to be gutted like a fresh trout because they disagreed in principle. He felt betrayed by a man who should have been eternally grateful for all the times Raoul had been there to watch his back.

With a determination bordering on obsession, Raoul picked up his phone and called his old friend in Sonora. He and Mario didn't see each other often, but they Skyped or texted all the time. Their shared childhood and successful business dealings forged a level of trust and respect that continued to flourish after several decades. It didn't matter if Raoul's Spanish was sprinkled with English words, and Mario spoke Spanglish so his friend could follow their conversation. Revenge and *vengansa* were impossible to misinterpret.

Mario assured Raoul he'd take care of the problem, but he surprised his friend by insisting he be present to witness the execution. There would be no satisfaction in hearing about Drake's death from a distance. He wanted to be an integral part of it, and they made the necessary arrangements. Tomorrow, two of Mario's trusted *sicarios*—hitmen and a *teniente*—lieutenant in charge of the operation, would arrive in Bruges. They would accompany Raoul to Sendorra under the pretext of attending the royal wedding. He'd take his own jet, the same one which rescued Drake when he was flailing in Prague, and this way Raoul would be able to recline during the trip while they avoided the meticulous security checks. Private airports were easier to navigate in terms of preflight checks, and a plane's hidden compartments were the perfect way to transport illegal weapons.

For the first time since he woke from the medically induced coma, Raoul thought of a future he almost squandered due to poor judgement. He wondered if he'd get a chance to visit Princess Charlotte while he was in Sendorra. She'd been the cause and effect of his altercation with Drake and thoughts of her had flitted through his head on occasion. Had she survived the trip home without repercussions? Was she still pregnant? Alain hadn't mentioned much other than she was fine, but Raoul remembered how fragile she'd been while in his care. Her tentative grasp on reality had been due to Drake gaslighting her for months. With more facts at hand, Raoul could see how the bastard had manipulated her from the beginning. He couldn't help feeling sorry for her and hoped he'd get a chance to visit. It would be nice to spend time with her in a friendlier environment.

IN THE EVENING Colin, Alain, and the royal couple met in the library for cocktails. Isabelle, having arrived safely, begged off due to a headache, which was just as well. They didn't need her input to start another argument. When Colin informed his fathers of Charlie's refusal to sign unless they removed the death clause—as she insisted on calling it—voices rose in protest.

"In my opinion," Colin said, "it's causing unnecessary tension in an extremely delicate situation. You have no idea what it took for Charlie to agree to a transfer in the first place. This clause has put a seed of doubt in her head, and there's no telling what she'll do next. We're fucked if she changes her mind."

"Alain?" Prince Sebastian asked. "You were the one who insisted on this measure, and although Errol and I are in full agreement, we also know the succession is in jeopardy if Colin doesn't give birth to those twins. He's refused to offer her marriage, so having the children himself is the only option. I hate to sound like my cabinet, who continue to harangue me about Colin's decision, but any child born out of wedlock is not entitled to inherit the throne."

"I can't believe you would sacrifice Colin for the sake of the crown," Alain said with disgust.

"It's Colin's choice," the prince objected loudly. "If I had my way, he'd be long married to the girl."

Astonished, Alain ventured, "To someone he doesn't love?"

"He cared enough to sleep with her."

"Love and sex don't always go hand in hand," Errol stated. "Ye ken that well enough, Sebastian. Our boy has the right to choose."

"Thank you, Da. And let me remind you all that I found a way around this conundrum until you guys messed it up with your doom and gloom. Let's take our chances and be done with this."

"It's easy to assume the procedure will go smoothly in the comfort of this room, but the body is a complex machine, and although Colin is in the best of health, we're fooling his organs into thinking he's pregnant," Alain pointed out. "What we're doing is unprecedented, and even Angela will agree a pregnancy will upset his body's natural equilibrium. To put this in the simplest terms, starting a race at a full sprint, with no warm-up and mediocre equipment, is inadvisable. There's no way to predict how this will end. I hate the idea of placing Colin in such jeopardy, so forgive me if I'd like some reassurance. His life means more to me than your damn succession."

After Alain's rant, things took a downward turn, and recrimination filled the air as Prince Sebastian railed at

Colin for being stubborn, Errol tried to keep the peace while Alain crossed his arms over his chest and refused to give in to the pressure.

Colin stepped outside to get away from the argument. Hearing Alain voice his fears out loud had unsettled him, and he called upon Andrew for his opinion on the debate.

What's up, Bro?

"Am I being foolish for attempting this transfer?"

I can't fault you for creativity.

"Seriously, Andrew. Am I going to die?"

Dunno, but I can promise I'll do everything in my power to shore up the foundation if it starts to crumble.

"Would you care to translate so I can pass along the good news?"

Turns out I can get inside Charlie's belly to check on the twins.

"No shit?"

For real. They are adorable by the way. Anyway, I digress. If I can do it now, doesn't it stand to reason I'll be able to get inside you after the transfer?

"Makes sense to me."

So, if something breaks, I'll fix it.

"You're not a doctor."

Angela can walk me through it.

"You're giving her a lot of credit."

She's awesome.

"And you're sure you'll be able to save the day if the need arises?"

I won't let my nephews die.

"What about me?"

You'll be fine.

"How can you be sure?"

You were meant to rule.

"So were you at one point."

Andrew shook his head. *No, I wasn't.*

"I'll tell Alain you vouch for my safety."

It won't mean anything to your guy. He's a know-it-all.

"It might persuade him to see things my way."

A blowjob might be more effective.

"Go back to wherever you came from."

Conversation stopped when Colin entered the library.

"We'll draw up a new contract without any stipulations," Colin demanded, brooking no argument. "It's the only way, and I'm not going to listen to any more debates. I know why you're doing this, Alain, and I love you for it, but I have it on good authority nothing bad will happen to me."

"Sure, you do," Alain retorted glibly, but the worried look on his face belied the words. "Did you stumble on a seer while you were outside?"

"Sort of," Colin said vaguely. "Come on. I'll explain over dinner."

"Are we included in the conversation?" Errol asked.

"Not tonight, Da."

They were much more accepting of magic and witchcraft, but learning their dead son was in constant communication with Colin would start a conversation he couldn't endure right then. Sometimes he couldn't believe the connection with Andrew even existed, and to convince his fathers that his twin could cross metaphysical barriers would be difficult at best, and it would certainly dredge up old wounds. Errol might use the reminder of Andrew's death to point out the danger Colin would be facing in the next four months.

"We'll talk again tomorrow morning," Colin

promised. "I need some quiet time with Alain."

They had a tray brought up to their suite, and over dinner, Colin recounted his conversation with Andrew.

"He assured me we'd get through this unscathed."

"Colin—"

"Stop right there," Colin begged. "I can't take any more of this. Instead of supporting me unconditionally, you're focusing on the worst-case scenario. I'm not going to change my mind, Alain. I don't care if the odds aren't in my favor. You'll have to hang on for the ride or walk away."

"Do you want me to leave?"

Colin threw himself at Alain and clutched him like he was the last available lifesaver on their sinking ship. He shook with emotion, exhausted from the mental and physical stress of trying to keep everyone on an even keel. There was no way he'd manage to hold it together if Alain walked away, but he wouldn't beg. Colin didn't reply, but he held his breath as Alain considered his decision. Fortunately, he didn't have to wait too long.

In one sweeping move, Alain lifted him in his arms and headed toward the four-poster. "I think you need a reminder of my commitment."

"God, yes."

Chapter Twenty-Six

A NEW CONTRACT was delivered by messenger the next day, minus the death clause, and after some deliberation, Charlie signed it with Angela as a witness. With the document safely in hand, the courier departed. Charlie was left wondering if she'd done the right thing. It made so much sense when Colin and Angela explained the necessity, but the chain of events leading to this momentous decision had her questioning everyone's motives, including her own.

Determined to live with her decision, she convinced Angela to let her take a shower and shampoo her hair. She was tired of the enforced bedrest, and sponge baths weren't as relaxing as warm water sluicing down her back. Her long hair could use a good scrubbing as well, and since the bleeding wasn't noticeable when they'd checked earlier, Angela gave the go-ahead.

She stayed under the pulsing spray longer than necessary, but after she stepped out of the enclosure and dried off, Charlie felt reborn. With her hair wrapped in a towel and dressed in a pink nightgown made out of the finest cotton, she sat on a chair by the window and finger combed her drying hair. She even thought about makeup for the first time in weeks. A little bit of blush and a dab of gloss might go a long way to lift her morale, which was at its lowest since she found out she was pregnant. It had been a long time since anyone had paid her a compliment or viewed her as more than a commodity—someone to fight over and ransom. She wanted her life back.

Angela left her in the care of Iris, her regular nurse, who'd grown fond of Charlie over the last week, and she did her best to protect her from the curious. Rumors swirled around the princess, reinforced by the comings and goings of the heir apparent and the royal guards policing the hospital. Charlie never ventured the truth but smiled mysteriously when Nurse Iris asked if Colin was the father of her precious cargo.

As she was helping Charlie back into bed, the door slammed open and a stranger stepped through. Charlie faltered and stared at the interloper. Dressed in a miniskirt over purple leggings, the blonde cocked her head, stuck her hip out in a contrived pose, and surveyed the room.

"May I help you?" Iris asked.

As the woman stepped closer, Charlie caught a whiff of musky maleness she only associated with one person. It was a repulsive odor and her bowels clenched. Was she so befuddled that everyone reminded her of Drake?

"I'm here to see Charlie," the stranger replied.

The voice was female, but there was something definitely off, and Charlie slowly backed away.

"You must be mistaken," she said haughtily. "I don't know you."

Drake's mask slipped and unmistakable malice glinted from his eyes.

Charlie gasped and put out a hand. "Get away from me."

Iris quickly stepped between them and tried to block Drake's path while calling out for help, but Drake already had a dagger in his hand and swung wildly, catching the unsuspecting nurse by surprise. Iris shrieked when the sharp blade slashed her arm, but she was still determined to keep him away from Charlie. She struggled with Drake to get control of the dagger, which gave Charlie the opportunity to slip out the door and run.

Two of her security guards were slumped on the floor, but Charlie didn't waste time checking to see if they were dead or alive. She sprinted down the long hallway, and when she heard Drake laughing in the background, she glanced over her shoulder and was horrified to see him closing the distance. He'd ditched the wig and the high heels and was running on bare feet, looking like a deranged psychopath intent on harming her and the twins.

This sudden activity after weeks of bed rest was a strain on her body. She was already winded and the movement in her belly was a sure sign the twins weren't thrilled by this unexpected jog. She spied the door to the stairwell and rushed forward, hoping there was a lock on the other side to keep Drake out, but she didn't find one. She sped down the stairs, taking each rise two at a time to try to increase the distance. Her heartbeat thudded in her chest, and the maniacal laughter in the background made every hair on her body stand on end. Drake was having way too much fun, deliberately slowing his pace, like a hunter drawing out the chase for sport.

The sound of doors banging open and boots clomping down the stairs spurred Drake into action, and Charlie screamed at the top of her lungs so her security would know they were on the right track. Keeping her eyes on the floor to avoid tripping, she didn't realize Drake was close until he grabbed her arm and yanked. She fell on the hard concrete and he straddled her. With one hand collaring her neck, he got within kissing distance and hissed, "Shush, my sweet Charlie. They'll never get to you in time."

"Get off me, you insane motherfucker!"

His grip never faltered, only grew more determined, and Charlie felt her breaths getting thinner as he squeezed her throat, cutting off her air supply. He used the point of the dagger to lift her nightgown and pressed the sharp edge against her belly button.

"I can't wait to see the little bastards wiggling around on the floor like maggots."

"Please," Charlie rasped. "I beg you."

A shot sounded and Drake jerked back, loosening his grip on Charlie. He howled in anger as blood oozed from the shallow trench where the bullet had grazed him on his forehead. Crimson drops slipped down over his eyebrow and into his eye, turning the sclera a macabre shade of red, while he rapidly blinked to clear his vision. Charlie squirmed to get free, but Drake was much stronger, and he pinned her down with one arm, and raised his other hand—the one holding the dagger—above his head to gain momentum. The blade glinted under the harsh neon lights, and Charlie deflected the downward swing, screaming in agony when the dagger sliced through the tendons in her forearm. Her rounded belly rippled as tiny arms and legs flailed in silent protest.

Drake muttered a curse and slapped her viciously.

She struck back with all the force she could muster, pushing hard against Drake's chest, and when she felt him give, she rolled away and staggered to her feet. Clutching her belly protectively, she waited for Drake's next move, but the royal guard who'd winged him drew closer and put the gun against Drake's temple.

"Drop the knife."

"I don't think so," Drake sneered.

"I'll shoot if you don't comply."

In a theatrical flash of lights, Drake evaporated out of sight just as the gun went off. The guard stared at the empty space in shock before he helped Charlie to her feet.

She'd fallen on the floor and blood dripped from the cut on her forearm. When the guard picked her up to carry her back upstairs, the pink nightgown caught the first drops of blood trickling from her vagina.

The corridor leading to her bedroom was a hive of activity as emergency personnel and more security guards swarmed in after the fact. Charlie felt lightheaded and background noises faded as her blood pressure dropped. She caressed her belly, which no longer undulated, and felt a sense of peace knowing she'd done her best to save the children. Now it was Angela's turn to take over.

THE DEMON WAS waiting for Drake when he materialized in the hospital parking lot. He looked unhappy and Drake started making excuses as soon as he saw his nemesis.

"I did my best with the hand I was dealt."

"You fell short."

"Give me another chance, and I'll bring you those babies on a silver platter."

"We don't give second chances where I come from."

"Come on," Drake whined. "It took a while for the grimoire to arrive, and I had to study it to get through the protective wards. At least give me an A for effort. I almost had those little bastards."

"You'll wish you had."

Before Drake could think of another excuse, the demon was gone, and he was amazed his life had been spared. He'd half expected the creature to snatch his beating heart clear out of his chest in retribution, but he was still standing. Hesitantly, Drake crouched down and scuttled through the parked vehicles until he reached his motorcycle, which was parked at the edge of the lot near a grouping of trees. Miraculously, his helmet was still hanging on the handlebar where he'd left it. He positioned it on his head, hitched up the miniskirt, and threw his leg over to settle on the leather seat. Glancing in the side mirror before backing out of his spot, he stared at his reflection. The handsome face he'd been sporting since he made his deal with the devil was no more. In its place was the empty socket no amount of magic could restore. Adding to the mix was the new gash on his forehead making him look more freakish than ever. He'd had hopes of crashing the palace disguised as a journalist, and now he knew it was improbable unless he could figure a way out of this crisis. He wondered what other surprises were in store for him back at Ginny's apartment.

His day went from bad to worse when he drove down the familiar street and saw several police vehicles parked around the complex. Security in full combat gear littered the area like marauding rats. Making a quick U-turn, Drake headed out of town, back to the motel where he'd stayed the first time. Had the demon somehow managed to tip off the cops? Was this the beginning of the end?

As he drove down the highway, Drake took stock of his weapons at hand. He'd stuffed some cash in his pocket before leaving the apartment, so he could pay for a meal and his room for one night, assuming he could get past the clerk who'd take one look at him and turn him away, or worse, call the cops. A few miles before reaching his target, Drake pulled over and dismounted. Sinking down into the snow, he squeezed his eyes shut, and chanted the familiar disguising spell he'd learned as a child. It had never been a challenge in the past, but he could feel his powers deteriorating, and although he'd been warned this might happen, the demon had to know there was no way Drake could breach the palace gates in this condition. Giving it his all, he conjured up the image of the man he hoped to inhabit again. Colin's sparkling blue eyes and engaging smile emerged and took form. Calling upon his dead grandmother for support, Drake grabbed hold of the tantalizing image with shaky hands and tried it on for size.

A dark mist enveloped him, and the wind shrieked, but Drake held on to the mask he hoped to inhabit one last time. He couldn't allow fear to knock him off course. Slowly the tempest subsided and night fell, cloaking the countryside in inky blackness. Somewhere in the distance a wolf howled, and Drake braced for an attack, but the animal never approached. An owl hooted and for one dreadful second, panic set in as he recalled the moment his eye was gauged out, but all was calm except for his ragged breathing and thundering heartbeat. With a last burst of energy, Drake got off his knees and lifted his bike. He adjusted the side mirror which had shifted during the fall, and with more hope than he had any right to feel, looked at his image. Colin stared back at him, bright-eyed and as beautiful as ever. He almost wept with relief, but had no intention of messing up the hard-won façade. He'd save the celebration for the wedding banquet. Ruining Colin's special day had been on his agenda after he slaughtered the babes, but now it would have to take first place.

Mentally and physically exhausted, Drake's normally crafty brain was sluggish, and he didn't consider the implications when he walked into the motel with a face that was as recognizable as the Imperial Palace. The clerk, who'd been doing his job for years, and knew the importance of discretion, didn't utter one word when Drake asked for a room. He simply took the money and slid over the key card. As soon as Drake disappeared down the corridor, the clerk picked up the phone and called the police. They took down the information and relayed the news to the head of security at the palace who hand-carried the report to the Duke of Maitland.

ASHEN-FACED, ERROL approached Isabelle who thanked him for the alert. Earlier in the morning they'd heard from the hospital and knew the lull in between violent episodes was over. Drake had made another attempt on Charlie's life and failed, but the horrific attack had a ripple effect, and the princess was experiencing contractions.

They'd hoped Drake was on his way out of town, but they were devastated by this new information. Isabelle pulled Alain aside and gave him the bad news. Choosing to protect Colin, who already had enough on his mind, Alain suggested Isabelle and Raoul figure out the best way to stop Drake if he was stupid enough to make an appearance. The plastic surgeon, looking battered but determined to help, had been surprisingly forthcoming about his shady connection with Drake and admitted he and his henchmen were mainly in town to seek retribution. Since Isabelle shared the same bloodthirsty attitude, and Alain had no stomach for violence, he left them to it.

Colin had to be kept in the dark. Alain never questioned his fiancé's courage or determination, but he was about to put his life on the line and needed to be physically sound. Hand-to-hand combat with a deranged warlock was hardly conducive to a successful transfer.

Chapter Twenty-Seven

SINCE MEETING ALAIN and confronting one obstacle after another, Colin hoped they'd marry someday. Their engagement had been set in motion by a near-death experience and was meant to last five years. Charlie's surprising news almost ruined their plans, but she'd provided the solution to a complex dilemma which had plagued their relationship from the start. Granted, circumstances weren't ideal, and they had jumped through multiple hoops to get this far, but he was about to reap his rewards, except this day—which should have been the happiest of his life—was turning into a hellish nightmare, thanks to his insane cousin, Drake.

It had started with the frantic call from Angela, and it spiraled downward from there. Somehow, Drake circumvented security and slashed his way through Charlie's innermost circle. She'd escaped with her life, but the traumatic events left a mark, and now she was bleeding and experiencing contractions. They'd put her on some kind of drip to halt the progress, but so far it wasn't working.

Before Drake's sudden appearance, Charlie had signed the new contract, and it was safely delivered into the right hands. If things had gone according to plan, he and Alain would have been married at least one week before they attempted the transfer. Now, there was a time crunch, and carefully laid plans had to be moved up. It was imperative the marriage take place so there was no denying the legitimacy of the children he was about to carry.

David had thrown up his arms in frustration when Colin ordered him to move the event forward by several hours. He and Alain would marry in a private ceremony with only his fathers and Isabelle in attendance. Guests, when they arrived, would be routed directly to the ballroom, where they would be distracted with magnums of champagne and good food. If Charlie's condition continued to deteriorate, and immediate surgery became necessary, Sebastian and Errol would host while Colin and Alain quietly removed themselves from the celebration.

Adding to Colin's stress was the arrival of Dr. Davies and his entourage of three. He couldn't comprehend Alain's sudden interest in this new acquaintance, but he was going out of his way to make sure the doctor was comfortably ensconced in the palace. He'd even arranged a hasty meeting with Isabelle, which made no sense whatsoever. When Colin asked for details, Alain waved him off with platitudes, which did nothing to soothe his nerves.

Colin assumed the role of a nervous bridegroom, clearly infected by David's dramatic overacting. Perhaps Andrew had the right idea, and a blowjob might put him in a better frame of mind. Last night's lovemaking had done wonders for Alain, who was surprisingly unruffled, despite the chaos. Colin had high hopes for tonight, but the bad news from the hospital put a damper on everything, and now he wondered if he'd even get laid. When he last checked in with Angela an hour ago, he was told the contractions had stopped, but not the bleeding.

They dressed in separate quarters, in accordance with David's instructions. He'd insisted they at least try to stick to tradition, and not see each other before the ceremony. Colin hadn't disclosed his choice of wedding finery, wanting to keep it a surprise, and when he looked in the full-length mirror and viewed his own image decked out in full Scottish regalia, in honor of Errol and his Shetland roots, he was delighted with the decision.

He'd consulted online with the finest tailor in Edinburgh, choosing his colors and style of jacket and waistcoat from the vast array presented in vivid detail. The rest of the outfit was put together by the experts and delivered in person by the owner himself, who stayed to help him dress. The forest green and black was a hunting tartan and a good choice for his blond coloring. The kilt went over a pair of black hose with matching forest green and black plaid flashes. The traditional *sgian dubh*, or kilt knife, was tucked into the hose on his right leg. A pair of shiny black Ghillie Brogues provided the finishing touch. For his shirt, Colin chose a white winged linen with a black bow tie underneath his Prince Charlie jacket and deep-green waistcoat. His wedding sporran was custom made, and he'd tucked the wedding rings inside since they wouldn't have a best man to carry out the task. He'd let his newly shampooed hair fall loosely around his face, instead of tying it back as recommended. It was more in keeping with his normal appearance, and he wanted Alain to see the man he'd fallen in love with, not some store-bought mannequin.

Once he was dressed, the owner handed him the custom-made dirk, a long thrusting dagger which was an integral component of a highlander's outfit. Colin reminded him they were attending a wedding, not going to war, and the owner slipped the dirk into the leather sheath stamped with the prince's royal insignia and placed it on a nearby table.

Colin took the backstairs to make sure he didn't bump into Alain. The organ music started to play as soon as he walked through the chapel entrance. Alain waited for him at the altar, flanked by Isabelle to his left, and the royal couple to his right. Andrew hovered in the background with Bibi on his shoulder. His twin's smile was incandescent, and he'd even dressed for the occasion, ditching his ghostly rags for a trendy coat and tie.

Colin had never seen Alain in formal attire, and his breath stuttered when he caught sight of the stunning man, in a midnight-blue tuxedo, patiently waiting to marry him. Alain's arresting hazel eyes glimmered as he tracked Colin's slow progress up the aisle, filling him with profound joy. It didn't matter what the future had in store for them because right then, in the here and now, nothing was more important than their shared love.

They kept the actual ceremony as brief as possible, exchanging wedding vows in hushed tones, and when they slipped the rings on with shaky fingers, they laughed at their combined nerves. Errol lost his composure halfway through, and tears rolled down his whiskered cheeks, while Sebastian hid his emotion behind a snowy white linen handkerchief. Isabelle appeared unmoved, but Colin reached into her mind to reassure her.

"I will strive to make him happy."

She gave him the briefest of smiles and silently replied, *"You have my blessing."*

When the officiant pronounced them married, Alain didn't wait for further instructions. He wrapped his arms around Colin's waist and captured his mouth in a bruising kiss, leaving no doubt in anyone's mind that this was a passionate union and meant to last.

They posed for official photographs, several by themselves and others including the royal couple and Isabelle. It was a tedious business but necessary for personal and public record keeping. To everyone's combined amazement and immense relief, the ceremony had gone smoothly. Per their agreement with the press, David gave them the go-ahead to announce the wedding and start posting pictures online.

Colin called to check on Charlie, and Angela informed him she was stable. Waiting another twenty-four hours to begin the transfer wasn't going to pose a problem. "Stay and enjoy your wedding reception."

"Can I eat and drink?"

"By all means."

"What if we have to do emergency surgery?"

"There are other ways to anesthetize you if something untoward happens."

"Good to know," Colin said. "I don't relish the idea of choking on my vomit during surgery."

"Let me do the worrying, your highness."

The reprieve was a special bonus Colin and Alain hadn't expected. They had the traditional wedding feast and first dance, listened with blurry eyes as Sebastian toasted their long life and continued happiness, and watched Errol present them with a statue he'd secretly sculpted. The bronze would be featured in official stamps and take center stage on their mantel. He'd crafted it from a photo they'd taken while they were in the Seychelles, and he'd managed to capture the wondrous joy of new love. With their arms draped over each other's shoulders, and their foreheads pressed together, they smiled in perfect harmony. It was an artistic masterpiece and one they would treasure for the rest of their lives.

During dinner, Alain groped Colin's thigh and slowly inched his way toward his prize. He cupped Colin's balls and leaned over. "How did you know I have a thing for men in kilts?"

"I wasn't sure, but I'm glad you approve."

"Thank you for staying in character," Alain purred while he stroked Colin until he was hard and slick with precum.

Colin bit down on his lip to keep the moan in check.

Unperturbed, Alain continued to torture him. "Do you think anyone will notice if we slip away?"

"We'd better go soon, or I'll spill on your hand."

Alain chuckled and withdrew.

Ten minutes later, Alain nudged Colin, and they headed upstairs to their suite. Lovingly prepared by David, no expense was spared to make their wedding night as perfect as possible. Champagne was chilling in the silver bucket, a dozen oysters on ice were laid out for their midnight snack, and an assortment of finger foods filled two trays.

Colin excused himself for a minute to use the bathroom and, once inside, debated the wisdom of slipping into something more comfortable or letting Alain undress him. He opted for the latter and returned in time to see his *husband*—a dream come true—filling two crystal flutes with champagne.

Alain handed him a glass and they each took a few sips without taking their eyes off each other. Love and pride blazed through Alain's intense gaze, warming Colin from the inside out.

"Was it everything you hoped for?" Alain asked.

"More than I dreamed of, given the circumstances."

"Let's make sure we reward David and Sam for all they've done to make this a success."

Colin nodded.

Without another word, Alain put down his glass and tugged on Colin's bow tie. "This outfit is incredible," he murmured. "You've never been more attractive."

"I wanted to look my best for you."

"You made the right choice, *chaton.* I went to university in Edinburgh, and I always looked twice whenever I spotted a guy in a kilt. You were gorgeous before you put on this outfit but decked out like this...you take my breath away."

Alain kissed him and when they parted, he dropped the black silk tie. "We've come a long way in such a short time," Alain continued. "Five months ago, you were a different person. When I think of everything you've had to overcome to get to this point, I'm embarrassed to admit I had my doubts about our relationship. I was sure we'd fizzle out in no time, but your personal growth has been remarkable."

Colin bit his lower lip to keep it from wobbling.

"I've never been prouder to walk by your side and assume my role as consort. I intend to spend my life living up to your expectations."

"You only have to be yourself," Colin said with a lump in his throat. "I love you just the way you are."

They kissed again and Alain slipped a hand underneath the tartan and caressed Colin's lightly furred ass. "I'm almost reluctant to remove your clothes. I don't suppose you'd let me..."

"On our wedding night you can have me any way you choose."

"You *are* beautiful," Alain said huskily. "And giving me carte blanche is an unexpected treat. Would you turn around and bend over?"

Colin complied and Alain lifted the hem of the kilt, revealing the luscious globes Colin parted for him so lovingly.

"There's some lube in my sporran," Colin muttered helpfully.

"Always thinking ahead," Alain marveled. "It's no wonder I'm crazy about you."

Colin spread his legs, and Alain sank to his knees, pressing his face into the muscular curves. He speared the warm folds of Colin's quivering hole and relished the clean taste. Colin must have anticipated this scenario when he got ready earlier in the day, and he'd done his best to prepare himself for Alain's questing tongue. Eating him out was a guilty pleasure Alain hadn't enjoyed lately, and the image of Colin—a man with endless potential, leading his principality into a brighter future—squirting soapy water into himself for this special moment was as intoxicating as the sight of him bent over and holding his cheeks apart.

Alain spent the next few minutes alternately tongue and finger fucking his prince until Colin's knees buckled.

They spent the next couple of hours taking turns at giving and receiving, buoyed by the oysters and other libido-inducing snacks. It was truly a night to remember and one they'd always cherish.

During a lull, Colin snuggled against Alain and ventured a mood-altering question. "Will you still fuck me after I'm pregnant?"

Alain sighed. "Are we seriously having this conversation?"

"When else?" Colin asked. "Once things are set in motion, it'll be go, go, go until the twins are tucked away in my uterus."

"I will do whatever is safe, and if Angela says you're off limits for four months, then we'll live with it."

"Are you sure?"

"Abstaining won't kill us."

"And speaking of dying…"

"Colin, stop. I'm not having this discussion."

"You need to listen, Alain. I know it goes against your nature to leave things to chance, and I'm grateful you didn't insist on the death clause, but we wouldn't be lying here if you'd continued to play hardball. Charlie promised to follow your lead if we're faced with a life-threatening emergency."

"When did you talk to her?"

"Early this morning before the messenger arrived with the contract."

"How do you know it's not lip service?"

"I trust her to do the right thing."

"Apparently, Raoul does too," Alain revealed. "He keeps asking about her status in relation to you and the future heirs."

Surprised, Colin pushed away and sat cross-legged on the bed while Alain continued to recline on the pillows. "What's the real reason he's here?"

"Revenge."

"Christ." Colin looked disgusted. "He'll have to take a number if he wants a go at Drake."

"Raoul knows there's a long line of people who'd love to tear him apart."

"Are you one of them?" Colin asked.

"Only if your life is on the line," Alain admitted. "I'd rather job it out, if I'm being honest."

"I wouldn't hesitate to gut the motherfucker."

"You need to save your energy for the big fight ahead of you."

Colin unfolded his legs and dove back in place by Alain's side. Physical contact was more reassuring than words, and right then, he had to be pasted to Alain. "My dad had a terrible time during his pregnancy."

"I know, but you're not him," Alain soothed. "Plus, you have magic on your side. I'm certain Isabelle and I can ease the way to a safe delivery."

"You don't need to lie," Colin said. "I'm prepared to suffer."

"It's not a lie," Alain promised. "There's strength in numbers, and you have modern medicine, a loving husband, and a family of witches, ghosts, and doting fathers on your side. We won't let anything happen to you."

Colin straddled Alain and knee walked until his cock was inches from his open mouth. "Is it my turn to top or yours?"

Alain spread his hands over Colin's chest and pinched his nipples between thumb and forefinger, kneading them gently until he heard a soft moan. "Who's keeping score, *chaton*?"

Chapter Twenty-Eight

DOWNSTAIRS THE REVELERS continued to enjoy the feast, and no one paid any attention to the handful of photographers arriving and circulating through the crowd. They were expected at a wedding feast, and this one in particular would be on everyone's lips for the next few months. The heir apparent liked to keep a low profile, and his marriage to a celebrated scientist had come as a complete surprise. The citizens of this small principality would be craving any bit of information they could get on the new couple.

Drake had worked on his disguise with hardly any help from the demon who'd warned him this was his last chance to make things right. He would accept Colin's heart in exchange for the pair he'd been promised, but it had to be won in combat. He was in the mood for a good fight, the bloodier the better. If Drake managed to pull this off without magic, the slate would be wiped clean, his lost eye restored, and he could start a new life in some other part of the world.

Drake wore a ball cap marked PRESS and was sporting a pair of dark slacks and a sweater. A fancy camera hung from a leather strap around his neck, and he looked through the zoom lens, trying to spot Colin and Alain. He approached a footman.

"May I help you, sir?"

"Where's the new couple?"

"They've slipped away."

"Dammit," Drake cursed. "We were promised a photo op."

"Weren't you at the ceremony?

Drake shot him a disdainful look and blurted, "Go about your business."

The footman faltered, surprised by the photographer's demeanor. Palace regulars were usually friendly and respectful, knowing full well they were rarely allowed on the premises and only with the royal family's approval. This arrogant fuck must be new, and the footman wasn't going to take shit from anyone.

"You'd better watch your attitude, or they'll throw your ass out of here."

Heat flashed from Drake's eyes, and for one second his mask slipped. *What in the hell?* Behind the even façade lay something so foul the footman had to take a step back. Was this the fucktard stalking the prince and his fiancé?

Prior to the evening's celebration, David had called a meeting to inform the staff to be on the lookout for anything unusual. A madman was on the loose and the royals were worried he might try to crash the party. Although the authorities had a good lead on the guy, he supposedly had an uncanny ability to weasel out of tight situations and, thus far, had eluded arrest.

From a safe distance, the footman studied the photographer who continued to scan the ballroom with a disgruntled look on his face. If he hadn't been so unpleasant, he could have gone unnoticed, but the staff had been warned, and this guy was raising the footman's internal alarms. He went in search of the event planner, who was in the kitchen discussing something food related with his husband, Sam. The footman broached his concerns, and after listening intently, David poked his head out the swing door and looked around. He spied the alleged photographer hanging by the bar.

"The bloody nerve," David muttered. "Thank you for paying attention. I'll handle it from here."

"Do you want me on standby?"

"Yes, but don't do anything to arouse his suspicion."

David took one last look at the man and headed straight for Isabelle. She was sitting at a table with the royal couple, and the doctor from Belgium, who'd disrupted the meticulously arranged seating plan at the last minute. David whispered in her ear.

"Someone who looks a little like Colin is posing as a photographer and enjoying the free booze."

"You think he's Drake?"

"Our footman got a bad feeling when he confronted him."

"I see." She gazed at the stranger and tried to feel him out, but he had his back to her. Nonetheless, her skin prickled, and she had to take the warning seriously.

Turning to Dr. Davies, Isabelle leaned in. "It appears we won't have to look much farther."

Like a bloodhound picking up a scent, Raoul followed Isabelle's line of sight. "He must be desperate to show up here."

"I'm certain he's running out of options."

"Do you have your cloak within reach?"

Isabelle had spent hours creating a spell-binding garment to throw over Drake if he ever got close enough. Keeping his magic under wraps was the only way to subdue the warlock until they could apply stronger methods to keep him in check. Raoul didn't even blink when she mentioned her supernatural skills.

"It's upstairs in my suite."

"Go and get it."

"Don't approach him until I return," Isabelle ordered. She slipped out a side entrance and vanished. Back in under ten minutes, with a black robe draped over one arm, she took her seat beside Raoul.

"Is he still here?"

"At the bar getting shit-faced."

"You can't be serious."

"Look at him."

Drake had a glass of something in one hand while the other gesticulated at the bartender who watched him warily. The entire staff was now on high alert after the footman mentioned they were dealing with an intruder. Isabelle whispered in Prince Sebastian's ear to warn him they were about to approach Drake. She asked if the royal couple would prefer to leave the premises in case things got ugly, but the prince was adamant. "I'd like to be around when you take down the bastard who killed my mother."

"Stay out of our way," Isabelle warned.

They moved as one, approaching Drake from behind, but his uncanny survival instincts made him spin around in time to spy Isabelle and her group approaching. He appeared surprised to see Raoul among the crowd, flanked by a pair of thugs with hate in their eyes. Drake sprinted for the main doors and, reaching the grand foyer, took the imposing marble stairs to the second floor.

Having never been inside the palace, Drake was at a loss. Footsteps and shouted orders to cease and desist were getting too close. He raced past glass-fronted display cases filled with priceless antiques, and old-fashioned suits of fine armor stood guard on either side of the long corridor. Dozens of ancestral portraits lined the walls and appeared to look down at him in disapproval as he deliberated his next move. There were so many doors leading to places he'd never been before. Desperate, Drake called upon the demon for help. "Which way do I go?"

The dreaded voice answered immediately. "Hang a right and go through the double doors at the end of the hall."

Drake obeyed, and when he parted the massive carved doors, he was faced with yet another long corridor and more doors.

"Now what?"

"Keep going until you get to the royal suite. It's got a red door with gold handles."

"Will I find Colin there?"

"And his consort."

"I should get some kind of bonus if I take them both out."

The demon lashed out, knocking Drake back several feet. "So far you've been all talk."

"There's no need to get testy," Drake remarked uneasily. He got rid of the camera and pulled a gun from an inside pocket.

"No gun," the demon ordered. "You promised me hand-to-hand combat."

"Like fucking gladiators?"

"To the death."

"Talk about getting your money's worth."

"You stopped amusing me a while back."

Drake stood outside the royal suite and took a deep breath. When he tried the knob it wouldn't give. "It's locked."

"No shit."

"Aren't you going to do something about it?"

"I'm not your personal assistant!" the demon roared. "Figure it out!"

Even though he was ordered to stave off magic tonight, Drake fell back on the familiar and conjured up a spell he normally used for breaking and entering. He knew Isabelle had laid a protection spell to safeguard her son and his new groom, but Drake was an accomplished thief, and this was child's play. When he turned the knob a second time, he stepped into a dark anteroom, which had been the scene of a celebratory dinner. Trays of food and a silver champagne bucket hadn't been collected by the staff yet, and Drake helped himself to a lobster roll. He hadn't eaten in several hours and could use the sustenance. He washed it down with a large gulp from the magnum bottle and prepared to break down the second set of doors leading to the actual bedroom.

Except the door swung open, and Colin and Alain stood at the ready.

With preternatural speed and strength, Drake seized Colin, dragging him away from Alain with savage intent. He wrapped his fingers around Colin's neck and squeezed, pressing down hard on the vulnerable Adam's apple which bobbed convulsively. Months of rage and frustration came to a head while Colin struggled to get free. At the same time, the demon goaded Drake, chanting *kill...kill...kill* like a blood-thirsty spectator in a Roman arena.

Alain screamed, "Let him go."

Drake sneered and pressed harder. Colin flailed, but he couldn't break the iron grip, and he was starting to lose consciousness. Exaltation surged through Drake's veins as he felt the life slowly seeping out of Colin. Soon he'd be dead, and he'd turn his attention to the coward, Alain, who was probably standing behind him with his thumb up his ass.

It was Drake's last coherent thought before Alain plunged the custom-made stainless-steel dirk into his liver and twisted viciously. He cried out in shock and released Colin, who sucked in a lungful of badly needed air. Drake's knees buckled, sending him crashing down on the carpet. Alain loomed, face mottled with fury, and he withdrew the dirk and raised his hand to deliver the death blow, but the door burst open and the room filled with past victims—Raoul, Isabelle, Sebastian, and Errol—looking grim-faced and determined to cut Drake off at the knees.

Raoul approached Alain slowly and reached for the dirk. "Let me handle this."

In a trance, Alain passed him the bloody dirk, and Raoul sliced Drake open from hip to hip, duplicating the transverse cut he'd experienced when Drake had left him to die. A hideous sound escaped Drake's throat as he watched his intestines slither out of him in a bloody mess.

"You're supposed to be dead," Drake gasped while he tried scooping the slippery coils back into his body.

"You'll wish I had died."

"My turn," Isabelle said, taking the dirk out of Raoul's hand. She swiped the forged steel across Drake's neck, severing his jugular, and deep red squirted out in rhythm with the beating of his dying heart. The group watched Drake's handsome features transforming in front of their eyes. The flesh peeled back, uncovering the empty eye socket, which was blackened with dried-out gore. Drake whimpered and begged for mercy, but the people surrounding him were unmoved. Prince Sebastian pried the dirk out of Isabelle's hand and thrust the steel directly into Drake's heart. "This is for my mother, and Princess Charlotte, and all the other people you've fucked over in your useless life."

Bibi and Andrew watched the well-deserved execution dispassionately.

The lights in the bedchamber flickered, and the air grew foul with the stench of loosened bowels and a combination of sulfur and charcoal, usually associated with burning flesh. Out of the darkness, something indescribable materialized and covered Drake's body possessively. The feeble warlock tried fighting it off, but the lifeblood had drained out of him, leaving an empty husk incapable of fending off the creature only he could see, but the others could sense with horrific fascination. A gust of wind swirled through the bedchamber, and a dark gray thermal plume lifted Drake's bloody remains off the floor and hurled him toward the fireplace, where he disappeared in a spectacular explosion of fire.

The demonic laughter filling the room brought the Mexicans to their knees, and they frantically made the sign of the cross and murmured prayers while Isabelle lifted both hands in the air to ward off the unspeakable evil drenching the enclosed space.

Colin and Alain held each other as the nightmare unfolded, and when the noises quieted and the smoke cleared, there was nothing on the floor, where Drake had lain, but a small pile of black ashes.

"Holy Mary and Saint Bride," Errol muttered, looking around in disbelief. "What on earth just happened?"

The stark look on Isabelle's face said it all. "The darkness took back its son."

"If Drake was in cahoots with the devil, it explains a lot," Raoul said pragmatically. "I just wish I had more time to torture the son of a bitch."

Prince Sebastian snorted. "What happened to your Hippocratic Oath?"

"It doesn't apply to snakes like Drake."

"When you associate with reptiles, you're bound to get stung."

"Truth," Raoul said seriously. "It's time I reevaluated my choices."

"I hope so," the Prince replied.

A valet had wrapped Alain and Colin in warm robes, since they'd been naked when they'd heard Drake break into their suite. The boxers they'd pulled on in haste did nothing to warm their trembling bodies, but the soft velvet went a long way to ease some of the shock.

Prince Sebastian urged them to move to another suite, and no one protested, glad to be far from the ghastly scene. As Colin and Alain silently padded down the hallway, Isabelle stayed back to confer with the royals on the best way to spin this attack for the general public. Although it was clearly self-defense, the less said the better, and she didn't want the royals' reputation tarnished in any way. Now that her peace-loving son was a part of this distinguished family, it was more important than ever to come up with an explanation the coven would accept as the truth. No one would miss Drake, least of all his Wiccan brothers and sisters, but leaving out the gory details would be prudent.

The color was coming back to Alain's complexion, thanks to the restorative powers of single malt whiskey and the warm body of his new husband pressed to his side. The alternative was too awful to contemplate. He'd acted on pure instinct, grabbing the dirk he'd admired earlier, and didn't think of repercussions as he drove it into Drake's unsuspecting body. He was grateful Raoul had taken over. Remorse, however misguided in Drake's case, would have followed him for the rest of his life if he'd delivered the death blow. Now there was nothing to feel but gratitude.

"I'm safe for the first time in months," Colin said quietly. "Thank you for saving my life. I know murder isn't part of your job description."

"My only regret is it ruined our wedding night."

Colin glanced at a clock on the mantel and shook his head. "We have hours before it's time to go visit Charlie."

"I can't promise any action."

Colin shook his head and whispered, "We're alive—that's what matters."

"I love you," Alain said gruffly.

"Love you, too," Colin vowed. "Don't ever forget it."

"Promise."

Chapter Twenty-Nine

THE STEADY BEEPING of a heart monitor broke through the fog before Colin opened his eyes. He moaned softly and tried to move, but a sharp tug on his penis held him in place. His eyes fluttered open, and he looked around the unfamiliar room trying to get his bearings. There was an IV stand beside his bed with a half-empty bag of yellowish fluid hanging from it. Steady drops of liquid slid down the clear plastic tubing and into his body through the needle taped in place to the back of his hand. He tried to sit up, but the annoying tug on his privates reminded Colin he was attached to something. He reached to adjust himself when his hand encountered hard plastic sticking out of his slit. His breath quickened and bells went off, which alerted someone at the nurses' station. Soon his room was crowded with people in white uniforms checking his vital signs to see what was happening to set off the monitors.

"Get this thing out of my dick," he slurred angrily.

"No need to fret, your highness," an unfamiliar voice soothed. "It's just a catheter."

"Get rid of it," he ordered. "Now."

Colin grimaced while the nurse carefully worked on his request, and when she removed the catheter, he rubbed his sore cock in a reflexive move. "I want to sit up."

"Slowly," she cautioned. Supporting his back, she pressed the mechanical control and adjusted the bed to a sitting position. Plumping the pillows behind Colin's neck, she waited for further instructions.

Colin inspected his surroundings. The hospital room was similar to the one he'd visited when Charlie was a patient, but this one was larger, and vases filled with flowers covered every available surface. The overpowering aroma of roses, gardenias, and God-knows-what permeated the atmosphere, forcing Colin to sneeze several times. The sharp pain in his abdomen that accompanied this simple maneuver made him wince. They'd warned him he might experience temporary memory loss after general anesthesia, and they were right. He couldn't remember much beyond counting backward.

Giving the nurse a side-eye, he asked, "Did I die last night?"

She chuckled. "No, your highness. Well-wishers have been sending flowers since the news got out."

He frowned. "Donate them."

"Even the roses from your husband?"

"Those can stay," Colin said. "Where is Alain?"

"He went home to shower and change."

"I'm ready to stand," Colin demanded. "Will you help me?"

"Of course," she replied immediately. "Swing your legs over the side of the bed and let the blood flow for a few minutes. You'll be a little wobbly at first."

Colin did as instructed and sighed as the room spun slightly. He knew this was a natural reaction to a change in position, but any form of weakness irritated him. If this was a prelude to the upcoming weeks, the nursing staff would be dealing with a shitty patient.

"I'm a little dizzy," he complained.

"Not to worry," the nurse said cheerily. "How about a sip of orange juice?"

Colin took the proffered glass and gulped the tangy beverage. He felt better within a few minutes, and after returning the empty glass into the nurse's hands, he insisted on getting out of bed.

Grabbing onto her arm, he stood on shaky legs. His gaze strayed to his stomach, which had been as flat as a board two days ago. A noticeable bump looked out of place and felt even weirder. There was also an unfamiliar and unsettling weight in his lower abdomen. When he felt the first flutter of movement, he gagged involuntarily. Holy. Fucking. Christ. He was pregnant!

The door swung open, and Alain strode in with a large box of chocolates in hand. He panicked when he saw the look on Colin's face and rushed to his side. "What's the matter?"

Colin fell into his arms and muttered, "Is this really happening?"

Alain supported him easily and shored up the embrace with a sympathetic kiss. "Yes, and you're doing great."

"I can't remember a thing."

"It'll start coming back in bits and pieces," Alain ventured.

"Can we unhook the IV?"

"We'll ask Angela when she comes to check on you."

Alain guided Colin back to bed, and after he and the nurse got him settled, he suggested she leave them alone for a while. "You can return when Dr. Whittaker makes her rounds."

"Call if you need anything."

"Thank you."

After she left them alone, Alain gripped Colin's hand and kissed his open palm tenderly.

"I'm so glad to see you," Colin voiced emotionally.

"No more than me," Alain replied. "You scared me half to death last night."

"What happened?"

"You don't remember?"

Colin shook his head.

"Charlie went into labor, and they had to airlift you to the hospital so they could do emergency surgery."

"Yikes. Sounds harrowing."

"You have no idea," Alain said. "One of the twins went into cardiac arrest but miraculously recovered once the transfer was completed."

"I wonder if Andrew had anything to do with the save."

"What do you mean?"

"He says he can get inside my uterus to keep an eye on the boys. Maybe he gave Drew's heart a little push?"

"Drew?" Alain asked, mystified.

"I'd like to name one of the twins after Andrew, but we'll call him Drew for short. This will avoid confusion."

Alain stared at him for a few moments.

"Are you okay with my suggestion?" Colin asked.

"Whatever you decide is fine with me," Alain said. "I don't know what Andrew did or didn't do. I can only tell you what happened. The fetal monitors were screaming angrily, the doctors were losing their minds; then it all stopped, and everything went back to normal."

"Are they doing okay now?"

"Yes. We heard two strong heartbeats the last time Angela checked." Alain pointed at the fetal monitor.

"How does it work?"

"Electronic discs called transducers are attached to a stretchy band they place on your abdomen. It acts like a stethoscope, transmitting a signal to the computer monitor, but you're disconnected at the moment. It would tether you to the bed, like the IV pole, if they left it indefinitely."

"I'd like to hear them for myself."

"We'll ask Angela to hook you up later."

"Sounds good. And how's Charlie doing?"

"She's in good spirits and already discussing a tummy tuck with Raoul."

Colin rolled his eyes. "Vanity, thy name is..."

Alain snorted. "She's obviously glad to have passed along her burden. She can't wait to get back into the swing of things, and Raoul has been most attentive."

"Charlie has always had a thing for bad boys," Colin griped. "I hope she finds some happiness this time around. Isn't he married though?"

"I'm not sure, but Charlie's future is no longer your concern," Alain reminded him.

"Probably not," Colin admitted. "But focusing on her will take my mind off my new normal, which feels peculiar, in case you want to know."

"I'm certain you'll get used to it in time."

Colin poked at the box of chocolates. "Presents already?"

Alain grinned. "This is just the beginning. Your wish is my command until you run out of cravings."

Colin looked amused. "No one mentioned this part."

"People usually focus on the bad stuff," Isabelle said as she entered the room and caught the tail end of the conversation. She handed Colin a small box of French pastries. "There are definite perks to pregnancy, and turning into an eating machine is one of them."

"Do tell," Colin said enthusiastically.

They chatted for over an hour, and when Isabelle left the room, Colin felt marginally better. He knew it would take time to feel comfortable with his situation, but the relief of a successful transfer trumped his other concerns. When Angela walked in later, he asked her several questions Isabelle couldn't or wouldn't answer.

"I hope you don't think I'm being ridiculous," Colin said apologetically.

"Of course not," she assured him. "Your body is going through changes at an incredible rate. Tell me what's on your mind?"

"Are the twins doing okay?"

"Surprisingly well after their bumpy ride."

"I heard one of them went into cardiac arrest?"

"We're not labeling the event since his little heart started up within seconds."

"But he's going to be okay going forward?"

"I don't anticipate any problems now that Drake is out of the picture, and we won't have to worry about any unwelcome intrusions. Your life will be boringly normal."

"Can I listen to their heartbeats?"

"Of course."

Angela flipped a toggle on the machine and attached the transducers to his belly. The steady gallop of two strong hearts was reassuring, and Colin beamed. "How exciting."

"It certainly is," Angela enthused. "Do you want me to leave the band in place?"

"No," Colin said. "Go ahead and unhook me. And can we ditch the IV as well?"

"The bag is almost empty. Let it run its course, and you'll be done with it."

"What's in it?"

"Antibiotics."

"I see. What else do I have to worry about?"

"Your worst fear will be weight gain."

"I've never had to monitor my food intake," Colin protested.

"You've never been pregnant," Angela said with a wry chuckle. "Snacking will take on a new meaning, and you'll pack on the pounds before you know it."

"A few months of indulgence shouldn't make a difference."

"Talk to me when the scale starts moving up too fast."

"When can he go home?" Alain asked.

"Another twenty-four hours should do it. He's got the long incision we need to monitor before we release him into your fine care. Are you planning on hiring a caregiver or nurse for Colin's daily needs?"

"What? No!" Colin protested. "I don't need a babysitter."

"Just until your incision has healed."

"Is it nasty?"

"Haven't you looked at it?" Angela asked.

Colin shook his head.

"Do you want to?"

He nodded.

Angela untied Colin's hospital gown from behind and pushed it down his arms and torso. The soft cotton lay bunched over his groin, which he appreciated, but displaying his junk was the least of his problems when he saw the classic vertical incision down the center of his rounded belly.

"Didn't you tell us I'd have a bikini cut?"

"We didn't anticipate the emergency surgery, and esthetics was the last thing on the surgeon's mind. He needed easy access to get the job done."

"It brings Frankenstein to mind."

She smirked. "It'll look better once they remove the staples, and silicone gel will help with the redness. This is why I'm suggesting a caregiver."

"I can do it," Alain maintained.

"The area needs to be cleaned and moisturized daily."

"It's not a problem."

Colin rubbed a hand over his distended belly. "Feels weird."

"You'll get used to it," Angela remarked.

"I'm not so sure." Colin looked dubious. "Won't my incision split as my tummy gets larger?"

"There's always a risk, but it's rare. Another reason you should keep your skin hydrated and free from infection—to prevent this sort of thing."

"And in four and a half months, you're going to cut me again?"

"Yes."

"Good times," Colin griped.

"You'll be so happy to get them out of your body you won't mind the surgery."

Colin yanked up the gown and slipped his arms through the openings. "Showtime is over."

Alain tied the strings in back to hold the gown together.

"Thanks," Colin said.

"You're welcome." Alain kissed him on the neck when he was done. "Whatever you need, *chaton*."

"I'd like to go home."

"Can we get him discharged any sooner?" Alain asked.

"No." Angela refused to give an inch. "I'm not going to risk any complications because you're impatient. Tomorrow will get here soon enough."

There was a knock on the door, and Prince Sebastian came through with Errol trailing behind. They were carrying bouquets of flowers, causing Colin to sneeze several times. Angela pressed a pillow to his stomach when he grimaced in pain.

"Hold this against your belly," she recommended. "It'll lessen the sting."

"Get rid of the damn flowers," Colin ordered.

"Sorry," the prince said hastily. He signaled for his bodyguard to remove the vases and baskets as quickly as possible. "I didn't know you were allergic to flowers."

"He's not," Alain explained. "But the concentration of different bouquets in the closed-in atmosphere is overwhelming."

"Aye," Errol agreed. "Too much of a good thing. How are you doing otherwise?"

"I'm fine," Colin said. "Eager to go home."

"Is he fit to travel?" Errol asked Angela.

"I want him to stick around for another day."

"I'm going to obey for now, but once I'm out of here, I'd like you to stop treating me like an invalid."

"You've been through a lot," Prince Sebastian reminded him.

"I was there, Dad."

"Just saying."

"How's the public dealing with the news?"

"No issues that we know of," he replied.

"And parliament will accept the twins as legitimate heirs once they're born?"

"Absolutely."

"And the countdown begins," Colin said, voice trailing. "I'm tired."

"We'll leave you to it then," Errol said. He bent to kiss Colin on the head. "Get some rest, son. You'll need all your strength in the next four months."

"Alain, will you see that he has everything he needs?"

"I've got this, your highness."

"Isn't it time you called me something other than your highness?"

"Call him Father," Colin said sleepily.

"And I'm Da," Errol said.

Bemused, Alain nodded.

Epilogue

THE FAMILY OF six were lying or sitting on colorful blankets, shielded from the harsh sun by blue-and-white beach umbrellas. Plastic buckets, shovels, and miniature fishing nets lay abandoned close to the water's edge. Several wicker baskets containing an assortment of picnic fare were open for inspection, and three toddlers sat cross-legged in a circle, munching on string cheese and animal crackers. Isabelle, dressed in a gauzy white shirt over pink capris, reclined on a beach chair, straw hat and sunglasses firmly in place. She was recovering from cataract surgery, and her eyes were still sensitive to the harsh rays that were difficult to avoid in this tropical climate. Alain and Colin lay sprawled underneath the other umbrella, sipping frosty mojitos, while they nibbled on deep-fried plantains sprinkled with sea salt.

They were celebrating their fifth wedding anniversary in the Seychelles with their three children, Isabelle, and half a dozen servants. The islands had played a significant part in their romance, and it felt fitting to share this milestone in a beautiful locale with the people they loved most. Prince Sebastian and Errol were unable to join their party, but Andrew had come along, in part because of his devotion to Colin, but mostly to keep an eye on the children, who had given his ghostly existence a new purpose. He'd protected them since they'd been transferred into Colin's womb, and his duties hadn't ended with their birth. Andrew was particularly fond of Emilia, Alain's biological daughter. She was the first one who'd seen his nebulous form, and their special bond was rock solid.

Not surprisingly, the twins loved and protected their little sister, but they also enjoyed teasing her, even though the little girl with abundant dark curls and arresting hazel eyes, usually managed to hold her own. Andrew and Alexander—Drew and Alex—had inherited Colin's blond looks and blue eyes, along with some of the magical Bradford gene, but they were no match for Emilia, who was Isabelle's blood relative, and possessed strong elemental powers that were slowly manifesting. Andrew only intervened when the little one turned to him for help, but she rarely did, having also inherited her grandmother's fierce independence.

Right then, he watched the twins prodding her with a large crab they'd caught and refused to throw back. This incurred their grandmother's wrath, and a long lecture on the concept of catch and release. Emilia retaliated by coaxing particles of sand into a miniature funnel that hurled toward her brothers, who screeched in protest.

Isabelle doted on all three and had stepped down from her position as High Priestess of the Simon Coven to become a full-time grandmother. She never dreamed it was possible to find something more engaging than coven politics, but the first time she'd held the newborn twins and recognized the magic in their blood, she knew her role in life was about to change. It didn't matter whose genes the babies carried; they were Alain's in every way but blood. A year later, Colin had offered to carry Alain's child, stubbornly ignoring the risks, and refusing to listen to reason.

After long debates with parliament, who were consulted to make sure the future child would be accorded royal status, they'd gone ahead with their plans, choosing an egg donor from a long list Alain had procured and studied diligently. After making his choice, the egg was introduced to his sperm in a petri dish and then implanted into Colin's waiting uterus. Isabelle had been ecstatic to learn she would have the longed-for granddaughter, after all, and Colin's status was elevated to godlike proportions in her eyes.

Alain had never imagined Isabelle in this role. They'd persuaded her to take up residence at the palace, so she would be closer to the children. She agreed to stay for months at a time, but maintained her home in the foothills on the border of Spain and France. As much as she loved her grandchildren, and she was fiercely maternal about her young charges, there was such a thing as overload. When her nerves were frayed from being around them constantly, she'd escape to the peace and quiet of her mountain fortress to bask in the solitude. Eventually, she'd miss the sweet hugs and sticky kisses, and fly back to Sendorra, refreshed and excited to be "Nana" again. Isabelle was the strong female presence who was a lot more attentive than Princess Charlotte had ever been.

To be fair, Charlie didn't like her role as single mother despite the fancy new title of Princess Mother. She'd moved to Brussels after Raoul divorced his wife to pursue something more permanent with Charlie. Colin had warned her of Raoul's shady past, but Charlotte was happy and scheduled her visits with the twins the same way she planned vacations and shopping sprees.

Which worked out in Isabelle's favor. The idea of leaving her gifted grandchildren in the hands of someone so flighty was unimaginable. Some women weren't made to be mothers, and Charlie fell into this category. Isabelle's biggest competition for the children's affection were Colin, Alain, and their grandfathers—which was only fitting in her estimation. Errol was particularly fond of the children and spoiled them shamelessly. Sebastian was more reticent but managed to convey his love with sporadic outings and magnanimous gifts. Lately, ponies were cropping up in conversations.

"Nana, can you teach me how to fly?" Emilia asked in her tiny voice. "I want to explore with Bibi and Uncle Andrew, but they can't carry me, so I have to do it on my own."

Isabelle's eyebrows shot up. *She was most certainly not going to teach a three-year-old to fly.*

"No, my darling girl. Nana won't teach you this particular skill until you're old enough to read and write. It's far too soon to be traipsing about the countryside with a couple of ghosts."

Emilia stuck out her lower lip, and fat tears rolled down her cheeks with hardly any effort.

The girl should be on the stage, Isabelle muttered to herself.

"But I wanna," Emilia wailed. "It's not fair that Alex and Drew get to play Tarzan, and I can't 'cause my arms are too short."

"It's got nothing to do with your arms," her brother Drew retorted. "Tarzan is a guy, and you're just a dumb girl."

Emilia's eyes narrowed. "Take it back."

"I agree," Isabelle scolded the firstborn twin and heir to the throne. "There's nothing wrong with being a girl, and your sister is far from dumb."

"But she's *not* like us," Alex lisped. "She can't run as fast, and she complains when sand gets in her shoes. And she has to sit to pee."

Blessed goddess. Spare me the dick wagging for another decade at least.

"I can pee standing up," Emilia said angrily. She pushed down her bikini bottoms and showed her brothers what's what.

Alex screamed and scooted back to avoid getting drenched.

Emilia burst out laughing and yanked up her pants. "I'll race you to the rocks over there."

Over there was an outcropping of rocks at least half a mile away. Emilia, named after Colin's grandfather, who feared magic and witches, took off like a wind nymph, curls bouncing and chubby legs pumping. At one point, Isabelle could have sworn the girl hovered over the sand, but it might have been her imagination. Or not. Emilia's blood positively sang with magic, and it wasn't hard to imagine her flying over the coconut trees in the not too distant future. She'd have to tether the girl before she got into trouble.

"Well?" Isabelle asked her grandsons. "What are you waiting for?"

Goaded into competing, the twins darted away with Andrew and Bibi bringing up the rear.

"Way to stir the pot, Maman," Alain scolded mildly. "The boys don't need any encouragement."

"I disagree," Isabelle said. "You don't want to raise a couple of misogynists who think women are only good for one thing. Wait till they find out Emilia can run rings around them. It's better for them to realize she can not only keep up, she'll best them if she sets her mind to it."

"Hey," Colin interjected. "The twins are not women haters. Alex adores his little sister and Drew—"

"Tolerates her," Isabelle reminded him. "He's a bit standoffish when it comes to females."

"I hesitate to say this, but I think the boy has mommy issues," Colin said. "Just the other day, he asked why Charlie doesn't come to visit more often."

"You need to work on her," Isabelle replied sternly. "Before it's too late. I'd hate to see our beautiful boy grow up with any kind of hang-ups."

"She has a point, *chaton*. Maybe Charlie can be persuaded to keep a schedule. Even if the visits are weeks apart, at least the children will feel she actually gives a damn when she shows up as planned."

"You know Charlie loves her boys," Colin defended. "She almost died for them."

"There's loving and there's doing," Alain pointed out. "It's not healthy to grow up wondering if your mother cares enough to give up her scintillating social life in Brussels to spend time with you. I wonder if Charlie even realizes her boys have magic."

"After her experience with Drake and Maura, I don't believe she considers magic a desired trait."

"Nevertheless," Isabelle intoned. "She needs to step up."

"I promise to sit down with her and work something out," Colin said.

"Maman," Alain said, suddenly alert. "Take a look at Emilia."

Their little princess was standing on the rocks facing the ocean, using her right hand like a baton. In the water, dolphins stood on their tails swaying in time with her movements, chirping and whistling in their unique dolphin way. Drew and Alex flanked Emilia, chortling with excitement. Soon all three were clasping hands and dancing around in circles while the dolphins mimicked their moves and whirled around in the water. Andrew and Bibi hovered in the background.

Alain and Colin exchanged long glances and smiled. Isabelle smirked and clapped her hands in delight. It was another ordinary day on the beach with their trio of magical children. She couldn't wait to see what the future had in store for them.

Author's Note

2019 marks my ten-year anniversary as a published writer. When my first novel released in April, 2009, I never expected my writing career to take off, but I was lucky to ride the first huge wave of Kindle, and the m/m genre was on the rise. Since then, a lot has changed in publishing, the universe at large, and my personal life. Writing has been the one constant in this uncertain world and the reason I get up in the morning. The wonderful people I've met along the way, and the countries I've visited in pursuit of a story, have kept me motivated and happy to be alive. My readers have played a huge part in my staying power. I know you have choices, and each day the market is flooded with exceptional books that deserve to be read. I can't thank you enough for picking one of mine and letting me into your heart and home. It's been an honor and a privilege.

Acknowledgements

Many thanks to my dedicated team of beta readers—April, Jason, Sharon, and Shaz—for their continued support and honest feedback. A special shout-out to my NineStar editor, BJ Toth. Thank you for the helpful suggestions that turned this novel into a more polished read.

About the Author

Mickie B. Ashling is the pseudonym of a multifaceted woman who is a product of her upbringing in multiple cultures, having lived in Japan, the Philippines, Spain, and the Middle East. Fluent in three languages, she's a citizen of the world and an interesting mixture of East and West. A little bit of this and a lot of that have brought a unique touch to her literary voice she could never learn from textbooks.

By the time Mickie discovered her talent for writing, real life got in the way, and the business of raising four sons took priority. With the advent of e-publishing—and the inevitable emptying nest—dreams of becoming a published writer were resurrected and fulfilled in April 2009.

Mickie discovered gay romance in 2002 and continues to draw inspiration from the LGBTQA community and their ongoing struggle to find equality and happiness in this oftentimes skewed and intolerant world. Her award-winning novels have been called "gut-wrenching, daring, and thought provoking." She admits to being an angst queen and making her characters work damn hard for their happy endings.

Email:mickie.ashling @gmail.com

Facebook: www.facebook.com/mickie.ashling

Twitter: @MickieAshling

Website: www.mickieashling.com

Instagram:@mickieashling

Blog: www.mickiebashling.blogspot.com

Other books by this author

Third Son
Through My Own Lens
"Once Upon a Mattress" within *Once Upon a Rainbow,*
Volume One
A Tangled Legacy

Also Available from NineStar Press

Connect with NineStar Press

www.ninestarpress.com

www.facebook.com/ninestarpress

www.facebook.com/groups/NineStarNiche

www.twitter.com/ninestarpress

www.tumblr.com/blog/ninestarpress